RIDING SHOTGUN
And Other American Cruelties

Andy Rausch

Crime Wave Press
Flat D, 11th Fl. Liberty Mansion
26E Jordan Road
Yau Ma Tei, Hong Kong
www.crimewavepress.com

ISBN 978-988-14938-3-5

The story "Riding Shotgun" was previously
published by Burning Bulb Publishing as "Bloodletting."

Contents

EASY-PEEZY

Dedicated to Leo Rausch

A decent cowboy does not take what belongs to someone else, and if he does he deserves to be strung up and left for the flies and coyotes.

—Judge Roy Bean

I rob banks for a living. What do you do?

—John Dillinger

1933

CHAPTER ONE

OUTLAWS NEVER DIE

Emmett Dalton, notorious bank robber from the Old West, was now long retired from his life of crime. After the 1892 dual bank robbery in Coffeyville, Kansas, which had made him a legend, he'd done a fourteen-year stretch in the pen out in Lansing. That stint had provided him with plenty of time to reflect on all the mistakes he'd made as a younger man, and he had vowed never to make them again.

But damned if he wasn't jealous of these youngsters. When he read about these kids like John Dillinger, Baby Face Nelson, and Bonnie and Clyde in the newspapers, he found himself longing to raise a little hell. But he was an old man now. He was sixty-two, and robbing banks was a young man's game. Who the hell had ever heard of a geriatric bank robber?

Today Emmett was an author with a couple of autobiographies under his belt, and was also a bit movie actor. Life was pretty damned good. He had no time for such nonsense as robbing banks, but that didn't stop him from daydreaming about it every now and again.

He was sitting at a table in the Brown Derby Restaurant across from his would-be biographer, Harrison Bennett. Harrison, whom Emmett guessed to be in his mid-thirties, worshipped him as some kind of a hero.

"Look," Emmett said, chewing a piece of steak. "Those stories are great. They make me out to be the greatest thing since Moses parted the Red Sea. People call me a living legend. But the truth is, those stories have been greatly exaggerated over the years. They're bullshit. Sure, I've managed to make a living trading on those old tales, but they just ain't true. I'm no more a hero than you are, son. I was a very bad man, Harrison, and I don't deserve to be seen as anything more."

Harrison scribbled in his little notepad.

"Why don't you take a break and eat your food," Emmett suggested. "It's getting cold."

"What was it really like pulling that bank robbery—the one that ended the Dalton Gang?" asked Harrison.

Emmett looked at him, a grim expression on his face. "Two of my brothers were gunned down in the street. It wasn't the best day of my life. It's the one day I'm always gonna be remembered for, but I've seen better days than that one."

"But the robbery itself—was it a rush?"

That was when Harrison saw a glint in the old man's eye. "It was a hell of a time robbing those banks. For the record, I was against it from the start. I said, 'Robbing two banks at the same time is just plain stupid. And on top of that, it's greedy.' But you know how bank robbers are, they don't listen. In the end, everyone in the gang wanted to do it but me, so I figured what the hell and went right along with 'em."

"Do you regret it?"

"Hell yes, I regret it," said Emmett. "The robbery itself was as fun as could be, but when we got out of that bank… That was a whole 'nother story. There must have been thirty men out there with guns trained on us."

"And you got shot," said Harrison. "Is that right?"

"You're damned right I got shot. I got shot twenty-three times. Can you believe that? The Lord must have been lookin' out for me. Hell, I'll bet every one of those sons of bitches that was standin' out there caught me with a bullet that day. Twenty-three bullets! Can you believe that? Here we are all these years later, and I still can't believe it."

Harrison took a drink of his coffee. "I'll bet that hurt like hell."

"I can't even begin to tell you how badly those wounds hurt," said Emmett. "And you know what? When I got to the doc's office, he was talking about me like I wasn't even there. They were all saying how I was already as good as dead. One of 'em said something to the effect of, 'Piss on 'im. Who cares if he lives anyway?' It was a really rough time. But I'll be damned if I didn't show 'em all. I lived, goddammit. Here I am sitting here with you all these years later, drinking this terrible fuckin' coffee, and I'm still alive."

"Is there anyone else from the Dalton Gang who's still alive?" asked Harrison.

"Shit no," said Emmett. "I am, as they say, the last of the Mohicans. I'm the last man standing." Now he turned the questioning around. "So tell me about this book you're writing. What's it gonna be called?"

"I was thinking about titling it *Outlaws Never Die*. What do you think?"

"I think that's one hell of a misleading title. Outlaws *do* die, and the Daltons were proof. We, and I mean as a group now, did that better than anything else—die. Well, everyone but me, I guess. I never was good at much of anything." Emmett laughed.

"Should I change the title?" asked Harrison, a concerned look on his face.

"You can title it that if you want. Hell, it's got a better ring to it than the titles of the books I wrote," said Emmett.

Harrison smiled. "I really enjoyed your books. Especially *Beyond the Law*."

"Thanks, but like I said, it was all crap."

"All of it?"

"Enough of it."

"Well, I wanna tell the truth in this book," said Harrison. "I want to tell it the way it really was."

"They'll never buy it," Emmett said flatly. "People don't want the truth. They'd rather have the legend."

Visibly uncomfortable, Harrison changed the subject. "So what do you think about all these robbers running around today?"

"You mean like Johnny Dillinger and all those folks?"

"Yeah," said Harrison. "People like Ma Barker's gang and so on."

"There sure are a lot of them all of a sudden," observed Emmett. "It's just like it was back in our day…" He stared off out the window for a second, and then turned back to Harrison. "I forgot—what was your question?"

Harrison smiled, chewing a bite from his rock-hard dinner roll. "I asked what you thought about these contemporary bank robbers?"

"For the most part I don't like 'em," said Emmett. "You know why?"

"No, why?"

"Because they got no style. They got no panache. You take a guy like Baby Face Nelson or Pretty Boy Floyd. They carry tommy guns, and they can shoot fifteen, twenty sons of bitches at a time with those things. They got no finesse. Boy, if we'd had tommy guns when we came out of that bank in Coffeyville, we'd have gotten away scot-free. No question about it. But you know what? Nobody's gonna remember any of 'em the way people remember us; the way they remember Jesse James' gang; the way they remember the Wild Bunch."

"You think so?" asked Harrison.

"I know so," said Emmett. "One of these days Johnny Law is gonna catch up with 'em and plant 'em all in their graves. And you know why? Because that man Melvin Purvis and those G-men of his, they got tommy guns, too. And when that day comes, you mark my words, people are gonna forget all about these contemporary outlaws of yours. Why? They got no style." He paused and took a sip from his coffee. "But you know who I do like?"

"Who?" asked Harrison.

"That goddamn John Dillinger. Now there's a bank robber's got some style about him. They say he robs banks and he tells 'em they should be thankful to have been robbed by him because, as he tells it, he's the greatest bank robber ever lived."

"You believe that?" asked Harrison. "That he's the greatest bank robber of all time?"

"No, and I doubt he believes it either. But the man's got style, and he has confidence. People just might remember him someday the way they remember us. We'll just have to wait and see."

"I think you might be right," said Harrison, agreeing with him as usual.

"So when do you wanna meet up and talk again?" asked Emmett.

"How about Wednesday afternoon?"

Emmett nodded. "Wednesday should be fine. It's not like I'm gonna have anything to do."

But he was wrong.

* * *

That night, with visions of bank robbers still dancing around in his head, Emmett read an account of John Dillinger's latest exploits in the *Los Angeles Times*. In the same issue, Emmett also read a story about a former Old West outlaw like himself named Jimmy McDaniels. McDaniels had run with the Jesse Evans Gang, robbing banks and stagecoaches back in the 1870s. According to the "where-are-they-now?" piece Emmett was reading, McDaniels was now seventy-eight years old and staying in a place called Seven Rivers, New Mexico, where he was living as a retired real estate agent.

"I'll be damned," said Emmett aloud.

"What?" asked his wife, Julia, who was sitting next to him, reading the latest issue of *The Reader's Digest*.

Emmett turned to her and said, "Nothing, dear."

And the wheels in Emmett's head started to turn.

* * *

After listening to "The George Gershwin Show," Emmett and Julia retired to bed. Julia fell asleep within a matter of minutes, but Emmett found himself restless and unable to sleep. Thoughts of Jimmy McDaniels, John Dillinger, and his own legacy kept racing through his head.

And he knew.

At that moment he knew with absolute certainty that he wanted to rob another bank or two before he died. This was significant because it was the first time he'd ever considered such a thing as a real possibility. He'd always missed the thrill of robbing banks, but he'd just assumed that life was now behind him.

But what if it wasn't?

What if he was to go down there and meet with old Jimmy McDaniels? What if he was to ask McDaniels to join him in robbing banks? Would McDaniels do it? The answer was likely no, especially since McDaniels was getting up there in years. But what could it hurt to go and meet with the man? Emmett had always believed himself to have good luck, as evidenced by his surviving the Coffeyville fiasco, and he felt confident he could persuade that old outlaw to join forces with him. If McDaniels were to say yes to his proposal, then maybe the two of them could show these young fellas how it was really done.

Emmett lay there considering all this for a number of hours. Finally, just after three, he got up and went to the kitchen. There he brewed some coffee and sat down and read that article about Jimmy McDaniels again. *Perhaps*, he thought. *Maybe this could really work.*

After considering this for a few moments, Emmett stood and went to the closet in the living room and pulled out a suitcase. He crept to the bedroom where Julia was sleeping and removed several sets of clothing, bringing them back out into the kitchen and packing them in the bag.

It was now just after four.

Emmett went to the bathroom and ran himself some water. He then took a quick bath in preparation for his impending trip. Once he was finished, he climbed out of the tub, dried himself off, and put on a fresh set of duds. He wrote out a long letter to his wife, telling her he would be gone for a while. The letter was intentionally vague, as Emmett didn't want her to put two and two together. He positioned the letter prominently on the dining room table so she would be sure to see it.

Emmett snuck back into the bedroom and kissed his sleeping wife's forehead. "I'll see you soon," he whispered. He turned and went back into the bedroom closet, retrieving an old shoebox from the top shelf. He held the box closed in his hands for a moment, knowing full well that once that particular Pandora's box was opened it could never be closed again.

He opened the box and removed his .44-40 Colt single-action revolver. He held it up, looking at it. He felt at home with the gun in his hand. It felt as though he had never even put it away.

CHAPTER TWO

HOOLINGANISM AND CAMARADERIE

It was roughly a thousand miles to Seven Rivers, New Mexico, and Emmett hoped to make it all in a single drive. He stopped his black 1931 Ford Model A coupe a number of times to purchase gasoline or stretch his legs, and he made the drive in roughly twenty-three hours.

When he got to Seven Rivers, he had no idea where the hell Jimmy McDaniels lived. It was still the middle of the night and there was nothing going on in town, so he napped in the car until nine. He planned to go to the newspaper office to inquire about McDaniels' whereabouts, but soon learned that Seven Rivers did not have its own newspaper. Instead, it relied on publications from surrounding cities Artesia and Carlsbad. He stopped at a filling station and offered the pump attendant ten bucks for information on McDaniels.

"Hell, everyone knows old Jimmy McDaniels," said the attendant. "He's kind of a big deal around here."

The attendant took the ten and gave Emmett directions to the real estate office where McDaniels had once worked. Ned Fremont, the agent working at the office, was more than happy to give Emmett directions to McDaniels' home.

Emmett drove a few blocks over to where the former outlaw now resided. When he got there, he pulled the coupe into the circle driveway, parking it next to another Model A. He straightened his suit, checked out his reflection in the automobile's window to make sure he looked right, and stepped up to the porch.

He knocked on the door several times. Finally, an elderly man with a pot belly and a bulbous nose opened it. Emmett recognized McDaniels from the photograph that had run alongside the man's profile in the *Times*.

"Can I help you?" McDaniels asked, still standing half in and half out the door.

Emmett extended his hand. "Pleased to meet you, sir. My name is Emmett Dalton."

McDaniels' eyes grew big as saucers. "Emmett Dalton?" he asked. "As in *the* Emmett Dalton?"

"I sure hope I'm *the* Emmett Dalton," said Emmett, grinning. "I don't believe this world could handle two of us."

For a moment, McDaniels was a child again. He reached out and grabbed Emmett's hand, pumping it hard. "I'm pleased to make your acquaintance," he said. "You can call me Jimmy."

He then opened the door and stepped back, allowing Emmett entrance. When Emmett walked into the house and got a good look at it, he instantly felt at home. The walls were covered with framed photographs and newspaper clippings about Jimmy's exploits as a bank robber. His old cowboy hat was hanging there, and his Colt .45 Peacemaker was on display in a glass cabinet.

"I love what you've done with the place," remarked Emmett.

"I kept *everything*," Jimmy said. "My dear departed wife, Sally, used to say I was a pack rat. I guess she was right."

As Emmett surveyed Jimmy's own personal outlaw museum, he came to a bookshelf filled with books on the Old West. Scanning them, he saw his own books, *Beyond the Law* and *When the Daltons Rode*.

"Yeah," Jimmy said happily. "I got both your books."

"Well," managed Emmett, "I guess there's no accounting for taste."

Jimmy walked into the next room. "Why don't you follow me in to the kitchen so we can talk." He turned back to Emmett. "Can I get you something to drink?"

"Please."

"What would you like? Coffee? Tea?"

Emmett asked, "You got any spirits?"

"It's only ten o'clock," said Jimmy. "You start that early?"

"For what I got to say, we're gonna need spirits."

Jimmy tilted his head, wondering what was coming. "Well, you've certainly piqued my interest, Mr. Dalton." He motioned for Emmett to sit at the table, and he went to the cabinet to get the Scotch and a couple of glasses. He sat down and poured them both a drink.

Emmett downed his immediately.

Jimmy grinned. "Some things never change, I guess."

"You don't know the half."

"So what can I do for you?"

"I want to talk to you about something."

"I surmised as much."

Emmett looked him in the eyes. "Do you ever miss it?"

"Miss what?" asked Jimmy, now sipping his own drink.

"Being an outlaw," Emmett said. "The hooliganism and the camaraderie."

"Of course I do. Those were the greatest times of my life. How about you?"

Emmett smiled. "Every goddamn day."

Jimmy smiled, too.

"I wanna talk to you about startin' a new gang," said Emmett.

Jimmy almost fell out of his chair. *"What?"*

"I'm serious as a heart attack."

"My God, man," said Jimmy. "I'm seventy-eight years old!"

"I know. That's why it's perfect. They'll never see us coming."

Jimmy stared at him, pouring himself another Scotch. He downed it.

"You're serious, aren't you?"

"Yes, sir, I am," said Emmett. "What do you think?"

"I think you're out of your damn fool mind, Emmett Dalton."

"So that's a 'no' then?" asked Emmett.

Jimmy raised his hand. "Now I didn't say that. It just so happens that I'm just as crazy an old fool as you are. This is an interesting proposition, Mr. Dalton. Yes, indeed. But how did you choose me?"

"Everyone else was dead."

Jimmy chuckled. "You can say that again." He poured them both another drink and raised his glass in toast. "To dead outlaws!" Emmett raised his glass, and they both threw back their drinks.

"So you're gonna do it?" asked Emmett.

"Are you kidding? I been waitin' forty years for you to walk through my door and ask me this."

Emmett couldn't believe what he was hearing. He'd been prepared to try and convince Jimmy, and it turned out the man didn't need persuading. "You don't need to mull it over?"

"What's to mull over?" asked Jimmy. "I got nothing else to live for, and I'm damn near dead. Docs say I got cancer in my bones. I won't live more than two or three years at best. So let's do this thing, Emmett Dalton. Let's go out there and show these little bastards robbin' all these banks how real bank robbers do it."

* * *

After Jimmy McDaniels had packed all his clothes, he said, "Just one thing left to pack."

"What's that?" asked Emmett.

"Come on," said Jimmy, leading him through the house. "I'll show you."

He led him down the hall, past the bathroom and his own bedroom to what would normally be a guest bedroom. Jimmy opened the door and walked in. Emmett followed.

The room was filled with guns of all shapes and sizes, mounted on the walls. There must have been fifteen different shotguns and thirty-five, forty pistols there. This crazy son of a bitch Jimmy had his own little armory here.

"Would you look at that," managed Emmett.

"Yeah, it's a hobby of mine. I been collecting guns for more than twenty years now."

Emmett couldn't believe his eyes. "They're beautiful."

"Take what you like, partner," said Jimmy, beaming like a proud father. "I'll be taking my old Colt .45 Peacemaker from the front room, as well as this Colt Dragoon here and a coach gun or two."

Emmett scanned the collection of shotguns, looking as beautiful as the day on which they'd been produced. "Mind if I take this sawed-off 10-gauge?"

"Take whatever you like. So long as we're partners, you're free to use anything I got. What's mine is yours, Emmett Dalton."

Emmett said, "That sounds damn fine to me."

"One more thing."

"What?"

"We're gonna need a few extra guns."

"Why?"

Jimmy grinned. "That's what I wanna talk to you about."

* * *

The two men were back in the kitchen, sitting at the table, finishing off the bottle of scotch. There were guns all around them, pistols on the table, pistols on their person, shotguns leaning against the wall.

"I got a friend by the name of Tom Pickett," said Jimmy. "You ever hear of him?"

"Can't say as I have."

"Tom was an outlaw like us."

"Who'd he ride with?" asked Emmett, pouring himself a drink.

"He rode with Dave Rudabaugh."

Emmett asked, "Dirty Dave Rudabaugh?"

"Same. Then later he rode with Billy the Kid."

Emmett nodded, turning it over in his mind. There were definitely advantages to having a third man in the gang. The main disadvantage was that they'd have to share part of the money. But hell, neither of them was doing this for the money. No, they were doing it to regain a piece of their youth, and a man couldn't put a price on that.

"How old is this guy?" asked Emmett.

"He just had a birthday," said Jimmy. "I think he turned seventy-five, but don't hold me to that. He might be seventy-six."

"What else can you tell me about him?"

"He used to be a lawman—part of the Dodge City Gang out in Vegas. After that, he was a lawman here in New Mexico."

"He still live here?"

Jimmy smiled. "No, he doesn't. That's the other thing I wanted to talk to you about."

"Okay," said Emmett. "What is it?"

Jimmy was lighting his pipe, and he waited until he had it going well before he spoke. Finally he said, "He lives in Joplin, Missouri. Ever hear of it?"

Emmett nodded. "Yeah."

"Well, think of it this way—all the banks a gang could knock over are out there in the Midwest," said Jimmy, puffing on his pipe. "In fact, there's a bank there in Joplin that's been hit three or four times this year alone. I believe Machine Gun Kelly, Dillinger, and the Barrows Gang all knocked it over."

"You sure it's safe to hit it again?"

"Those stupid bastards don't learn," said Jimmy. "They keep thinkin' surely they won't get hit again, and then they do. It's an easy job. Easy-peezy."

Emmett thought about it. "So you wanna go get this guy Pickett in Joplin?"

"I do," Jimmy said. "We're gonna need a third man anyway. It takes two men to hit the bank and a third to drive."

"Times have changed. Last time I robbed a bank, we were riding horses."

Jimmy laughed. "Me too. But horses die when they get shot."

"And automobiles explode," said Emmett. "That's not really reassuring."

"Well," said Jimmy, "I reckon we could take horses to do the job, but I think the law would catch up to us pretty damn quick."

Emmett laughed now. "I was just joshin'. I love horses, but I don't miss ridin' 'em everywhere. Seems like I always had sore balls back then."

Jimmy laughed. "I don't miss that either."

"So I guess we're heading to Missouri," said Emmett.

"Yeah," said Jimmy. "I guess we are."

"There's one place I wanna stop on the way. One bank I wanna knock over."

"With just the two of us?"

"Yeah."

"Where's that?"

Emmett grinned. "Coffeyville, Kansas."

CHAPTER THREE

COFFEYVILLE, KANSAS

The long journey from New Mexico to Coffeyville took two full days, with each of them taking turns at the wheel. Emmett was driving when they passed through Tulsa, Oklahoma. He was now only about eighty miles away from the town where he'd made his mark. As he drove on, his mind turned to Julia. He was sure she would be sick with worry, and he now felt bad for having left her in the dark about all this. But the truth was, Julia was a God-fearing Christian woman, and she would not have approved of all this craziness.

Having been asleep for the past six hours, Jimmy began to stir. "Where we at?"

"We're close," said Emmett. "We just passed Tulsa."

"I never been to Tulsa," remarked Jimmy. "I woulda liked to have seen it."

"You ain't missing much. It's a big city, sure, but it's changed so much since I was there last. It don't even look like it could be the same city."

Jimmy nodded. "Everything's changed."

"Everything but us."

Jimmy smiled at this truth. "So what's it like in Coffeyville?"

"Well hell, I ain't been there in forty-one years. How the hell should I know?"

"Isn't Walter Johnson from there? I seem to recall he was."

"Walter Johnson, the ball player?" asked Emmett. "He's from Coffeyville?"

"Seems like I read that somewhere."

"Well, I guess everybody's gotta be from somewhere."

"You a baseball fan?"

"Just in passing," said Emmett.

"Does Walter Johnson still play?"

"He's a manager now."

"With the Senators?"

"Used to be, but now he's over there in Cleveland."

They drove on, soon approaching the Vedigris River, which meant they were close now. They came to the small suburb of South Coffeyville, and Emmett could feel his anticipation building with every passing minute.

"What do you wanna do in Coffeyville, aside from the obvious?" asked Jimmy.

"We could go to a show," said Emmett. "Man on the radio said that *King Kong* picture is pretty good."

"Supposed to be scary?"

Emmett said, "I guess."

"Let's rob the bank first."

"Then go to a show?"

"Why not?"

And on they drove.

* * *

Last time he'd been in Coffeyville, Emmett and his brothers had attempted to rob the First National Bank and the C.M. Condon Bank at the same time. But now, all these years later, the C. M. Condon was gone, leaving only the First National to rob.

Now here they were, sitting outside the bank in the coupe.

"We really need a third man to drive," said Jimmy.

"Third man shit," said Emmett. "We can do this with just the two of us."

"You think?"

"Hell yes. We were built for this, son."

"We just leave the Ford running?"

"Yeah."

In the old days, both men would have spent the minutes leading up to a robbery getting themselves psyched for the event. Today, however, they were older and wiser, and each man remained calm and collected.

Emmett had the big .44-40 Colt revolver in his hand, ready to go. Jimmy had both of his pistols holstered in a fancy black two-gun rig and was carrying the 12-gauge.

Now was the time.

"You ready for this?" asked Emmett, his hand on the door handle.

"Ready as I'm ever gonna be, I reckon."

The two old outlaws stepped out of the Ford. There was no one on the sidewalk, and no cars moving in the street around them. This was gonna be a piece of cake. Easy-peezy, just as Jimmy had said.

Moving towards the entrance, Emmett said, "I'll take lead." He swung the door open and rushed inside. Jimmy was right behind. There were only three customers in the place. Everyone in the room saw them at the same time.

Emmett raised the Colt. "Alright everybody, this here is a robbery!"

No one knew what to do. All the people in the bank looked around for cues. Finally Jimmy yelled out, "Everyone down on the floor! *Now!*"

Emmett rushed ahead to the front counter with Jimmy standing back at the door. Just when Emmett reached the counter, another bank employee, a frumpy, middle-aged woman wearing too much makeup, stepped out of the vault to see what was happening.

"You!" Emmett said, catching her off guard. "Take out all the money from the drawers and put it in a bag." He looked back at Jimmy, who was surveying the room. So far so good. Emmett turned back to the woman. "Who's the bank manager?"

The woman pointed down at the floor where a skinny, balding man in a suit was lying. "That's Lenny right there," she said. "He's the manager."

"Lenny, get on your feet," said Emmett.

Lenny looked up nervously, slowly raising himself off the ground.

"Take me to the vault now."

Lenny turned towards the open vault. Emmett briefly considered trying to jump up and over the counter, but he knew he couldn't make it. As Lenny the bank manager stood waiting at the mouth of the vault, Emmett walked down around the counter.

Old Lenny here was nervous as all hell, but he didn't put up a fight. He just unlocked the door and walked inside the vault.

So far so good, Emmett thought.

"I want you to take as much cash as you can get ahold of and stick it in a couple of bags," said Emmett. Lenny nodded and went to work. Emmett waited nervously as the bank manager filled two bags with cash. Finally, the man handed over the bags, filled to the brim with cash.

"Thank you, sir," said Emmett. "Now you stay here."

"In the vault?" the man asked.

"In the vault."

Emmett walked back to the woman at the counter and picked up the third bag of money, holding them all in the same hand. "You didn't hit the alarm, did you?" he asked.

She shook her head.

Emmett raised the Colt into the air so everyone could see it and said, "You have just been robbed by the Emmett Dalton gang! So when someone asks who it was that took your money, you can tell 'em proudly it was Emmett Dalton and Jimmy McDaniels."

When the customers and employees heard the name Dalton, they all gasped collectively.

"Hey," someone said. Emmett looked over and saw the fat, old security guard lying on the floor near Jimmy's feet. He was looking up at him.

"What do you want, fat man?" asked Emmett.

The man was grinning. "You're Emmett Dalton?"

"Yes, sir," said Emmett proudly.

"I was working here way back when you sons of bitches robbed this bank the first time," the security guard said.

Emmett and Jimmy exchanged a look. Jimmy racked the shotgun.

"Didn't you learn your lesson the first time?" the security guard asked.

Emmett frowned, not liking any of this.

"Say that again," dared Emmett.

"I'll say that and more," said the security guard. "I'll say that you're a worthless no good pile of shit. And I'll say you shoulda learned your lesson when you and your dumbass brothers got all shot to hell back in '92."

"Shut your mouth," demanded Emmett.

But the security guard kept right on yammering. "You're gonna foul this all up again. You couldn't do it forty years ago, and you can't do it now. You're just a hopeless screw up."

Emmett told the man to stand.

The security guard stood, not the least bit afraid of him.

Emmett turned the Colt on him.

"You stupid bastards shot a lot of good men that day," the security guard said. "I take pride in knowing that two of them slugs you took in your hide came from my gun, Emmett Dalton."

Emmett wasn't prepared for this. He hadn't planned to shoot anyone today.

Fuck it.

Examples had to be made.

"You shot me?" asked Emmett incredulously.

The security guard grinned big. "I shot your stupid ass twice."

Emmett looked down the barrel of the Colt at the security guard, still showing no fear. Emmett's finger tightened around the trigger.

This is it, he thought.

This man had to go.

Watching the man's face with the hopes of seeing his smug expression change, Emmett squeezed the trigger.

Click!

He squeezed it again.

Click!

Emmett stomped his foot. *"Goddammit,"* he said.

"What is it?" asked Jimmy.

"I need to borrow your Peacemaker."

"Why?"

The security guard laughed heartily. "Because this stupid sumbitch forgot to load his goddamn pistol!"

Emmett heard a smattering of laughter around the room.

He slid the gun back into its holster.

Jimmy pulled out the Peacekeeper and tossed it to him. Emmett caught it, and pointed it at the security guard.

"Not so funny now, is it?" he asked.

The security guard just kept grinning. "Nah," he said. "It's still pretty damned funny."

Emmett squeezed the trigger.

Blam!

The volley struck the security guard in his left eye, and the man and that stupid smile of his were no more.

Emmett and Jimmy ushered everyone into the vault and locked them inside.

* * *

The two bank robbers had gotten out of the First National Bank and made their way back to the Model A without a hitch. The street was still empty and there was nary a soul around. There were no police sirens blaring in the distance. In fact, it was dead silent. Emmett stomped on the gas and the automobile roared off down the street.

"Sorry about that," said Emmett. "I didn't want to shoot nobody."

"No problem. If he'd kept his damn fool mouth shut, he'd still be alive."

This made Emmett feel better.

"We gotta get this car off the street for a little while," he said.

Jimmy pointed. "There's a movie theater. Pull in there in the back lot."

And the two men went inside and watched *King Kong*, and no one ever showed up at the theater looking for them.

They had gotten away with it.

CHAPTER FOUR

THE WHEELMAN

On the hour and a half drive from Coffeyville to Joplin, Emmett and Jimmy discussed the robbery they'd just pulled. The two of them were like enthusiastic schoolchildren as they recounted it all.

"I didn't even have to tell the bank manager what to do," said Emmett. "He already knew."

Jimmy sat, smoking his pipe. "Sorry bastard didn't wanna join that security guard. Yeah, he knew what to do. That's the thing with these little banks in the Midwest; they been hit so many times most of 'em won't even put up a fight. They just hand the money over. The Barrows Gang and all them other robbers just made our job a little bit easier."

"Hell, even robbing banks has changed," observed Emmett. "I ain't never seen a bank manager just go for the vault without being asked. Back in the day, those bank managers acted like the damn money was theirs. A lot of 'em woulda died for money that didn't even belong to them."

"We were young at the wrong time. Just imagine if we were young right now. We'd be knocking 'em dead," said Jimmy.

Emmett stared down the road, finally saying, "Hell, we're gonna do that anyway, Jimmy. We're gonna show 'em all what a gang of old codgers can do. By God, they're gonna know our names."

"Everyone already knows your name," said McDaniel.

Emmett smiled, momentarily basking in his fame. "Well, if they didn't know us by now, they're damn sure gonna."

"I got a question."

"What is it?" asked Emmett.

"I'm not complaining or nothin' like that," said Jimmy. "But why are we the Emmett Dalton Gang and not the Jimmy McDaniels Gang?"

ANDY RAUSCH

"On account of it being my idea. Besides, and I mean absolutely no offense here, my name is more famous than yours," said Emmett. "And I did tell 'em your name, too. I said we was Emmett Dalton and Jimmy McDaniels."

"I know. Again, I ain't complain'. I was just wonderin', was all."

"Don't worry. I promise we're gonna make you famous, Jimmy. You and me, we're gonna be the next Barrows Gang, the next Dillinger… We're gonna own this world one of these days."

Emmett drove on, puffing on a big, fat cigar.

"We're almost to Joplin," said Emmett. "Where does your friend Tom Pickett live?"

* * *

Jimmy explained the situation to Emmett—Tom was a broken-down old man, living in a rest home. He was suffering from emphysema, and he wasn't doing all that well.

"He lives in a damned rest home?" asked Emmett, irritated. "You could have mentioned this detail earlier."

"I wasn't sure you'd go along with it," said Jimmy. "But we gotta spring the man. He doesn't wanna be there anymore. He wants the same thing we want—to go out with a bang… To rob banks again. He wants to be an outlaw again."

Emmett chomped on his cigar. "Is there anything else I need to know about Tom Pickett?"

"Well," said Jimmy sheepishly, "I might have forgot to mention one other detail."

Emmett turned and looked at his partner. "What?"

"He's in a wheelchair."

Emmett sat upright. *"What?"*

"I suppose I shoulda mentioned that sooner."

"Yes," said Emmett. "I suppose you should have."

"I promised the man I'd get him out of there. We owe it to him."

"I don't owe the man shit. Hell, I don't even know him."

"But he was one of us," explained Jimmy. "He was an outlaw. That life he's livin' in that rest home, that ain't no kind of life at all. We gotta do this."

"If I was to help you get Tom out of the rest home, how the hell is he supposed to help us rob banks in a damned wheelchair?"

Jimmy shrugged. "I didn't think it would be a big deal. After all, he's just gonna be the wheelman."

Emmett laughed.

"What is it?"

"When you originally referred to him as the wheelman," said Emmett, "you forgot to mention the man actually comes with his own wheels."

Jimmy smiled. "Are we gonna break Tom Pickett out of that rest home, or what?"

"How's he gonna do security?" asked Emmett. "Third man, he usually pulls security outside the bank. Can your man do that?"

"I reckon he could. We'll just park right out front and give him a pistol. Then, he sees anybody coming, he can shoot 'em or fire off a round to let us know."

Emmett looked down for a moment, considering the matter. "Ah, what the hell," he said. "Let's do it."

"Really?"

"Sure. I wouldn't wanna live like that either. Let's go get the poor bastard out of there."

* * *

Sunnyvale Rest Home was the kind of place that featured all the amenities of home without actually feeling anything even remotely like home. The place was overly-sanitized and had the feel of a hospital more than a home. The rest home's advertisements touted it as a place to begin a new life, but the truth was apparent the moment Emmett and Jimmy walked in—this was a place where people went to die.

Emmett passed a pretty young nurse as he walked in. He smiled at her, and she gave him a sideways glance. "Hello," he said, stopping her. "Could you tell me where a patient named Tom Pickett might be staying?"

The pretty young thing smiled back, but Emmett didn't know if it was because of his good looks or that he reminded her of her grandfather. "Sure thing. You just go straight down this hall to the front desk. They'll get you fellas signed in and then you can see Mr. Pickett. How does that sound?"

Emmett told her that sounded fine with him, and the two men proceeded down the hall to the front desk. When they came to the desk, no one was there. They waited for a few minutes, and finally a man approached them. "How can I help you?" he asked.

"We're old friends of Tom Pickett's," said Jimmy. "We're here to see him."

"Too bad you fellas just missed his birthday," the man said. "It was a shame—no one came to visit." The man picked up a pencil and opened a notebook. "What are your names?"

"My name is John Smith," said Emmett. "And this handsome young devil here is Joe Johnson."

The man raised his face, looking them over. The crap aliases were probably a dead giveaway, but hell, Emmett had been forced to come up with them on the spur of the moment.

"Could you guys sign here?" asked the man, handing them the notebook.

Emmett signed in, handing the notebook to Jimmy. The second outlaw turned and whispered to Emmett, "What's my name again?"

Emmett whispered back, "Joe Johnson."

Jimmy scrawled the name. He then handed the notebook back to the man.

"Mr. Pickett is in room 105," said the man, pointing down the hall. "It's just three doors down on your left."

Emmett looked down the hall, then back at the man. "We just go on down?"

"Sure."

Emmett and Jimmy walked down the hallway, the place smelling simultaneously of disinfectant and death. When they got to Tom's room, Jimmy led the way seeing as how he knew the man.

Jimmy knocked.

Tom was a frail little man with paper-thin flesh draped over a pile of bones. He had liver spots all over his body. Jimmy had been

26

right—Tom was on his last leg, so to speak. He looked bad. He turned his wheelchair to face them.

"Who is it?" asked Tom.

This was a bad start.

"It's me, Jimmy McDaniels."

"I didn't recognize you, Jimmy. How are you?"

Jimmy said, "I'm fine. How the hell are you?"

"Terrible," said Tom. "The bastards won't let me smoke in here. Can you believe that?"

"That's terrible," said Emmett, still puffing on his cigar.

"And who are you?" Tom asked Emmett.

Emmett extended his hand, and Jimmy introduced them. Tom shook his hand.

"Emmett Dalton?" he asked. "Are you the same Emmett Dalton that robbed those banks over in Coffeyville all those years ago?"

Emmett grinned. "I used to be."

"Well, it's damned fine to meet another old outlaw," said Tom, grinning a toothless grin. "What are you boys up to?"

"We're gonna spring you out this place," said Jimmy.

"You mean it?'

"Yeah."

Tom put his hand over his heart. "Thank you, sweet Jesus," he said. "I been prayin' for this for a long, long time. This here is surely the answer to my prayers."

"Is there anything you need to take with you?" asked Emmett.

"No, they can burn it all," said Tom. "I just want a damn cigarette."

* * *

Emmett and Jimmy tried to walk out of the rest home with the man, but they were stopped as they attempted to leave. "Where you taking this man?" asked the **heavyset** heavy-set nurse.

"We're just going for a walk," said Emmett. "It's a lovely day outside."

The nurse frowned. "This is most irregular. The residents can only go outside if they're accompanied by one of our staff members."

Emmett was already tired of this bullshit.

He reached into his jacket and pulled out his revolver, aiming it at the nurse. "We're gonna be leaving with this man, and there's not a damned thing you're gonna do about it."

The woman was visibly shaken.

She kept her mouth shut.

The two men wheeled Tom out to the Ford. Jimmy opened the coupe's door, and Emmett hefted Tom into the vehicle. "Damn, Tom, what the hell you been eatin'?" asked Emmett.

"He heavy?" asked Jimmy.

"Shit yes. He's like a sack of bricks."

Once Tom was in the backseat of the automobile, Jimmy folded up the wheelchair and stuffed it into the back beside him.

"Now what are we gonna do?" asked Tom.

Emmett smiled, looking at him in the rear view mirror. "We're gonna rob us a few banks, Tom."

Tom lit up. "Then this really is the answer to all my prayers." Tom sat there silently for a moment before asking, "You don't think we're too old?"

"Hell no," said Emmett. "I think we're just fine."

"I'm gonna need a gun," said Tom.

Jimmy turned to him. "I brought you a Colt .45 revolver. That work for you?"

"Sounds great," said Tom. "There's just one more thing."

"Yeah?"

"How the hell am I supposed to be the getaway driver?"

Emmett looked in the mirror again. "What do you mean?"

Tom laughed. "I'm paralyzed from the waist down. How the hell am I supposed to drive a car?"

CHAPTER FIVE

MISERY IN MISSOURI

The three old bank robbers checked into a place called the Hotel Connor. Emmett had originally planned to rob the Farmers Bank of Joplin just after breaking Tom Pickett out of the rest home, but he had reconsidered. Robbing two banks in one day would be an amazing thing, but that's what got him into trouble the first time around. No, there was no need to get cocky. Besides, they had a major problem. Their getaway driver couldn't use his legs, so how in the hell was he supposed to drive? Sure, Emmett and Jimmy had pulled the Coffeyville job alone, but that wouldn't really work more than once or twice. Jimmy had been right—they needed a third man.

And they had one—kind of.

But he was paralyzed.

What the hell have I gotten myself into here? Emmett asked himself. But being the good sport that he was, Emmett decided to make do with what they had. He decided to adapt to the situation. He went down to the lumber yard he'd passed on the way into town and purchased a single two-by-four. He then brought it back to the hotel.

"What the hell's that for?" asked Jimmy.

"This here is how Tom's gonna drive for us," said Emmett proudly.

Tom, choking on a cigarette, asked, "How?'

Emmett held up the two-by-four. "You can hit the accelerator with this. That allows you to use your arms. Then you don't have to worry about your legs. What do you think?"

"I think you're crazy," said Tom. "That's what I think."

The man wasn't joking.

"What makes you say that?"

"What the hell kind of gang would want a crippled getaway driver?" asked Tom. "That shit don't make sense."

Emmett had to admit that the whole thing did sound crazy, especially when you said it out loud. But Emmett was as loyal as the day was long, and besides, they were in desperate need of a third man, and it wasn't like they could just go and run an ad in the *Joplin Globe*.

So they were stuck with old Tom Pickett.

"Should we plan out the robbery?" asked Jimmy.

"What's to plan?" asked Emmett. "We'll check the place out in the morning before we pull the job, just to make sure everything looks good. You know how it is—we just go in there, guns blazing, and rob the damn place. It don't take a lot of leg work. Besides, this is Joplin. This is the Farmers Bank. Remember, they been hit three or four times already this year. Like you said, easy-peezy."

Jimmy nodded, puffing on his pipe. "What do you wanna do now?"

"I figure we'll go and get some dinner, maybe go to another show."

"Another show?" asked

"Sure," said Emmett. "We'll get our minds off the thing. I mean, it's not like we have anything to worry about anyway. This is Joplin. What could go wrong?"

* * *

Emmett didn't like the way the day was starting. Today's issue of the *Globe* had come out, and they'd done a write-up on the Coffeyville robbery. The article didn't sit well with Emmett one damn bit. In the article the reporter referred to them as "the Old Timers Gang" instead of the Emmett Dalton Gang. Apparently the Coffeyville Police had given them this mocking moniker, and the media seemed to be eating it up.

"Goddammit," Emmett muttered, rereading the article for the third time. "We can't have this. This is bullshit. How are we gonna get respect if we can't even get the bastards to call us by our rightful name?"

Emmett decided he would telephone the editor of the *Joplin Globe* and personally inform him of his mistake. Maybe, just maybe, the damage to the gang's collective reputation could still be salvaged.

"I need to talk to the editor," said Emmett, using the telephone in the hotel hallway. "I need to know, what's that sumbitches' name?"

The woman on the other end of the phone said politely, "Alvin Cobb is the editor. Hold on and I'll get him for you."

Emmett put his hand over the receiver and turned to Jimmy, standing behind him, smoking his pipe. "She's going to get him now." He then turned back to the telephone and waited for Alvin Cobb. A moment later, Cobb picked up the telephone.

"Hello, this is Alvin Cobb," the man said. The second Emmett heard his voice he immediately pictured Cobb as a portly, well-dressed, arrogant prick.

Emmett raised his mouth to the telephone, a cigar in his mouth. "My name is Emmett Dalton. I robbed that bank in Coffeyville yesterday."

"Is this really Emmett Dalton?"

"Yes, sir, it sure is," said Emmett.

"What can I do for you, Mr. Dalton?"

"I just called to tell you that your facts were all wrong in that story you did in the paper this morning."

"Oh?" asked Cobb. "How so?"

"Your paper called us the Old Timers Gang, and that ain't our proper name."

"Is that right?" asked Cobb, a lightness in his voice suggesting he was trying not to laugh.

This irritated Emmett. "We're the Emmett Dalton Gang."

"Surely you must know every newspaper in the country is now calling you the Old Timers Gang. I'm afraid the damage has already been done, Mr. Dalton. Now everyone's gonna call you the Old Timers Gang from here on. You might as well get used to it."

"Hell's bells," muttered Emmett.

"Can I interview you while I have you on the telephone?"

Emmett looked at Jimmy. He wasn't sure this was a good idea. He put his hand over the receiver and asked Jimmy what he should do. "Tell the man yes," said Jimmy. Emmett figured what the hell and agreed to be interviewed.

"You're an author and a motion picture actor now, Mr. Dalton," said Cobb. "What made you decide to pick up where you left off and start robbing banks again?"

So Emmett told him the truth. "Other than John Dillinger, these younger bank robbers got it all wrong. They got no style. They tote around those big goddamn tommy guns, shooting up the place. Where's the grace in that? Where's the style?"

"I got you. No style," repeated Cobb. "So what made you decide to rob the First National Bank of Coffeyville again?"

"I figured where's a better place to start than where I left off," said Emmett. "And I felt like I had a score to settle with Coffeyville. Last time we was there, they shot and killed my brothers. The sons of bitches shot me full of holes, and I spent fourteen years behind bars for that robbery."

"So this was payback?"

"You're damn right this was payback. The name Emmett Dalton is a name those sons of bitches aren't likely to forget any time soon, I'll tell you that."

Cobb said, "I'm sure you're right, Mr. Dalton. When you were in that bank, you shot and killed a man. Hold on. I'll have to look it up…" Cobb got quiet for a minute before returning. "A Mr. Jeb Murtree, a bank security guard. What do you have to say about that?"

"I ain't got much to say about it," explained Emmett. "If the damn fool had kept his stupid mouth shut, he'd still be alive today. But no, he had to go runnin' off at the mouth. He had to talk shit. Well, look where that got him."

"May I inquire as to where you are currently?" asked Cobb.

Emmett rubbed his moustache. "No comment."

"Are you in Joplin?"

Emmett stared at the telephone, not knowing what to say.

Shit. This was a mistake.

"Mr. Dalton?" asked Cobb.

Unsure what to do to cover his tracks, Emmett hung up the phone. He turned to Jimmy. "Come on," he said. "We gotta move fast if we're gonna rob that bank. That son of a bitch knows we're in Joplin. I guarantee you he's gonna call the cops."

"And we're gonna rob the bank anyway?"

"Yup."

"Right now?"

"Right goddamn now," said Emmett. "Help me get Tom's wheelchair down the stairs, so we can get him propped up behind the steering wheel."

"We're gonna go and rob the Farmers Bank without doing any leg work?" asked Jimmy. "That sounds like a bad fucking idea."

"We'll be fine."

* * *

Seven minutes later Tom Pickett pulled the Model A right up in front of the bank. It was just after nine.

"I got a bad feeling about this," said Tom.

"Yeah," said Jimmy. "Me too."

This got Emmett steamed. He held up his Colt. "Are you bastards backing out on me? 'Cause I'll rob this goddamn bank all by my lonesome if I have to."

"Of course not," said Jimmy. "Let's do it."

"Am I still the leader of this gang?" asked Emmett.

"We ain't got time for dick measuring," said Tom, smoking his cigarette. "You dummies got to get in there now if we're gonna rob this fucker."

The man had a point.

* * *

When Emmett and Jimmy entered the bank, there were no customers in the place. It was just the bank employees.

The bank manager—a little redheaded fella—spoke up. "The police just telephoned," he said. "They're on their way now. If I were you boys, I'd get out of here while you still can. Here in a few minutes this place is gonna be crawlin' with cops."

Emmett was nervous. He looked back at Jimmy, who just shrugged.

"Get down on the ground," said Emmett. "Anybody moves or hits the alarm, they die. You get it?"

Nobody said a word.

Emmett ordered the bank manager to fill a couple of bags with cash from the drawers. This time Emmett figured he'd just skip the vault what with the cops coming and all. The bank manager agreed, and he leaned forward to get the bags. When he came back up, Emmett saw at once that he didn't have a bag in his hand—he had a pistol.

Goddammit, Emmett thought.

Emmett didn't want to kill anyone, but he had no choice.

He was on auto-pilot now, those old senses coming back to him.

He fired the .40-44 shooting the bank manager in the Adam's apple. The manager dropped the pistol and reached for his throat, blood seeping out between his fingers. The man was all wigglin' around, on the verge of convulsing.

Emmett put him out of his misery.

This time he shot him in the cheek, killing him instantly. The bank manager's eyes rolled back in his head and he crumpled to the floor.

Jimmy yelled, "Come on, let's get out of here!"

Emmett knew there was no time. He couldn't hear sirens yet, but he knew damn well they were coming. "Stay on the floor," he yelled. "Anybody gets up, they die!"

And he turned for the door.

＊ ＊ ＊

The three bank robbers were now speeding away in the coupe. They passed a couple of police cars going in the opposite direction.

"What the hell kind of robbers are you guys?" asked Tom.

"You weren't there," said Emmett. "It got ugly fast."

"So let me get this straight," Tom said. "You shot and killed a man and then got out of there without so much as a goddamn dollar? What kind of bullshit half-assed gang is this, Emmett?"

Emmett was pissed. "Just shut up and smoke your damn cigarette, pops."

CHAPTER SIX

GOOD AND LOYAL SERVANTS

Wanting to put as much road between themselves and the Joplin robbery, Emmett and the gang headed down US 54 to St. Louis. The air was turning colder. Halloween was about a week away, and the wind had picked up tremendously. It looked as though it might snow at any moment.

Emmett and Jimmy had scouted the bank while Tom stayed back in the room and read through the Bible as he was trying to become better friends with God "on account of how we might be seeing him soon." This irked Emmett a bit. Not just that Tom was implying they might be shot and killed any day, but also that he now talked about nothing else but God. The thing that made such conversations with Tom interesting was that he always laced each sentence about Christianity with profanity of some sort. His heart was in the right place, but he wasn't the brightest guy who ever robbed a bank. He'd say things like, "Jesus Christ was one tough son of a bitch" or ask if anyone knew how big "Noah's goddamn ark" was. Emmett had nothing against religion. Hell, he'd been raised in church and had married Julia, a good God-fearing woman who had dragged his ass into church each week. But Tom wanted to talk about God all the time. He seemed to know no other subject.

So when they walked into the hotel room in St. Louis and were confronted by Tom about their lack of "goddamn religion," they weren't really all that surprised.

"I been thinkin'," said Tom, taking a drag from his cigarette. "It's high time you boys found our Lord Jesus Christ. Now I know both of you been to church a time or two, but you need to really study the Bible and pray more. That might help us to be better goddamn bank robbers. You know, if God is on our side, then who can be against us?"

Emmett asked, "You think a fella could really pray to God about things like committin' robberies?"

"Why, sure I do," said Tom. "Jesus helps with all things, even some things that ain't so good. Besides, all we're doing is takin' money away from the rich people. That ain't so bad. In a way, we're doing a good thing. You know what the Bible says about the rich man? It says a camel would have an easier time passing through the hole in a goddamn needle than a rich bastard would have of getting' into heaven."

Emmett nodded. It made sense.

Jimmy said, "Maybe we should start prayin' before every job we do."

"That's exactly what I was thinking," said Tom. "It's like God went into your mind and filled you with the same thought he filled my head with."

＊ ＊ ＊

The next day they were sitting idly in the Ford, right there in the middle of the street. Automobiles were passing by them and tooting their horns, but they didn't pay them any mind at all. They were in the middle of prayer.

"Dear God our Lord Jesus Christ we speak unto you," said Tom, leading the thing. "We look to you and ask as your humble goddamn servants that you come down off of your seat up there in heaven and watch over us as we rob this place. Please don't let none of these stupid sons of bitches try anything in here, and don't make Emmett and Jimmy have to kill anybody, oh God, oh wise one. We promise that, aside from robbin' banks and occasionally killin' folks, to be good and loyal servants. We are your sheep, and you are our—"

This was when the prayer was interrupted by a knock on the window.

The three bank robbers opened their eyes and looked up, seeing the cop standing there. Emmett rolled the window down.

"You boys can't park here," said the cop. "You're stopping the flow of traffic."

It was at this point the cop saw the pistols and the sawed-off Greener. He stepped back and reached for his gun. "What are you boys doing here with all these guns?" This time it was Tom that acted. He raised the short barrel of the coach gun past Emmett's head and squeezed the trigger, blasting the cop back a good foot. Lucky for them there were no pedestrians around. Emmett jumped out of the automobile and dragged the cop's bloody body back into the coupe.

"Ah, Jesus Christ," he muttered.

"What?" asked Tom.

"My upholstery," said Emmett. "I'm gonna get blood all over it." He paused for a moment before adding, "Stupid goddamn cop."

Jimmy looked at Tom. Emmett was still standing half in and half out the automobile door, and the dead cop was sitting up in the seat between him and Tom.

"Let's hurry up and finish our prayer," said Tom.

And so they did.

* * *

Emmett and Jimmy walked into the bank, business as usual, and they felt they were right back in the swing of robbing banks. It had all come back to them just as it's said about riding a bike. Their pistols were down beside them, and they were wearing long coats. The place was packed.

Nobody noticed them at first.

Everyone just went about their business.

And then someone screamed out, "He's got a gun!" People started freaking out, turning and screaming and holding their children.

"Everyone get down on the damned floor!" screamed Emmett. "Anybody moves and we start shooting. We're the Emmett Dalton Gang. Maybe you heard of us. Well, we're here to rob this here bank today. Anybody got any questions?"

There were none.

Jimmy covered the front doors as Emmett stalked towards the front counter. "I should mention that if anybody trips the alarm, we're gonna start killing folks," said Emmett to the teller. "Now kindly start sacking up all the bills in those drawers." He turned towards a man still standing, obviously the bank manager, ready to go down with his proverbial ship.

"You," said Emmett. "You the manager?"

"Yes," said the man nervously.

"Let's go open your vault." Emmett walked around the counter towards the bank manager, but the man didn't move an inch.

"I won't do it," said the bank manager.

"Yes, you will," said Emmett. "Or else my little gun makes a big noise, if you catch my drift."

"I do, but I won't do it."

Emmett turned and shot a man lying on the floor in the head, his brains and blood spraying a good foot away from him.

"Let's try this again," said Emmett.

"No, I still won't do it."

Emmett turned and shot a bank teller, and then looked back at the bank manager.

"I still won't do it," said the bank manager.

This was when Emmett heard a woman's voice say, "Oh, Jesus Christ, Charlie."

Emmett turned and saw a woman—a bank employee—coming towards them. Before he could swivel his pistol she said, "To hell with you, Charlie. I'll open the goddamn safe."

The bank manager looked disgusted by all this. Emmett raised the pistol and shot the man. "We don't need you anymore, Charlie," he said. He followed the woman to the vault. She turned the dial a few times and the safe came open.

"The money's already bagged up in there," said the woman. "Just grab it and go."

Emmett took two steps into the vault before he realized what he'd done. The woman closed the door on him, locking him inside.

"Open this goddamn door right now!" screamed Emmett, but no one came.

Shit, he thought. *What am I gonna do now?*

Emmett Dalton's comeback wasn't turning out quite the way he'd envisioned it.

Emmett sat inside the vault in darkness for about five minutes before he heard gunshots outside. He'd be damned if it didn't sound like sub-machine gun chatter. Then he heard the dial of the vault again, and the door opened.

There was a man standing there, dressed in a fancy suit, carrying a tommy gun.

"Come on out of there," he said.

Emmett started to walk out, but the man said, "Don't forget the money."

He went back and grabbed the two bags of bills that were inside the vault and then walked out.

"We can shake hands later," said the man, smoking a big, fat cigar. "My name's George Nelson. Everybody calls me Baby Face."

"Pleased to make your acquaintance, Mr. Nelson," said Emmett.

Baby Face chuckled. "I'm sure you are."

Emmett looked around and saw that there were two more robbers, along with his pal Jimmy. The rest of the robbery went without a hitch until they were leaving the bank. As they were walking out, Baby Face sprayed into the crowd with his Tommy gun, wounding and killing a handful of people. It was, as Emmett would later recount, the most gruesome thing he'd ever witnessed.

Emmett was still carrying the money when they got outside.

"You go ahead and carry that," said Baby Face. "Just follow me. I'll be in that Studebaker right in front of you boys."

* * *

The three members of the Emmett Dalton Gang followed Baby Face and his boys to a rundown shack about thirty miles outside St. Louis. Once they were all inside, Baby Face introduced them to the other three members of his gang. They were: Homer Van Meter, Tommy Carroll, and Eddie Green. Then Baby Face said, "And boys, these are the members of the Old Timers Gang."

The band of outlaws looked as though they were genuinely impressed.

Emmett was not.

"We don't go by that name, the Old Timers Gang," said Emmett. "We're the Emmett Dalton Gang."

Baby Face put out his hand for Emmett to shake, and Emmett did so. "Pleased to make your acquaintance."

Baby Face smiled. "Likewise, Mr. Dalton."

"So what do we do about the money, since we both sort of robbed that bank?" asked Jimmy.

"We'll split it, fifty-fifty," said Baby Face. "After all, we got nothin' but respect for you old guys."

The feeling was not mutual. Although Emmett was glad Baby Face came along and saved his ass, he was not particularly pleased about his having shot a handful of innocent people. Sure, Emmett shot people when he needed to, but this was something else; this was a fucking bloodbath, and Emmett wanted no part of it.

But what was done was done, and there wasn't a goddamn thing Emmett could do to change any of it.

CHAPTER SEVEN

MEETING DILLINGER

"Why don't we just go ahead and divide up the money now," said Emmett, lighting his cigar. "Then we'll be on our merry way."

"Don't worry about it," said Baby Face. "We can divide up the money in a bit. For now, why don't you boys kick back and relax. There's someone comin' that I want you to meet. I know he'll want to meet you."

This made Emmett uncomfortable. He liked being in control; he liked knowing what was happening. "What do you mean you want us to meet someone? Who?"

Baby Face said, "Relax, it ain't a trap or nothin'. We all look up to you older guys. I wouldn't set you up or nothin'. It ain't like I'm gonna be workin' with the Feds… I just robbed a bank today, and on top of that I done killed more of their FBI men than anyone in U.S. history, so I ain't no friend of Melvin Purvis and his goddamn G-Men."

"I wasn't thinkin' that," said Emmett. "I just don't like being in the dark here. I wanna know who I'm meeting."

"This guy's a bank robber like us. A real big fan of yours. Hell, we all feel the same way. I hope I'm still as spry and as crazy as you sons of bitches are when I'm your age."

Emmett enjoyed being complimented; it was nice hearing these things from a fellow bank robber with as much notoriety as Baby Face Nelson had.

"So, are you gonna tell me who we're meeting with, or not?" asked Emmett.

"Fine," said Baby Face. "I wanted it to be a surprise."

Emmett said nothing. He just puffed on that big old cigar of his.

Baby Face said, "His name's John Dillinger. Maybe you heard of him? He's gonna be here for a day. He uses this hideout sometimes, too."

* * *

Emmett and Jimmy sat and played cards with Baby Face and his boys. Tom mostly just sat in his wheelchair and smoked his cigarettes, telling everyone about the impending return of Jesus Christ. Nobody much wanted to hear about it, but everyone got a real kick out of hearing him curse as he did it. He was telling everyone a story about "that motherfucker Moses" when Eddie came in and said, "Dillinger's here."

Baby Face sat down his cards. "He just got here?"

"Yeah," said Eddie. "He's parking the car around back now."

Everyone stood up to greet him. A couple minutes later, Dillinger entered the room. He was as dapper and charismatic as Clark Gable, only more handsome, and with smaller ears. This was a man who could have been anything he'd wanted to be, and all he wanted was to be a bank robber. Emmett respected a man who had respect for the craft.

At first Dillinger didn't see Emmett and the boys standing there. He came in, hugged Baby Face, and said his hellos to Baby Face's crew. When he looked up and saw Emmett standing there, his expression was one of genuine awe. "Holy shit," he said. "You're Emmett Dalton."

Dillinger put out his hand for Emmett to shake, and Emmett did.

"You've said an awful lot of nice things about me in the papers," said Dillinger. "And I want you to know, I have a mutual respect for you old boys. You fellas been at this for a long, long time, and I just respect the hell out of that."

Before long, everyone had gone back to playing cards. Emmett and Dillinger sat facing each other, away from the card game, trading stories of past robberies.

"What kind of advice could you give a young buck like me?" asked Dillinger.

"I'm not as sharp at this shit as I used to be," said Emmett, "so I don't really know that I'm one to give advice. But I will say this—you shouldn't be using that tommy gun to shoot everybody up."

"I shouldn't?" asked Dillinger, smoking a cigarette.

"No, and I'll tell you why. You're too good for that. You're too classy for that. No offense intended to our present company, but the Thompson sub-machine gun is a classless weapon. Sure, it's handy in a wartime situation, but to take it into a bank and shoot the place up? It just reeks of classless amateurism."

Dillinger glanced over at Baby Face, lost in his card game. "Baby Face loves to shoot people," said Dillinger. "I don't much care for killing folks, but I've had to do it on occasion."

"Me too," said Emmett, puffing on his cigar. "But I always use a revolver. It's a more noble, more respectable weapon."

"I suppose you're right," said Dillinger, nodding. "Speaking of revolvers, I was wondering something: did you ever have a showdown with anybody back in the day? You know, one of those duels out in the dusty street like they always have on those cowboy radio shows."

"Nah, nothing like that," said Emmett, chuckling. "But I did have a second cousin, Lester, who got involved in one of those."

"What happened?"

"Lester ended up out in the graveyard," said Emmett. "The son of a bitch that shot him put a hole right through his eye. They had to have a closed-casket funeral. I never did like Lester that much, seein' as how he was kind of soft in the head. But it ain't right for a fella to shoot a man who ain't right in his head, you know?"

Dillinger nodded in agreement, hanging on Emmett's every word.

"Now I got a question for you," said Emmett.

"Okay," said Dillinger. "What is it?"

"'That story about your escapin' from the hoosegow with a gun made from a bar of soap—is that true?"

"Nah," said Dillinger. "It was actually a gun made of wood. Soap's a better story though."

"Still a neat trick."

"Thanks," said Dillinger. "Is it true you got shot more than twenty times when you and your brothers tried to rob them banks out in Kansas?"

"Yes, sir, it is. I took twenty-three bullets."

"And you lived. How remarkable."

"You boys," said Emmett. "You're a lot like we were. The 1890s and the 1930s ain't a whole lot different if you think about it. You guys are out here robbin' banks, same as we were. The only difference now is the technology. You boys got fancier guns and you get to drive away in an automobile instead of on horseback."

Dillinger, still looking at Emmett with admiration, asked, "Do you ever miss those old days?"

"Every fucking day," said Emmett.

"What do you miss most?"

"I know this is gonna sound silly comin' from an old bank robber like me, but it seems to me that people used to have more respect for one another. People said things like 'please' and 'thank you.' You ask me about things changin', where the hell do I begin? There's been so many big changes in these past forty years or so I can hardly keep up."

"I'm sure," said Dillinger. "I'll bet those Gatling guns were really something to deal with back in the day."

"Those were like our Thompson sub-machine guns," Emmett said. "Except you couldn't carry those sumbitches around with you. They had to sit on a tripod, but if you came face to face with one of those—like the Wild Bunch—you were deader than hell."

Dillinger said, "I love hearing these old stories, Emmett. You boys are really something. What the hell made you want to go back out there and rob banks again? Hell, it looked like you had it all—steady income, legendary status, pretty wife… Why'd you do it, Emmett?"

"Maybe I'm just too stupid to know any better," said Emmett, a big grin on his face.

"I'm serious."

"Well, I just missed it," said Emmett. "There ain't nothin' in this world like that thrill you get when you run into a bank with your gun out and you tell all those people what to do. There's nothing like that sense of control… It's just an incredible rush that's unlike anything I've experienced doing anything else. People used to say, Emmett, you've made it—you're a movie actor. People think that's the pinnacle of the thing, but the truth is, it ain't nowhere as fun as robbin' those banks was."

Dillinger nodded in agreement. "I know exactly what you mean. Hell, I've already made enough money to retire from this game, but it's in my blood now."

"Right," said Emmett.

"It's there, and it don't leave. You know, I even have dreams about robbing banks when I go to sleep at night. I tell you, that kind of thing makes my pecker harder than a pretty woman."

Emmett chuckled. He knew exactly what Dillinger meant. He felt exactly the same way.

CHAPTER EIGHT

MELVIN PURVIS TAKES A STAND

FBI special agent Melvin Purvis was just a regular guy, just like anyone else. Sure, the newspapers made him out to be some larger-than-life crime-buster, but he was just a normal blue-collar working man. One time a newspaper reporter had asked Melvin, "What makes you tick?" To this, Melvin had replied, "I love my job." And he did. Not because it made him feel powerful or because it gave him the sense of control robbing banks gave Emmett Dalton. No, he just loved doing something he was good at.

And he *was* good.

He was the best when it came to apprehending the nation's most wanted robbers and killers.

His boss at the Federal Bureau of Investigations, J. Edgar Hoover, wasn't his biggest fan, and Melvin had no idea as to why. He sensed it was because Hoover wanted all the recognition and glory Melvin was getting. And Melvin really couldn't understand such a thought, considering he himself hated that particular aspect of his job. He wasn't a particularly gifted speaker, so he loathed talking to the press. And when people told him their children looked up to him as a hero, he only shook his head in dismay.

He was no hero.

Babe Ruth was a hero.

Franklin D. Roosevelt was a hero.

But Melvin Purvis was just a regular man who happened to be very good at his job. End of story.

Today word had come down directly through Hoover that Purvis was to now move the Emmett Dalton Gang up into the FBI's top ten most wanted list, as they had only yesterday been responsible for a handful of deaths in a bank robbery down in St. Louis.

"Geez, how old are those guys?" Purvis had asked.

"Age hasn't got shit to do with it, Purvis," said Hoover. "Those rotten S.O.B.s are running around in cahoots with Baby Face Nelson, which makes them just as deadly as he is. These are men who kill with no remorse, and who rob whatever they can get their greedy little hands on. They must be stopped at once. Surely you can accomplish this, Purvis. As you said, they're old men."

Melvin hated when Hoover talked to him like that. Hoover always spoke with disdain and a holier-than-thou haughtiness Melvin couldn't abide. Here he was, out here doing everything in his power to accomplish every goal Hoover set out for him, and Hoover showed no appreciation whatsoever.

Fuck Hoover.

Melvin didn't do this because he wanted to please his boss.

He did it because he loved his job.

* * *

It was three o'clock in the afternoon when they held the press conference. There were a good twenty-five reporters in attendance, all of them there to hear what Melvin Purvis had to say.

"Today we're here to announce that we're adding the bank robbers known as the Emmett Dalton Gang, a.k.a. the Old Timers Gang, to the FBI's most wanted list," explained Purvis into the microphone. "We will begin a manhunt at once to apprehend these cold-blooded killers, who just this week were responsible, or at least partly responsible, for the deaths of nearly twenty people in a bank robbery down in St. Louis, Missouri."

"How old are those guys?" asked one reporter.

"It is true that these men are older," said Purvis, "but age has nothing to do with this. Certain privileges come with advanced age, but the right to rob and kill people is not one of them."

Another reporter spoke up. "Will there be a reward set for these men?"

"There will be a reward for any information leading to the arrest of these fellas," explained Purvis. "The amount has yet to be determined, but it will be substantial."

"Are these the oldest men ever to be put on the FBI's most wanted list?"

Purvis smiled. "I think that's safe to say." Everyone in the room laughed.

"How many murders are these men responsible for?" someone asked.

"We figure them for about twenty-five murders," explained Purvis.

"And how many robberies have they committed so far?"

"They've committed at least four robberies."

"How can you be sure you'll get them?" asked one reporter. "I mean, no offense, but you haven't been able to catch Baby Face Nelson or Dillinger or the Barrows Gang yet."

"We're very close to apprehending all these different groups," said Purvis. "Because of the secretive nature of our investigations, I can't really divulge much more than that at this time."

A reporter in the back asked, "How do you intend to catch these groups of killers and robbers?"

"We will ultimately win this war on crime," said Purvis, "through highly-sophisticated scientific techniques and superior leadership. The FBI will not stop hunting these groups of wanted felons until they are dead or in prison, I assure you that."

* * *

Emmett was sitting on the bed in a hotel in Chicago when he read about Melvin Purvis' declaring them as wanted fugitives on the FBI's most wanted list.

"Well, shit," he said. "At least they got our name right."

Jimmy sat in a chair, smoking his pipe. "I don't like it. This is serious. When the FBI gets involved, that's the big time. That's a whole 'nother animal there. Those G-Men don't stop coming, don't stop trying, until they catch their man. No, sir, I don't like it one bit."

Tom, enveloped in a cloud of cigarette smoke, said, "Maybe if somebody had kept his goddamn gun from going off, we wouldn't be in this predicament."

"What the hell is that supposed to mean?" asked Emmett.

"It meant maybe you should have kept your spurs from jingle-janglin' so much and tried not to shoot anybody and everybody that got in your way," said Tom. "I don't see Jimmy here blastin' up the

48

place, shootin' motherfuckers willy-nilly. No, sir, that's just you. I only shot one sumbitch and that was because I had no other choice."

"I didn't shoot anybody I didn't have to shoot," said Emmett, becoming defensive.

"How about that security guard back there in Coffeyville?" asked Tom. "Why'd you shoot him? Because of your pride? Because you couldn't let an old man talk a little shit without putting a goddamn hole in him?"

"I'm listening to you talk shit," said Emmett, "and I haven't shot you yet."

Tom just stared at him. "I suspect the day will come when you do."

"You know," said Emmett, "I resent this bullshit. It's not like I shot up all those people back there in St. Louis. That was Baby Face."

"And why'd he shoot 'em?" asked Tom. "Because your dumb ass got locked inside the vault. All of this is your fault. Do you see a recurring theme here, Emmett? Everything fucked up that happens is always your fault."

Emmett took a deep breath and tried to diffuse the situation. "Why don't you just smoke your cigarette and get some rest," said Emmett. "I'm sure everything will look a whole lot sunnier in the morning."

To this, Tom said, "Why don't you go fuck yourself?"

And that was that.

CHAPTER NINE

THE CHICAGO JOB

"There's lots of banks in Chicago," observed Emmett. "We should be able to find one and make a nice payday for ourselves."

"Where you figure we'll head after this?" asked Tom, smoking his millionth cigarette of the day.

"I dunno," said Emmett. "Maybe we'll take a vote."

When they reached Chicago, they drove around looking at all the banks, finally settling on one called the West Town State Bank. This decision wasn't based on anything more than Jimmy and Tom's saying it "felt right," but Emmett figured he'd let them have their way since they were starting to question his decisions.

After that, they went back to the Drake Hotel, where they were staying. Emmett parked the Model A in the lot beside the hotel. He and Jimmy then assisted Tom with getting out of the automobile and getting situated in his wheelchair.

"What do we do with the bags of money?" asked Jimmy.

"We'll leave 'em in the Ford," said Emmett.

Jimmy scratched his head, unsure about this. "You think that's a good idea?" "I think it'll be just fine. We'll just push the bags down under the seats where they're out of sight. Besides, in a swanky place like this, no one's gonna be after our money."

* * *

As they were walking into the hotel, Jimmy asked Emmett, "What are you gonna do with your share of the money?" Emmett had no answer for it. "I already got money. Maybe I'll give it to the poor people. God knows with this depression on, there's enough of 'em out there."

"Piss on 'em," said Tom, rubbing his yellowing stubble. "Maybe they wouldn't be poor if they'd get off their asses and do something to fix their situation. That's what Jesus says."

"Jesus says 'piss on 'em'?" asked Emmett.

No response.

"Well, I'm gonna buy a new Stetson," said Jimmy. "One of them nice fedoras all the dapper dandies are wearin' now. How about you, Tom? What are you gonna buy?"

"I don't know that I need anything money could give me other than a little companionship with a pretty lady, and even then, I'm seventy-five fuckin' years old, so what good's that gonna do me?" He paused, thinking for a minute. "I don't reckon there's anything I really need that I don't already have."

* * *

They idled the car up in front of the West Town State Bank at just after ten. Tom was using the two-by-four to drive, with a sawed-off shotgun sitting between his legs. Emmett and Jimmy prepared to jump out, pistols in their hands.

Tom led the group in prayer. This time there were no interruptions.

"Alright, old man," said Emmett. "We'll be right back. You stay here and keep watch. You see anybody doing anything they shouldn't oughta be doin', you either blast 'em with this shotgun or fire off a round so we'll know something's goin' down. Got it?"

Tom looked annoyed. "This ain't my first trip to the rodeo, sonny."

Emmett looked at Jimmy. "I guess it's time."

The two men climbed out of the Ford, their pistols down at their sides. They managed to slip through the pedestrians on the street unnoticed, and soon they were entering the bank. There was an old security guard, probably about Emmett's age—*why were they all so damned old?*—sitting in a wooden chair to the right. Emmett pointed his pistol at the guard, and the guard did nothing; he just sat there. Once Jimmy was in the door and had the security guard covered, Emmett announced, "This is a goddamn robbery! Everybody get down on the ground now! Anybody don't do what they're supposed to be doin' catches a bullet, you got it?"

Everyone got down. There were only a handful of customers, all men and women, no children, in the place. There were approximately ten employees counting the security guard now lying on the floor by the door.

51

Emmett approached the counter. "Where's the bank manager?"

"Hello," said one of the men, smiling. "I'm Edward."

"You're the manager?"

"Yes, sir," said Edward.

"Okay, Ed, what I need you to do is to open that vault and get us as much money in bags as you can within a minute." Emmett turned around to address everyone else. "Anybody hits the alarm, Edward here buys the farm. Any questions?"

No questions.

Emmett came around the counter and walked to the vault with Edward, who was still smiling. He unlocked the old vault, and pulled it open.

"You probably shouldn't be doing this, mister," said Edward.

"No shit," said Emmett. He waved his pistol at the man. "Get in there and get me my money."

Edward just grinned. "If you say so."

Edward entered the vault and bagged up the money. As he did so, Emmett turned and scanned the room. Everyone was doing exactly what they were supposed to be doing.

Now this is how you rob a goddamn bank, thought Emmett.

Emmett looked down at his watch and told Edward, "Time. Gimme what you got." Edward handed over three sacks of cash.

"Now what?" asked Edward.

"You stay here in the vault," said Emmett, closing the door on him. He then turned to the rest of the room. "You all just got robbed by the Emmett Dalton Gang. When the cops come and ask you who done this, you be sure and tell 'em that—the Emmett Dalton Gang, you got it?"

And Emmett and Jimmy went out the door. They ran through the pedestrian traffic on the sidewalk, carrying guns and bags of cash. No one paid them any mind whatsoever.

* * *

After the robbery, Emmett and the boys went to the show and watched *Duck Soup*. Then they went out to eat at a place called the Triangle Restaurant. As they dined on celebratory T-bone steaks, they talked themselves up about the job they'd just pulled.

"I thought that went pretty well," said Jimmy.

"It seemed a little too easy," said Tom. "I dunno, just didn't feel right."

This pissed Emmett off as the entire reason they had robbed that particular bank had been because Tom and Jimmy thought it "just felt right." But now Tom was saying it felt wrong. Here Emmett had done a good deed in breaking Tom out of the rest home, and all Tom ever did was bitch and moan about anything and everything. Hell, he had even complained about the picture show they'd selected, saying Jesus Christ didn't like comedies.

Fuck Tom, Emmett thought. *Who gives a shit what he thinks?*

From now on, things were gonna be different. From now on, Emmett was gonna make it clear who the goddamn boss was around this place. This was his gang, and by God he wasn't about to take any crap off an old washed-up, never-was asshole like Tom Pickett.

"What do you mean it doesn't feel right?" asked Emmett.

"Didn't you notice how no one put up a fight?" asked Tom. "That ain't normal. They just stared at you and handed over the money."

Emmett felt himself getting short with Tom. "Look," he said, "we finally had a good robbery, and here you are complainin' about it. That ain't exactly normal either."

"I'm not complaining," said Tom. "I was just pointing out that it all seemed a little too easy. It made me feel funny, that's all."

Emmett was still annoyed. In fact, he wasn't really in the mood to be around either of the old men. Both of 'em acted like they knew every damn thing, and Emmett was still peeved at Jimmy for not telling him about all the baggage that came with Tom's grouchy old crippled ass. Although he had barely touched his steak and baked potato, Emmett dismissed himself from the table. "I'm gonna step outside and get some air," he said. "Have me a cigar."

Emmett stood up, folded his napkin, sat it over his plate, and walked out of the restaurant.

Jimmy looked at Tom. "Something's the matter with him."

"Well," said Tom. "He'd better get it corrected real fast, or else he's liable to get us all shot to hell in one of these piss-poorly-planned robberies of his."

"Agreed."

And that was all they said.

CHAPTER TEN

THE SYNDICATE

The morning started out shitty, and only managed to get worse from there. First, Emmett had gone down to the lobby to get a copy of the *Chicago Daily News*. The story about yesterday's bank robbery was splashed across the front page. The headline read: "OLD TIMERS GANG STRIKES AGAIN!" Right off the bat this irritated Emmett; the newspapers were still referring to them as the Old Timers Gang.

Jimmy was sitting on the edge of the bed, looking at the article. "Maybe we should just go with it," he said. "There are worse things to be called than the Old Timers Gang."

"To hell with that," said Emmett. "We're not the Old Timers Gang, goddammit. We're the Emmett Dalton Gang."

"Why does this matter so much to you?" asked Tom, smoking a cigarette.

Emmett felt the blood rushing to his face. "It just does," he said. "I did everything I was supposed to do. I'm supposed to be a legend now. People are supposed to know my name."

"Oh, they know your name," said Jimmy. "They think of you as the leader of the Old Timers Gang, the guy who forgot to put the bullets in his gun—the guy who got locked inside a vault."

"I don't wanna think about that right now," said Emmett.

Jimmy gave him an unhappy look. "Neither do I."

"What are you saying?"

Jimmy shrugged. "It's a little bit embarrassing."

Emmett was getting heated. "What? You don't think I'm cut out to be the leader of this gang?"

"I never said that," said Jimmy.

"Nah," said Tom. "He didn't say that."

Emmett said, "But you were thinking it."

"God as my witness, I wasn't. I swear."

"Maybe it's you who thinks you ain't cut out for this," observed Tom.

Emmett could feel himself becoming more and more angry by the second. He was embarrassed, and as a proud man, this made him feel even more angry. Unsure what to say, Emmett stormed out of the room and went back downstairs to the lobby.

I'm cut out to be the leader, he thought. *I'm the one that put this damn gang together.*

* * *

"The man's got issues," said Tom. "I'm not sure he's cut out for this."

Jimmy didn't want to talk about it. "I think he's fine. He's just a little rusty is all."

"A little rusty?" asked Tom, laughing now. "A little rusty don't explain robbin' that bank without any bullets. Bein' rusty don't explain rushing into a robbery without any planning whatsoever. And what about the vault thing? It's more than that. These mistakes he's makin' are big goddamn mistakes. Back in the day, those mistakes woulda got the man shot."

Jimmy looked at him. "What are you saying? You think we should shoot him?"

"Hell no," said Tom. "Shit, I'm too old for that. I'd rather just relax and not shoot anybody."

"So you think we should just go along with him?"

"How bad do you wanna be a bank robber?"

Jimmy said, "Real bad."

Tom tried to blow a smoke ring, but messed it up and it dissipated. Then he turned back to Jimmy and said, "I guess we go along to get along. We let Emmett be the boss, and hope to hell he don't get us locked up in the damn hoosegow or worse."

Jimmy looked down at the newspaper again, thinking that the Old Timers Gang wasn't really so bad a name after all.

* * *

Emmett and the boys were packing to leave the Drake when someone knocked at the door. Jimmy walked over to the door, his Peacemaker out, ready for the cops if it was them. He opened the door. There were three Italians standing there, all wearing gaudy suits. Jimmy knew at once they were gangsters.

"How can I help you?" asked Jimmy.

The short, fat one, obviously the leader, said, "You can start by letting us in."

It was at this moment Jimmy noticed one of the men was holding a gun, trained on him.

"And if I say no?" asked Jimmy.

"You won't like what happens next," the man said. "Let us in and everybody gets to walk out of here alive."

Tom spoke up from behind Jimmy. "Let the bastards in."

Jimmy lowered the Peacemaker and moved out of the way so the three men could enter.

"We need you to come with us," said the wop.

"Where we goin'?" asked Emmett.

The goon with the pistol held it up. "Does it matter?"

"I guess not," said Emmett. "Not when you put it like that."

Jimmy started to pick up the suitcase, but the man said, "Leave the suitcase."

"Why?"

The wop grinned. "Cause I said so. That a good enough reason for you?"

Jimmy shrugged.

"Now, we're all gonna take a walk down the stairs," said the wop, looking at Tom. "At least all of us that can walk. How the hell do you guys get him down there with his wheelchair?"

"There's an elevator," said Emmett.

"Ah," said the wop. "Okay, we're all gonna take the elevator and go downstairs. Then we're taking you to see the boss."

"Who's the boss?" asked Emmett.

"If you can't figure out who we are by now, then maybe you're as dumb as they say in the newspapers," said the man, sneering.

Emmett felt embarrassed and infuriated, but he kept his mouth shut.

The six men went to the elevator, got on, and rode it down to the first floor. They then left the hotel, and walked to two black

Model As. Emmett and the boys were instructed to split up, and they accompanied the gangsters. Where the hell they were going was anybody's guess. Nobody spoke in either vehicle, so there weren't a lot of clues.

* * *

Finally the vehicles stopped, one behind the other, outside a place called the Metropole Hotel on Michigan Street.

As they were getting out of the automobiles, Emmett asked, "This is where your boss is?"

The wop just muttered, "Shut your mouth and do as I say."

Once everyone was out of the Model As, the wop commanded them to walk. They went through the lobby, where no one so much as glanced at them walking with a pistol out, and got on the elevator. When they got to the top, they walked to a closed office door with a man standing outside.

"Hey Louie," said the wop. "We're here to see the boss."

Louie, a great big fella that looked like Jack Dempsey, nodded and opened the door for them. He then stood there in the door frame, taking up half of it, and none of the boys could see who was waiting inside. Just before entering, Tom had a strange thought—he wished Al Capone hadn't gotten shipped off to prison for tax evasion two years before because, as Tom thought, if they had to die, at least they could have met Al Capone first.

When they entered the office, which looked as nondescript as any office ever did, there was a man with big, broad shoulders sitting behind a desk, smoking a cigarette. To his left was another guy, who looked a little too intelligent to be just another dumb goon.

The man behind the desk stood and walked around it with his hand out for Emmett to shake. "Hello, Mr. Dalton."

"Hello," said Emmett, shaking his hand.

"Have a seat," the man directed. "My name is Frank Nitti." He then turned to the man on his left. "And this is my associate, Paul Ricca."

"Why are we here?"

Nitti smiled, and waved at the seats. "Like I said, have a seat, fellas."

Nitti sat back down at the desk now, his hands folded in front of him, staring at them with a big smile on his face. "The way I see it, you owe me $20, 376 plus the vig."

Emmett sat forward in his seat. "Why's that?"

"Because that's how much you stole from me."

"At the bank?" asked Jimmy.

"At the bank," said Nitti.

Emmett said, "We got $20,376? Hell, we hadn't even counted it yet."

Nitti just kept smiling. "If you know who I am, or know who we are, then you'll understand why this is a predicament. When people steal from us, examples have to be made."

Emmett and Jimmy looked at each other.

"We had no idea that was your money in that bank," said Emmett. "Honest."

Nitti asked, "How would you have?"

"No way we could have."

"Occupational hazard, I guess," said Nitti.

Now Tom spoke up, jonesing from not having had a smoke in twenty minutes. "So what the hell is it you want?"

"Just the money," said Nitti.

"We don't have it here," said Emmett. "It's back at the hotel."

"We already have the money."

Jimmy asked, "You do?"

"Yes, Mr. McDaniels, we do," said Nitti. "It was in your car, which I might add is an awfully stupid place to leave that much money."

Emmett had a thought. "How much did you take?"

"All of it," said Nitti. "Every last dime."

"What?" asked Emmett. *"You took all our money?"*

"As I said, Mr. Dalton, the $20,376 was the amount you owed us."

"And the rest?" asked Tom.

Nitti grinned big. "Let's call it a little something extra."

Emmett asked, "For what?"

"For not killing you fellas right here," Nitti said dryly.

Now Nitti's partner, Paul Ricca, spoke up. "Remember, you stole from the Syndicate. You got any idea how many men have died for doing the same? We're giving you the opportunity to walk away from here in one piece."

"Without our money?" asked Tom.

"Why would you allow us to live?" asked Emmett.

Nitti said, "Out of respect. You boys have been in the game for a long time, and we respect that, so we're gonna let you live."

Tom said, "Fuck you, Mr. Nitti," and spit on the floor.

The smiles fell away from Nitti and Ricca's faces.

Ricca pointed at Tom and turned to Emmett. "You better control the old man."

"Or else what?" demanded Tom.

Now Ricca sat forward, opening his jacket to reveal a pistol. "Or else you all get dead. What do you think of that?"

"I think you're nothing but a two-bit hood all dressed up in your father's fancy clothes," said Tom.

Ricca didn't say a word.

Nitti said, "I think we'd better end this meeting now so Mr. Pickett doesn't say something he might regret."

"So that's it?" asked Emmett.

"Pretty much," said Nitti, smiling again.

Emmett asked, "So you just brought us here to tell us you took our money?"

"I brought you here to tell you I wasn't gonna kill you," said Nitti, reaching into his jacket pocket. He then produced a leather wallet. He reached into the wallet and took out a twenty-dollar bill, tossing it on the desk.

"This should pay for a cab to take you boys back to your hotel," said Nitti. "Now do us both a favor and get the fuck out of here before I murder your old asses."

CHAPTER ELEVEN

BULLETS AND PRAYERS

A few months passed by, and Emmett and the boys became better robbers. The rust started to chip away, and they finally managed to get their shit together. But the thing that Emmett was most proud of was that he hadn't shot anybody since St. Louis. He'd winged a fella in Wichita Falls, but that was it. Things had gotten better with Jimmy and Tom, too. Their last six or seven robberies had gone off without a hitch, and nobody questioned Emmett's abilities any longer.

Jimmy had purchased himself a Stetson fedora, and Tom had gotten closer to "the Lord almighty, Jesus fucking Christ." Emmett had called home and learned that Julia was divorcing him on account of his robbing and killing people.

With both Jimmy and Tom alone and sick, and Emmett without a wife, none of them had anything else to live for but robbing banks. It was what they did, and it was who they were. Emmett had been an author and an actor; Jimmy had been a real estate agent; Tom had been a lawman. But today, they were all no-good bank robbers, and they loved every minute of it.

After Melvin Purvis had announced their inclusion onto the FBI's top ten most wanted list, the media had stopped making fun of them. No one called them the Old Timers Gang anymore, and nobody ever mentioned the mistakes Emmett had made when he'd first returned to the life.

All in all, things were good.

* * *

The Emmett Dalton Gang was about to rob the Federal Reserve Bank in Kansas City, Missouri. Here they were, in a stolen Ford coupe (they had to change vehicles as they weren't sure they could go on using Emmett's automobile, even with fake tags), brandishing several guns apiece, preparing to rob the place.

Again they sat idly on the curb in front of the bank, saying a group prayer. The bank would be opening in ten minutes, and they wanted to hit it right off the bat, bright and early.

"Dear God, we are your humble servants," lead Tom, drawing on his cigarette. "We love you and will obey you. Sure, we rob banks, but we try not to hurt anybody when we're doin' it. Hell, God, we haven't shot anybody in months now. So please watch over us, be with us, and be in us, as we prepare to rob these miserable sons of bitches of all their money. We know this is your will that the rich people lose their cash. So it is written, so it shall be done…"

And so on.

* * *

At that exact same moment, a fleet of cars containing members of the Federal Bureau of Investigations was heading towards the bank. Melvin Purvis was in the lead car, a Pierce-Arrow Silver Arrow, along with his right-hand man, Redd White.

"Let us say a little prayer before we go and catch these robbers," said Melvin. He and Redd both closed their eyes in prayer; Davis Demont did not, as he was driving through Kansas City traffic. "Dear Lord our father who art in heaven," said Melvin, "We ask that you be with us as we chase these bad men. We ask that you protect us, as we are your humble servants. Dear Lord, we ask that this lead we are following be one that is right and correct, and that we are able to apprehend these robbers with very little bloodshed today…"

And so forth.

* * *

As was the norm, Emmett was out front, with his .44-40 caliber Colt single-action revolver out and in the air. Today he was also carrying a .10-gauge shotgun in his other hand; he couldn't say why exactly, but his gut told him to bring it along, so he had. There were only a few customers in the place, as the bank had only just opened its doors a couple minutes before.

Emmett rushed through the bank towards the counter, his gun up, saying, "This here is a robbery. Anyone who doesn't wanna die today better lie down on the floor now and keep his or her hands where I can see 'em." As everyone started moving towards the floor, Emmett motioned to a blonde-haired bank teller with the shotgun. "Not you, honey. I need you to get out a couple of bank bags and fill 'em up with all the cash in these here drawers."

He looked back at Jimmy, who was doing just fine back by the door, his shotgun to the head of the security guard.

So far so good.

* * *

Melvin, Redd, and Davis pulled up in front of the bank. Melvin stepped out of the automobile, putting on his trademark white gloves. Redd prepared his Tommy gun—checked it, made sure it was loaded properly—and placed the weapon into his boss' gloved hands.

The other cars were now pulling up behind theirs. Melvin walked towards the FBI officers, all armed to the teeth, now getting out of their vehicles. He motioned for them to take different locations on the street in preparation for the bank robbers' emergence from the bank.

* * *

Tom was sweating like a motherfucker. He was only a car's length ahead of that goddamn Melvin Purvis, and he could see him back there, directing his men to take their positions around the bank.

Dear Lord, thought Tom, *Please forgive me for what I am about to do.*

He then switched gears, shifting out of park, used the two-by-four to accelerate slowly, and moved out into the street. As he drove off, he could see Purvis and his men scattering in every direction. No one paid him any mind whatsoever.

* * *

Emmett had the bank manager, a Mr. Carter, up against the wall next to the vault, his revolver in his mouth. "So help me God," Emmett said, "I will shoot you deader than Garfield if you don't open this motherfucking vault and get me my money."

Mr. Carter had no idea how close he was getting to becoming a bloody brain stain on the wall.

Emmett heard a piercing gunshot behind him. He swiveled, his revolver still in Mr. Carter's mouth. He now saw that a customer had tried to rush Jimmy, and Jimmy had been forced to shoot him down.

Fuck it.

These things happen.

Streaks were meant to be broken.

As Emmett was in motion, turning back towards Mr. Carter, a man stood up on the other side of the counter, a pistol in his hand, and fired. The bullet grazed Emmett's right shoulder. The shock caused Emmett to squeeze the trigger, making him shoot the bank manager. Mr. Carter started to slide down the wall, leaving a streak of blood and brains as he did. Now there came a third shot from behind Emmett. He spun just in time to see Jimmy blasting the man who had shot Emmett. The man flew back and bounced off the counter, falling out of Emmett's line of sight.

Now what?

With the bank manager dead, their chances of getting into that vault were slim to none. Emmett walked briskly back towards the blonde woman, sacking the cash from the drawers. "Who else knows the combination to that vault?" asked Emmett.

"No one," said the woman. "Honest."

Emmett raised his bloody pistol in her direction.

"I swear!" she yelled out.

He squeezed the trigger, and the woman went flying back against the counter, inadvertently flinging the money into the air as she fell.

"Let's get the fuck out of here!" yelled Jimmy.

* * *

When Melvin Purvis heard the shots inside, he knew his tip had been a solid one. He was still standing by the automobile, having not yet found a place to hide, when he saw the two robbers—Dalton and McDaniels—come running out of the bank. With no proper place to hide, Melvin was forced to crouch down between vehicles just ahead of them.

* * *

Emmett didn't understand.

"Where the fuck is Tom?" he screamed.

Jimmy was the first one to notice the FBI men scattered all around them, beginning to move out of their hiding places. *"The goddamn FBI!"* he shouted. He raised his shotgun in the direction of a cluster of them, and was immediately shot down.

* * *

Melvin stepped out from between the parked cars now. He wanted to be the one who took out Emmett Dalton. Again, this wasn't about Melvin's ego; it was about doing the finest job he could possibly do. He started moving towards Dalton, who didn't yet see him.

And then Dalton did the unthinkable. He dodged the bullets flying at him from across the road and jumped into a moving automobile on the passenger side. Melvin started to run now, trying to catch up to him, but it was no use.

Emmett Dalton went speeding past him.

* * *

"Please don't hurt me, mister," said the man driving the automobile.

To this, Emmett said, "Open up your door and jump out or else you die." To his credit, the man didn't hesitate. He just swung the door open and jumped out of the moving vehicle, falling hard to the pavement.

Emmett scooted over and took the wheel, stomping on the accelerator as he did. He looked back in the mirror, and saw nothing.

CHAPTER TWELVE

FACE OFF

After Emmett Dalton had raced past him in a hijacked Ford, Melvin Purvis had jumped back into his own vehicle, with Redd now driving. Melvin was clinging to the tommy gun tightly now, and his teeth were chattering. He wasn't afraid—no, he was *excited* now, perhaps the most excited he'd ever been.

They drove for a moment, gaining speed, before they saw the stolen automobile ahead, swerving in and out of traffic.

"I'm gonna try and take him here," said Melvin.

Redd turned to him. "*Here?* It's awfully goddamn busy here, boss."

"Maybe, but it all stops today."

* * *

Emmett was weaving in and out of traffic, pushing the automobile up to its max at sixty-five miles per hour. He almost got nailed by oncoming traffic several times, but always managed to find his way back into his own lane at just the right moment to avoid collision.

He looked back in his rear view mirror now, and he saw them. The bastards were back there. Of course it was still a hell of a distance, but he swore it looked like Melvin Purvis himself there in the Silver Arrow. But what the hell was he doing? He could see clearly that the man was now hanging himself out the passenger side window.

* * *

The wind was in Melvin's face. He had to squint to see, but he could still make out that bastard Emmett Dalton up there ahead of them.

"Speed up," he ordered to Redd.

Redd said, "I'm going as fast as I can. This sucker won't go any faster!"

Now Melvin saw Emmett slow down for a moment to avoid a collision. Melvin raised the barrel of the Tommy gun, aiming it towards the stolen car, and he squeezed the trigger.

* * *

Emmett figured out what the hell Purvis was doing just a millisecond before the federal agent opened fire on him. A hail of bullets struck the Ford, but none of them touched Emmett. Stunned and confused, he swerved the vehicle, scraping up against an oncoming automobile on his left.

Emmett had to think fast now. He made himself focus. Once he had his bearings about him again, he pulled the steering wheel hard to the right. The Ford jumped up over the curb, scraping its side along several store fronts. Emmett very nearly struck a woman walking on the sidewalk, but luckily she dove out of the way at the very last second.

Emmett couldn't see shit from where he was.

He stomped the brake and slid the thing into park.

He jumped out of the car, the Colt in his right hand, the shotgun in his left. Seeing the entrance to a diner only a couple feet away, he jumped from the vehicle and ran towards it.

* * *

What the hell was Emmett Dalton doing? Melvin watched him swerve to the right and jump up over the curb. At first he thought he'd hit him, but then the Ford ground to a halt up ahead. Melvin squeezed the trigger again, and the Tommy gun sprayed bullets all over the automobile. Much to Melvin's chagrin, he didn't hit Dalton. Just before the spray of bullets reached the left side where Dalton had been, the robber leaped from the vehicle into a store.

As Redd and Melvin approached, Melvin could see now that it was a diner.

The cocksucker was in there.

"Stop here!" ordered Melvin.

He could hear screams from inside the diner.

* * *

No one in the diner knew how to react when they saw the commotion followed by Emmett's barreling in, carrying the two guns. Someone screamed, and several others dove onto the floor. A few people stood and ran towards the entrance.

Emmett reached out and snatched a heavyset woman trying to run past him. He put the Colt to her head and said, "Don't try anything funny. I'll shoot."

* * *

When Melvin got to the entrance of the diner, a smattering of people came running out past him. Through the crowd he could just make out Emmett Dalton moving back towards the back of the place with a woman in his arms.

Melvin turned to Redd. "You ready?"

"Sure thing, boss," said Redd.

Melvin led the way, walking calmly past people running, the Tommy gun out in front of him. He could now see Emmett Dalton clearly. He had a Colt revolver up to a woman's head.

Melvin kept moving towards him, slowly and confidently.

Dalton was backed into a corner. Right then and there Melvin decided that the hostage could live or die, but he was killing or apprehending Emmett Dalton today, no matter what.

Dalton panicked, readjusting the Colt so Melvin could see it clearly. "Try any shit and this woman dies," said Dalton.

"Let's you and I have a talk," said Melvin.

Dalton didn't know how to react to this. *"What the hell?"* he said.

"We're just gonna talk this thing out."

Dalton's eyes narrowed to slits, and he looked at Melvin, trying to figure out what the hell was happening.

"My name is Melvin Purvis."

"I know," said Dalton. "I saw you in the newspapers."

"And I see your picture plastered all over my office walls," said Melvin.

Dalton readjusted the pistol again. "I'm telling you—I'll shoot this broad."

Melvin smiled. "I believe you, Mr. Dalton."

"If you want this woman to live, you gotta let me outta here."

"That's never gonna happen."

The woman's eyes got big and she looked even more terrified now than she had before.

"This man to my right has the unfortunate name of Redd White," said Melvin.

Dalton looked at Redd, aiming a rifle at him.

"Old Redd here is a sharpshooter. If I tell him to take you out, he's gonna take you out. Do you understand?"

"Fuck you," managed Dalton.

At that moment the hostage elbowed Dalton in the ribs, and managed to break free. Before Dalton could react, both Melvin and Redd shot him. Caught in the hail of sub-machine gun bullets, Emmett Dalton's body danced rhythmically for a moment before finally falling to the ground.

And Emmett Dalton was no more.

THIRTEEN

CONCLUSION

After concluding his speech about the deaths of Emmett Dalton and Jimmy McDaniels, Melvin Purvis took questions from the reporters who filled the room. "How many members of the Emmett Dalton Gang are still at large?" asked one.

Melvin said, "We're not sure. There may be one man still out there, there may be two. We have no knowledge at this time as to who the other members of Emmett Dalton's gang were."

* * *

Tom Pickett had a hell of a time transferring himself out of the automobile into his wheelchair without assistance. It took over an hour, but finally he was back in his wheelchair, strapped in and safe.

He'd parked a block away so no one would see the stolen automobile. It took all the strength he had, but he managed to wheel himself around the block, smoking one last cigarette as he did so.

As he wheeled himself up towards the entrance to Sunnyvale Rest Home, he saw a familiar face approaching. It was Charlene, one of the nurses who worked there. "Tom Pickett, where in the blazes have you been?" she asked. "We been worried sick about you. We thought you was kidnapped."

Pretending to have dementia, Tom feigned ignorance. "Do I know you?"

And this is how Tom Pickett lived to be seventy-eight years old.

RIDING SHOTGUN

DAY ONE

Joe Gibson arrived home from his trip, exhausted. It had been a long fucking day. As he made his way through the house, he had no sense that anything was out of the ordinary. When his wife didn't answer, he thought nothing of it. Maybe she hadn't heard him.

When Joe walked into the kitchen, he had no choice but to see things the way they were. He saw the three men standing around her, pistols in their hands. He looked to Denise, tied up and gagged, sitting in the kitchen on a wooden dining room chair. Her hair still wet from her shower, she wore a silk robe, closed so Joe couldn't see if she had anything on underneath.

Caught off guard, he could do nothing to help his wife before being struck in the back of the head with the pistol of the fourth man—the one he hadn't seen. Joe fell to the floor, hitting his head on the kitchen cabinet as he went down. On the floor, confused, disoriented, in shock and in pain, no idea what the fuck was happening. He had blood in his eyes. He tried to raise himself, wiping away the blood with his arm.

The fourth man was on him again, kicking him in the side. More pain, and Joe found himself on the ground again. He looked up at the men through blurry eyes. "What the fuck?" he said, the men laughing at him.

Now Joe got a good look at the men for the first time, but recognized no one. They were dressed identically, each wearing an expensive-looking suit with no tie, a dress shirt beneath opened at the top. They each wore black leather gloves. The clothes looked out of place on these men, each of whom looked rough and rugged like cons. One of the men was a big muscular Mexican (about fifty years old) with a hideous v-shaped scar reaching down from above his left eyebrow through an apparently dead eye (complete with a tattooed teardrop) to his cheek and back up past the eyebrow to his forehead. Joe knew nothing concrete about this menacing man and yet he had the sense he was a stone cold killer.

The second man, a forty-something white guy with a pockmarked cop face and slicked-back black hair, was stocky with a build equal parts muscle and fat. He looked like a mean sonofabitch.

The third man was dark black with wild Don King hair and big, crazy wide eyes. Wiry, younger than the others, something about him suggested he'd just been released from prison.

The fourth man—the dirty bastard who'd struck Joe from behind and kicked him in the side—was a tall, gangly white guy with a high forehead, bug eyes, long hair, and a skinny head. He looked like Ichabod Crane from that old *Sleepy Hollow* cartoon. Joe figured him for about forty-five, and found him to be extremely creepy.

Looking at Denise, her beautiful eyes now big and afraid, filled with tears, staring at him, Joe felt re-energized. He scrambled to his knees in the hopes of rushing the men, but Ichabod kicked him back to the floor. Joe whirled around quickly to find himself face to face with the barrel of the man's pistol. His eyes moved upward to Ichabod's face. He could see clearly this man wanted to shoot him. "Do it," the man said, practically begging. "Go ahead and try that shit."

"Now, now," said Pockmarked Cop Face. "No need for that. I'm sure Mr. Gibson will do exactly as he's asked. Isn't that right, Joe?"

Joe looked at Denise sitting there helplessly, gagged and tied, her eyes pleading for him to save them both. He looked at Ichabod, his pistol still aimed at his face. Fuck. He felt like a pussy, but he could do nothing. Attacking the men now would be foolish and would only endanger Joe and his wife. No, he thought, he would wait until the right opportunity presented itself. Then, when he could get the drop on one of them, he would just have to hope for the best.

"All you gotta do is keep your fucking mouth shut and listen to what I have to say, Joe," Pockmarked Cop Face said, clearly enjoying the sound of his own voice. "Now I don't want to be unfriendly— especially when I'm a guest in someone else's home. It's just that we have a lot of ground to cover. So if I come across as anything less than cordial, I hope you'll forgive me. First we gotta get one thing straight—you make any wrong moves or try any Bruce Willis hero shit, things are gonna get real ugly real quick."

Pockmarked Cop Face caressed Denise's cheek with his pistol. "I'd hate to have to kill your wife, Joe."

The two men's eyes locked for a moment, Joe glaring so intently the man's smile fell away. "You hurt her," Joe said, "and I'll kill you. Maybe not today, maybe not tomorrow, but you will die."

This caused the other three gunmen to laugh hysterically. Pockmarked Cop Face didn't find it funny. "Big words coming from a guy who's on his knees with a gun to his head, don't ya think? We could all take turns raping your wife and I don't think there's a damned thing you could do about it, Joe." This caused the men to laugh harder.

The big Mexican spoke up. "I just got out of the joint, man. I could go for that." Pockmarked Cop Face looked to the Don King-looking motherfucker, who grabbed his crotch and said, "Sure, I'd fuck her." This caused the men to burst into laughter again. Finally Pockmarked Cop Face raised his hand, signaling them to stop.

He looked at Joe. "Let's skip the bullshit, Joe. No one's gonna rape your old lady. That's not why we're here. You keep cool and everything's gonna be just fine."

"Who are you?"

"Who I am is the asshole who's got you by the balls, friend. And I'm here to offer you an opportunity."

Joe's eyes narrowed. *"Opportunity?"*

"Yes. The opportunity for you to do something for us."

"Why would I want to do anything for you?"

"Good question. You know what interests me? Motives. The reasons people do the things they do. I'm big on motives, Joe, and right now you need one. Why would you do anything for us? I'll give you two reasons."

"Okay?"

"The first is right here." Pockmarked Cop Face aimed his .45 at Denise's head. "And the second reason? The second reason got out of school at three o' clock."

And for the first time since all of this began, Joe remembered his daughter, Emily. The realization washed over him, and he felt guilty for not having noticed her absence sooner. But he'd been startled, and a lot had happened in the passing of the last five minutes. Joe felt his eyes filling up with tears. "Where is she?"

"Don't worry," said Pockmarked Cop Face. "She's safe."

"Please don't hurt her." Joe heard himself speak, surprised by the desperation in his voice.

"If you do what I ask you, there shouldn't be any problems. You ever play *Simon Says*, Joe? Sure you have. Okay, I'm Simon. That pretty much makes you my bitch. That means I tell you to do something—*anything*—you better damned well do it. Normally there's no prize in Simon Says, but we got us here a high stakes game, Joe. Go ahead, ask me what the prize is." He stared at Joe, but Joe said nothing. "Maybe you're thinking it's a new car. Is it a new car, Don Pardo?"

"No," Ichabod said, getting into the act. "It ain't a new car."

Joe stared at his wife, making eye contact with her, trying to tell her everything would be all right.

"Maybe an all-expense paid trip to the Bahamas?" said Pockmarked Cop Face.

"No," said the Don King-looking motherfucker. "It ain't that shit, neither."

"You know what the grand prize is, Joe? It's your eight-year-old daughter's life. If you don't do exactly what I tell you, little Emily goes down for the dirt nap."

"What do you want me to do?"

Pockmarked Cop Face smiled. "I'm gonna leave you with a folder. It'll be inside your car, underneath the driver's side floor mat. Inside that folder you will find a photograph of a man—a very bad man—and the address and room number of the hotel where he'll be staying, as well as a complete itinerary of his visit to New York."

Joe didn't understand. "What does he have to do with me?"

"Nothing. And everything."

"What does that mean?"

"It means that, as of now, he has absolutely nothing to do with you. But your futures are inextricably intertwined, Joe. You see, you're going to kill him."

Joe didn't understand what he was hearing. *"What?"*

"Murder him. Terminate with extreme prejudice. Take his life. Cash in his chips. Make him have one really bad fucking day."

"Why me? I'm no killer."

"Precisely the reason. Who's gonna suspect you? You've never met the guy and you don't have a criminal record."

"But I'm just a writer."

"Yes, but a mystery writer. You think up these murders and then figure out where the killers make their mistakes. Who better to plan the perfect murder than a mystery writer?"

Joe shook his head and looked desperately at his wife. "That's ridiculous. Okay, at least tell me one thing."

"Okay?"

"Out of everyone in New York City, how did you select *me*?"

Pockmarked Cop Face smiled big. "Your lucky day, Joe. I'm told it was almost completely random."

"Why don't you just kill this guy yourself?"

"I represent a party who would love nothing more than to see this man's name in the obituary column. However, for business reasons, we cannot be directly involved with any attempts on his life. So we found you."

"The man you want killed, what does he do?"

"Fuck you care what he does? Your only concern should be getting your daughter home in one piece."

Joe looked at Denise. "What if I die trying to do this thing?"

Pockmarked Cop Face grinned. "You'd better not."

"Or what?"

"We'll kill Emily."

Joe kept his mouth shut, took a moment to collect his thoughts. "Will this man be alone when I go to the hotel?"

"No. He'll be surrounded by more dicks than Jenna Jameson in a gangbang flick."

"And what am I supposed to do about them?"

"Be resourceful."

"What does that mean?"

"Kill anyone who gets in your way."

"When is this supposed to happen?"

"You have a day to prepare. You kill him in two days. It cannot be the next day or the day after. No extenuating circumstances."

"And after I've killed him?"

"You wait by the phone. Once we've confirmed that you've taken him out, you'll receive a call telling you where to pick up your daughter."

"What do I tell the police about Emily? I have to tell them something."

"You tell 'em a bunch of niggers broke in and held you and your wife at gunpoint as they rifled through your belongings. Tell 'em they kidnapped your little girl but didn't say shit about where they were taking her or why."

"They're not gonna believe that."

"Why?"

"Because it sounds like bullshit. What was I supposed to be doing while all of this was happening?"

Pockmarked Cop Face laughed. "Same thing you're doing now. Tell 'em you tried to fight the men off and they shot you in the shoulder."

"*What—?*"

Before Joe could finish, Pockmarked Cop Face shot him in the shoulder. Joe screamed out, the force of the bullet knocking him back. The pain was excruciating.

"Now, are you clear on what you're supposed to do?"

Joe nodded, holding his bleeding shoulder. "Crystal."

"I want you to know that we're not fucking around."

"I don't think you are."

Pockmarked Cop Face grinned. "I think you do. Before I leave, I'm going to prove to you that we're serious." He paused for a moment. "Here's what you do: When the cops come, you tell them you got shot in the shoulder. Then you tell them the jigs shot your wife in the head and killed her."

In the brief millisecond between Joe's hearing the words and comprehending what they meant, the man raised his pistol to Denise's head. Joe lunged wildly, and again came the hard blow to the back of the head. And in that briefest of moments he saw the man fire a round into the side of Denise's head.

And the world went black.

DAY TWO

Detective Mertis Whitlock sat at his desk, nodding his head to *Tell Me Something Good* on the radio. He absently chewed at the ham-and-cheese loaf sandwich his wife had packed for him, occasionally dipping it in his cup of coffee, and looking at his new partner, Jillian, doing paperwork at an adjacent desk. A cute little white thing, twenty-six or twenty-seven years old, Mertis briefly considered flirting with her, but thought the better of it. Instead he said, "Something about Joe Gibson's report feels wrong."

Jillian looked up. "Which part?"

"Him saying he doesn't know who killed his wife and took his little girl."

"Yeah? Why?"

"I've been doing this job for a long time, and I can tell when someone's bullshitting me. Gibson was definitely bullshitting me."

"You think Gibson killed his old lady?"

"No, no, nothing like that. I think he's lying about it being four brothers, for one thing."

"Why is that?"

"The perps didn't steal anything," Mertis said. "They just came for the little girl."

"So?"

"In case you haven't noticed, brothers don't kidnap little white girls very often. It's not their M.O. And there's no ransom request. They just came by, popped Mrs. Gibson, and took the little girl? That shit doesn't make sense. Something doesn't add up."

"So what are you saying?"

"I think Gibson is full of shit. I think he can ID the guys who did this."

"Why would he lie?"

"Could be one of three reasons, as far as I can figure."

"Which are?"

"One, he's too scared to tell us the truth—afraid these guys might come back after him. Two, maybe he's working out a ransom deal with them in private. Three, maybe he's planning on going after these men on his own."

"He doesn't seem like the revenge type."

"No, he doesn't, which means it's gotta be one of the first two reasons. My gut tells me he's scared."

"Who could blame him?" Jillian asked. "Considering what they did to his wife, it's no wonder the guy is scared."

"No shit."

"So what are you gonna do?"

"I think I'll give him a day or so and stop back in and check on him, maybe try and get some answers."

* * *

Joe knocked on the door of his brother Billy's house. Billy wasn't home. He was upstate, serving out the second of a three-year B&E sentence. Today Joe was here to see Roberto, Billy's lover and sometimes partner in crime.

Roberto came to the screen door. Shirtless, with a big Puerto Rican flag tattoo visible on his chest, he opened the door just a crack and looked at Joe suspiciously. "What brings you to Red Hook, Joe?"

"I need some help."

Roberto's eyes narrowed. "We haven't heard from you in two years, man."

"I'm sorry. I've been busy."

"He's your brother. He misses you. You can't take an hour out of your busy schedule to go and visit him?"

"What can I say? I don't like seeing him behind bars."

"No one does. But you don't do it for yourself—you do it for Billy, so he knows we haven't forgotten him."

"You're right. I'll go see him."

Roberto opened the door just a little more. "You look like shit, Joe."

"What can I say? The past day has been pretty shitty."

"Everything okay?"

"Not really, but I don't want to talk about it."

"Fair enough. You said something about needing help?"

"I'm in a situation. I need guns."

Roberto laughed. "Then go to Wal-Mart."

"I'm serious. I need guns that are clean and untraceable."

"What you need guns for?"

"I'm going hunting."

"What kind of animal you hunting?"

"I can't tell you any more, Roberto. It's better for both of us that way."

Roberto nodded. "I'll set you up with a guy I know, he'll get you some guns. But you gotta promise to go see your brother soon."

"I will."

"You promise?"

"Cross my heart."

* * *

Joe met Roberto's friend, Bastard—presumably a nickname—at a seedy motel about ten minutes from Billy and Roberto's place. A heavyset black guy, Bastard looked like a defensive lineman. Inside the room, Bastard opened a big metallic case containing six different handguns. He removed each of the pistols, spreading them out on the bed.

Joe looked them over. He knew very little about guns, but two of them stood out, mainly because they looked badass.

Joe pointed to one of them. "May I?"

"Sure."

Joe picked up the big handgun, weighing it in his hand.

"You know anything about guns?" Bastard asked.

"Not a thing."

"That's a Smith & Wesson. They call that model the Governor. It fires either .45 rounds or .410 bore shotshells, your choice. It retails for about $700 new. I'll sell you this one for five bills."

"It's clean?"

Bastard grinned. "All my guns are clean."

"How powerful is this one?"

"The Governor is so powerful it'll drop a bear with a single shot, so just imagine what it would do to some knucklehead motherfucker on the street."

Joe nodded. With the gun still in hand, he pointed at another pistol. "And that one?"

"That there's the Beretta 96A1."

"Is it a .45?"

"Nah, the 96A1 is a .40 caliber handgun."

"As powerful as a .45?"

Bastard laughed. "She can knock a crackhead nigga out his shoes at a hundred feet."

"What does it cost?"

"The Beretta retails for about seven bills. I can sell you this one for $500, as well."

"I'll take 'em both."

DAY THREE

Joe finally nodded off early in the morning two days after the murder of his wife. He only slept for about forty-five minutes, but he slept nonetheless. His head hurt like hell, and he felt dull aches in both his shoulder and his heart. He missed his wife and daughter dearly. Just after waking, Joe allowed himself to cry for the first time since the men had shown up at his home and changed his life forever.

It rained heavily, which perfectly fit Joe's mood. Today would be the day he would kill a complete stranger. Joe recognized the man from the newspapers. Carlo Ventimiglia, an elderly man—some kind of Mafia boss from Chicago. Joe felt sick inside, and had serious doubts that he would survive to see his wife's funeral.

Two hours later, Joe found himself standing in the rain in front of the swanky hotel where Ventimiglia and his goons were staying. According to the file the bastards had left him, the gangster and his entourage had the entire second floor reserved. Joe looked at his watch and saw it was just after 10 a.m.. Noting a huge Catholic church on the corner, Joe turned and walked in that direction. He didn't consider himself a religious man, but he felt he could use a little religion on this particular day.

He stepped out of the rain and into the church, his heavy black raincoat concealing the two holstered handguns. Just after Joe entered the foyer, his coat dripping water all over the carpet, a young priest approached him. "Can I help you?" the priest asked.

"I'd like to confess my sins."

The priest smiled and said, "No problem," escorting him to the confessional. Joe stepped inside and sat down. The priest climbed into the opposite end of the confessional, speaking through the partition. "How long has it been since your last confession?"

"Forever."

"How long is that?"

"I've never confessed my sins before."

"Are you Catholic?"

"No, Father."

"What religious denomination are you?"

"I have no religious denomination."

"What brings you here today?"

"Special circumstances."

"Which are?"

"I'm about to kill some people, Father."

Joe could hear the shock in the priest's voice. "Excuse me?"

"I'm not happy about it, Father, but I have no choice."

"I see."

"So what do I do now?"

"Well, it's my hope that you might reconsider."

"No, I mean how many Hail Marys do I say?"

* * *

Joe entered the Hyperion Hotel just before eleven. According to the information he'd been given, Ventimiglia and his men would be leaving for a meeting at any moment. The hotel had a large lobby filled with seats and assorted plant life. Joe sat down in one of the plush seats, the only person in the lobby. A large baby grand piano sat silently to his left. A large fountain sat in the center of the room, nearly blocking Joe's view of the elevator. He kept to himself, watching the few people who littered the downstairs area of the hotel come and go. Thankfully, none of them looked like mob guys, and none of them seemed to pay him any mind at all.

Joe had been waiting for about ten minutes when the elevator doors opened and Ventimiglia's entourage came pouring out. Surrounded by goons—Joe counted four of them, all dressed in black suits—the feeble old man wore some sort of oxygen mask.

Now was the moment to act.

Do or die time.

Joe reached into his jacket, his right hand curling around the handle of the big Smith & Wesson. His other hand located the handle of the Beretta. He stood up, bringing out the guns in a single fluid motion. He still had not been seen thanks to the fountain.

Too frightened to think about what he was doing, Joe moved on autopilot. If he considered his actions, he would chicken out.

Joe moved to the right of the fountain, his right arm coming up, the Smith & Wesson settling on a target. He squeezed the trigger and the handgun came to life, dropping the gray-haired Mafioso walking just to the right of Ventimiglia. Joe moved his arm slightly to the left and squeezed the trigger again. The mobsters were aware of him now, and they were scrambling in different directions. A fat man to the left of Ventimiglia jumped in front of him, blocking Joe's shot. The bullet, intended for Ventimiglia, tore the man's throat apart.

A gunshot came from behind the old man, but it went wide and missed Joe by more than a foot. Joe fired his third shot. This one struck the old man square in the face. In an instant Ventimiglia was gone, replaced by a faint blood mist.

"*They hit the boss!*" someone yelled.

Another shot rang out. Joe heard it strike the piano behind him. Joe swiveled slightly, the Smith & Wesson settling on another target. Shot number four struck a retreating mobster in the back of the head, his brains coming to rest on the wall before him.

Only one man left now.

Joe's body moved on instinct. He wasn't aware of it, but every one of his shots had hit a target—and at a distance. This would have been considered exceptional shooting for a professional, but for a novice it was more like a miracle.

The last mobster tried to keep the fountain between Joe and himself. Joe moved to his right and popped off another shot, this one tearing into the metal elevator doors. Joe moved slowly toward the fountain, the Smith & Wesson still raised in his right hand. After a moment of silence, the guy ran out from behind the fountain to Joe's right. The man had a pistol in each hand, firing them both as he ran. Shots zinged off the walls and floor to Joe's left and right, but none of them touched him.

Joe squeezed the trigger and popped off the Smith & Wesson's last round. The bullet struck the guy in the chin and he dropped to the tile floor. As Joe moved toward him, he could see the man was still alive. He had fallen on his face and now tried to crawl. Joe holstered the Smith & Wesson and grabbed the Beretta with his right hand. Two feet from the wounded mobster, Joe raised the Beretta, aiming it at the top of the man's head. He squeezed the trigger and the man stopped crawling.

Joe looked over the bodies to make sure everyone was dead. Convinced they were, he started to turn. Just as he did, he saw one of them—the fat one with the torn-out throat—move his arm slightly. Joe raised the Beretta and fired a shot through the man's head.

On the way out of the hotel, Joe looked over at the two desk clerks—one male, one female—peeking over the top of the counter. He raised the Beretta in their direction and they disappeared beneath the counter once more.

Joe strolled out of the hotel nonchalantly, holding the front door open for an elderly woman entering the building.

* * *

Mertis Whitlock pulled the Crown Vic into Joe Gibson's driveway. He crushed out his cigarette in the ashtray and turned off the engine. The rain fell harder now than it had when he left the station, and he now wished he'd thought to bring an umbrella. He climbed out of the car, pulling the top of his raincoat up over his head, and ran toward the house. He raced up the steps and onto the front porch. He pulled the raincoat back down and rang the doorbell.

No one answered.

"Shit," he said to himself. He turned and looked around at the quiet neighborhood. Not wanting to battle the rain again any time soon, Mertis decided he'd stick around for a few minutes and wait for Gibson. He reached into his coat pocket and fished out the pack of smokes. He slid a cigarette out of the pack and put it to his lips. Letting it dangle there, he lit it.

After smoking two more cigarettes and having waited for about fifteen minutes, Mertis decided it was time to give up and head back to the station. Just as he came to this conclusion, he saw Joe Gibson's blue Ford Expedition coming down the street. Since Mertis had parked in the driveway, blocking the garage, Gibson parked along the curb in front of the house.

A moment later Gibson joined Mertis on the front porch. Mertis saw that Gibson was not wearing a coat. "Helluva day to leave your coat at home."

Gibson laughed halfheartedly. "I've had a lot on my mind."

"Makes sense."

"So what brings you out in this weather, detective?"

"I just wanted to ask you a few more questions."

Gibson nodded, but didn't seem to care one way or the other. He looked up at Mertis, lighting another cigarette. "Can you spare one of those?"

Mertis held out the pack. "You smoke?"

"I haven't smoked in a long time. Maybe seven, eight years. But now..."

Mertis nodded. There was nothing more to say.

Gibson put the cigarette in his mouth, and Mertis lit it.

"Your face is looking a little better," Mertis said.

Gibson rubbed his jaw. "Still hurts like hell, though."

"I'd imagine. And the shoulder?"

"Ditto. So what was it you wanted to ask me?"

"Look, Mr. Gibson, I know you're probably scared, and you know, you've got good reason to be frightened. But the men who shot your wife and kidnapped your little girl—"

"Yes?"

"Are you absolutely sure you can't ID them?"

"I told you, there were four black guys. They—"

Gibson was interrupted by Mertis's cell phone, now ringing. "Hold on a sec'," Mertis said, answering the phone.

"Hello?"

Mertis listened for a moment before saying, "At the Hyperion Hotel? I'll be right there."

He closed the phone and looked at Gibson. "I'm afraid I've gotta go. Duty calls."

Gibson put his hand out and Mertis shook it.

"I may come back around in a day or so," Mertis said. "Do you still have my card?"

"Yeah."

"Good. If you think of anything else, you give me a call. Okay?"

"Sure thing."

Mertis turned and prepared to run back into the rain, but Gibson stopped him. "Detective?"

"Yeah?"

"You think I could bum one more smoke from you?"

DAYS FOUR AND FIVE

A hell of a day for an outdoor funeral. The unrelenting rain came down from the slate gray sky. Joe sat front and center under the funeral canopy, Denise's closed coffin about a foot in front of him. Joe could feel the crowd's gaze upon him, all of them wanting to see him cry. But Joe had no tears. He was in a dark place so black it transcended tears and self-pity.

He could hear the minister droning on and on, reciting that old chestnut from Ecclesiastes about there being a time for everything under heaven. Joe had just been a million miles away from here, somewhere deep inside his own mind. But now he was back. He'd never had much use for religion and he'd never seen the Bible as being anything more than a collection of poetry and fairy tales, but the line about there being a time to die pushed a button.

What a crock of shit this was.

It hadn't been Denise's time to die at all, and any God who believed otherwise could be nothing more than a self-serving asshole. She was only thirty-five; she should have had her whole life in front of her. And here was this jerk-off minister—a man who'd never even met his agnostic wife—saying it was her time to die, as if that made everything better. And what did the minister care? He probably had five more of these things lined up for today. This, for him, was just another job, one as impersonal as the next.

"A time to be silent, and a time to speak," the minister said.

Joe didn't plan it, but he felt himself stand up.

He heard a few gasps behind him. The minister stopped speaking and stared at him, unsure how best to proceed.

Joe looked him in the eyes. "I'm sorry, but this is all bullshit."

Joe turned and walked out into the rain.

* * *

Joe waited patiently for the kidnappers' call, but it did not come. He wanted to pass the time, but nothing seemed relevant anymore. What, was he gonna sit and read a book while his wife moldered in the ground and his daughter was God knows where? Could he possibly be expected to sit and watch today's episode of *Jeopardy* and actually give a fuck about any of it? The world had lost meaning for him. With Emily's return, there was a slight chance he might find some shred of meaning once again, but for now there was nothing.

A few days before, he'd been roughly halfway through a new novel. He'd been on a tear lately, and the damned thing had just seemed to write itself. Joe believed it to be the best thing he'd ever written, which he found sad considering he knew he would never finish it. Maybe one day he would feel like writing again, but not on that particular book. No, that project would forever serve as a reminder of a life and time that no longer existed.

Joe sat on the front porch steps, chain-smoking Pall Malls and drinking Maker's Mark from the bottle, the telephone sitting on his lap. He stared at the dark sky, but found no answers. He looked around the quiet neighborhood through a veil of rain, his wounded shoulder aching.

It had now been almost two days and he hadn't heard from the kidnappers. Surely they knew by now Ventimiglia was dead. It was all over the news. How could they not? And now a different realization began to settle in—perhaps Joe had killed all those men for nothing. At this point, it didn't feel like much of a stretch to assume that Emily wasn't coming home.

The bottle of Maker's Mark went dry just before dark. Feeling drunk and lost in despair, Joe passed out on the porch.

The rain continued to fall.

And the phone refused to ring.

* * *

After waking the next morning and discovering the kidnappers still hadn't called, Joe decided to pay his brother Billy a visit in prison.

Visitation wasn't as bad as he expected. Rather than using telephones to talk to one another through a glass window, Joe and Billy were allowed to sit across from each other at a table. Other families visited at tables all around them. The screams of babies drowned out virtually all other sounds, and the stench of their piss-filled diapers hung heavily in the room.

"What's a nice guy like you doing in a place like this?" Billy asked, grinning.

"What, I can't visit my brother?"

"I guess there's a first for everything."

"I guess so."

"You look like shit."

"Funny, I feel like shit."

"Write any good books lately?"

"Not according to the critics."

"Yeah, the guy in the *Times* said *Everybody Loses* was derivative of your earlier work."

"Yeah, well, fuck him. What does he know?"

"Right."

"The reason I'm here—a group of men broke into my house. They murdered Denise."

Billy's eyes got big and he sat forward. *"What?"*

"And they kidnapped Emily."

"The baby?"

"Well, she's hardly a baby anymore. She's eight now."

"They asking for a ransom?"

"No."

"Damn. That's fucked up. The cops got any leads?"

"Fuck the cops. I'm gonna take care of this myself."

Billy looked around to make sure no one was listening. "You sure that's a good idea?"

"It is what it is."

"You need some help? I could get Roberto to help you out."

"I'm good. I need to do this one myself."

"Be careful, bro."

"The reason I'm here—I need your help."

"Anything," Billy said. "What can I do?"

"I'm trying to locate the men who did this." Joe then described each of the men in full detail. Billy could only be sure about the Mexican, the most distinctive of the bunch.

"His name's Hector. Hector Carrera. They call him Gonzo, like on *The Muppet Show*? He's a small-time hood, does B&Es, works as a heavy, sometimes a hitter. Last I knew he was doing a stretch up in Sing Sing. I guess he's out now. I'll call Roberto, find out where Hector's staying. Roberto'll call you tomorrow."

"What else can you tell me about this guy?"

"I pulled a couple jobs with him a few years back. We weren't partners, exactly—we were part of a team. But this fuckin' guy, this asshole Hector, fucked everything up the last time we worked together. I almost got my head blown off because of him."

"Anything else you can tell me about him?"

"You don't fuck around with a guy like Hector. You make one mistake and you're dead."

DAY SIX

Hector lived in the Meat Packing District, and not in those fancy new apartments like they show on *Sex and the City*. Hector's dilapidated piece of shit house was the last one standing on his block, and it was a doozie. Joe couldn't understand how the rat trap hadn't been condemned yet.

It was a few minutes before four in the afternoon when Joe drove by, checking out the place. He saw no sign of the big Mexican, but a great big motorcycle with a naked woman and flames painted on its tank was parked beside the porch. Joe figured it had to be Hector's.

Joe parked the Expedition a block down the street. This time he left the holsters in the truck, instead carrying the pistols in the front pockets of his slacks. With no prior experience, he wasn't very good at any of this, but he figured he would just walk right up to the door and knock. Then, when Hector answered, there would be hell to pay. When Joe got to the house, he walked quietly up the creaky steps and onto the even creakier porch. He slid the pistols from his pockets, and banged on the wooden door.

A dog started barking from somewhere inside the shack, and Joe could hear a man saying "fucking hold on a minute." About thirty seconds later, the door swung open.

And there was Hector—the same bastard who'd helped hold him and his wife captive.

One of the bastards who'd shot Denise and taken Emily.

Hector wore ratty jeans and no shirt, sloppy prison tattoos all over his chest and abdomen.

Joe raised both arms, the pistols aimed at Hector.

"You?" Hector said. "Fuck do you want?"

"What do you think I want?"

"If I knew, I wouldn't have asked."

Joe moved forward, making his way through the door. Once his arms were inside the door frame, Hector slammed the door shut against them, causing Joe to drop the pistols. *"Arrrggghh,"* Joe managed, sliding to the ground. Before Joe knew what was happening, he felt Hector's boot kicking him in the side of the head. Joe fell hard. As he did, Hector picked up the Smith & Wesson.

Hector chuckled, looking down the block to make sure there were no witnesses.

"Get up, asshole."

Joe rubbed his head before climbing slowly to his feet. Now his wounded shoulder, his arms, and his head all hurt like a sonofabitch.

Hector stood over him, motioning for him to go inside. Joe did. Inside, the strong stench of dog shit was overpowering. Trash piles towered everywhere, and the remnants of TV dinners past were lying all around.

Joe did not want to die here amongst all this garbage with that damned dog still barking somewhere in the house.

"I love what you've done with the place," Joe said.

"You think because you got a nice house and you some kind of big shot writer that your shit don't stink?"

"Not as bad as your house does."

Hector laughed again. There was a finality in his laughter this time, and Joe knew he would die soon unless he did something quickly.

"Sit down," Hector said, motioning toward a green recliner that looked like it had been purchased in 1976.

Joe did as he was told.

Hector raised the Smith & Wesson, aiming it directly into Joe's face.

"Got any last words, *puta?*"

Joe said nothing.

He watched Hector's finger tense. He pulled the trigger.

Nothing happened.

Joe had forgotten to switch off the safety!

A brief expression of confusion flashed across Hector's face. He turned the handgun sideways to inspect it, and Joe kicked him in the balls as hard as he could. Hector let out a squeal like an injured cat. He fell backwards, but managed to keep the gun in hand. Before he could get to the safety, Joe was on him again, kicking him in the side of the head.

He kicked him again.

And again.

And again.

Hector no longer moved, his eyes closed. Certain he'd killed the big Mexican, Joe took a moment to catch his breath. Then heard Hector laughing again. Joe looked up, noticed the huge, gaudy orange lamp—another holdover from the 70s—and grabbed it. He held it over his head just as Hector switched off the safety, and he brought the lamp down as hard as he could onto the injured man's face.

This time Hector lost consciousness.

Joe retrieved the Smith & Wesson. He climbed onto Hector's chest, straddling him, the pistol right in the man's face. He slapped Hector's cheek to revive him. This did the trick and Hector opened his eyes groggily.

"What the fuck, man?"

"I need answers."

"Not from me."

Joe cocked back the hammer.

"We killed your wife—you gonna kill me no matter what I say, right?" Hector said.

"Maybe, maybe not. You tell me what I wanna know, you just might make it out of here in a wheelchair or a coma. You don't, the only way you leave here is in a fucking body bag."

Hector chuckled. "Tha's good, the part about the wheelchair or the coma. You pretty good at this, Mr. Gibson. In another life, you coulda been me."

"I don't think so."

Hector's expression turned angry. "Why? You too good to be me?"

"Cockroaches are too good to be you."

Hector grinned. "Tha's a good one."

Joe repositioned the pistol in Hector's face. "Where's Emily?"

"Who's Emily?"

"My daughter."

"Oh," Hector said, a look of recognition washing over his face. "The little girl."

"Where the fuck is she?"

"I heard you killed that grease-ball Ventimiglia at that hotel. That was you, right?"

Joe nodded.

"And they didn't give you your little girl back?"

"No."

"Tha's fucked up." Joe read Hector's expression to be a sincere one.

Joe's eyes narrowed. "You telling me you don't know what they did with my daughter?"

"Man, I didn't know shit about the little girl. I didn't even know they was gonna shoot your old lady. They didn't tell me any of that shit. It was just a job, man. I ain't got nothing against you. It was, you know, just a job. It wasn't personal."

"It was pretty fucking personal to me."

"I guess, but man, you gotta understand how this kind of shit works."

"Explain it to me."

"I got a call."

"Who called you?"

"My man Jonesy."

"Was he one of the guys with you that night?"

The look on Hector's face made it apparent that he'd said more than he wanted to.

Joe pushed the barrel of the Smith & Wesson against Hector's nose. "I said, was Jonesy there that night?"

"Yeah."

"Which one was he?"

"The nigger with the fucked up hair, look like a skinny Don King?"

"He was the one who called you?"

"Yeah."

"So he put this thing together?"

"No, he didn't tell me who put it all together. He was just a hired hand like me. He said it was a need-to-know-basis kind of thing and if I needed to know, then I didn't need the job. I said, 'Shit, I need the work. My dumb ass ain't gotta know nothing about nothing,' you know?"

"Did you know any of the other guys who were there?"

"One of 'em, the white guy who looked like a cop."

"Yeah?"

"I saw him around when I was in Lewisburg a few years back. He hung out with the Aryans."

"You know his name?"

Hector shook his head. "I didn't associate with those guys."

"Are you sure you don't know who orchestrated this thing?"

"I'm sure, man. Scout's fucking honor."

"Do you know how or why they picked me?"

"No fucking clue. The white guy said something about it being random, but tha's all I really know."

"You don't know shit."

"No, man, I'm telling you."

"Why did they want Ventimiglia dead?"

"I dunno that either. Shit, man, I don't even know who I was working for."

Joe took a moment to collect his thoughts. Finally, he said, "Okay, how do I get ahold of Jonesy?"

Hector smiled. "No way, man. You ain't gettin' shit outta me."

"You sure about that?"

"Definitely."

Joe moved the Smith & Wesson, shooting Hector in the left shoulder. Hector wailed for a moment, but then went quiet. He was breathing hard. "Looks like no wheelchair or coma for me, man, because I ain't tellin' you shit. You gon' hafta kill me."

"This is your last chance, Hector."

Hector spat at Joe's face, but none of the spittle reached him.

Joe pulled the trigger and fired a round directly through Hector's dead white eye.

"Fuck, Hector, you coulda just told me what I needed to know."

As Joe took a deep breath of air, he glanced over at the table beside him where the orange lamp had been. There was a tattered

Southwestern Bell phone book sitting there, a few names scrawled on its cover. Joe picked it up and looked at it. One of the names was Jonesy, a Brooklyn address written just beneath it. Joe tore off the phone book cover and stuck it in his pocket.

He retrieved the Beretta from the floor by the door. Joe wanted to do one more thing before he left. He followed the sound of the barking dog back into the kitchen, where he found a bruised and battered, half-starved Rottweiler locked in a cage. He opened the cage and let the sickly animal go free. The Rottweiler then went immediately to its fallen owner and started sniffing his body. The dog hiked up his back leg and pissed in Hector's face.

DAY SEVEN

PART ONE

Mertis and Jillian examined the lobby of the Hyperion Hotel again. Mertis stood in the same place Joe Gibson had been standing four days before. He had his arms raised outward, fingers pointed like guns, reenacting the shootout the way he figured it went down. Jillian was looking at the bullet hole in the piano a few feet away.

Mertis was firing imaginary rounds. *"Bam! Bam!* Then the shooter apparently ran out of bullets in the Smith & Wesson and switched guns. He then moved in to finish them off at point blank range with the Beretta."

"I read this the same way you do," Jillian said. "There had to be two shooters."

"Otherwise it doesn't make sense. Why would the shooter fire two shots from the Beretta and then switch handguns again before popping the two desk clerks and the old lady?"

"Right, the Glock 9."

Mertis looked at the front desk. "For a job like this, you need a second man for crowd control. I'd bet you dollars to doughnuts he's the guy removed the surveillance tapes. The primary shooter wouldn't have had time for all that."

"And the way the desk clerks and the old woman were shot—"

"Execution-style."

"Those shootings seem inconsistent with the others."

"I can't put my finger on it, but something about the five wiseguys by the elevator feels funny, like the shooter was an amateur."

"His shots were pretty consistent for an amateur."

"Mighta been dumb luck. Thing is, this doesn't feel like a mob hit at all. Usually in a mob hit, the targets are taken out at close range so there's no chance of anyone escaping."

"So you think it was amateur night?"

"These guys, yes," Mertis said, pointing at the elevator area. He turned and motioned toward the front desk. "But those shootings—the desk clerks and the old woman—were done by a pro. But why would a pro sit back and watch the amateur gun down all the wiseguys by himself? It doesn't make sense."

"What are you thinking?"

Mertis bit his lip. "I'm thinking how odd it is that Denise Gibson gets murdered execution-style, and then three days later we have more execution-style murders here at the hotel. I also find it odd that we had what is possibly a group of pros there to take out Mrs. Gibson—a civilian—and then an amateur here to take out a Mafia boss. None of it makes a damned bit of sense."

"What does your gut say?"

"I think the two cases might be connected."

"How so?"

"I don't know yet. I'm still trying to connect the dots."

＊ ＊ ＊

Joe took a shower, hot water cascading down over his body, making him feel just the tiniest bit better for the briefest of moments. He hadn't slept more than a few hours in the six days following Denise's death, and it was starting to catch up with him. His head hurt like hell and he felt weak.

Joe had shaving cream all over his face. He had just begun shaving, and had removed only a single row of the cream, when a voice spoke to him from outside the shower curtain. "Turn off the water and get out. And don't try any bullshit or I'll shoot you."

What the hell?

Who could this be?

Joe didn't recognize the voice. He turned off the water and slowly pulled back the shower curtain. There was a man standing there with a Glock 9 aimed right in his face. The guy was Italian, probably about thirty, had jet black hair with a goatee, and wore a black suit just like the men Joe had killed in the lobby of the Hyperion Hotel. He was definitely a wiseguy, probably one of Ventimiglia's. If that was the case, Joe was as good as dead.

"Who are you?" Joe asked.

"I'm sure you've got a pretty good idea. We'll talk about that. We've got time. First things first, why don't you cover yourself with a towel or something? It's hard talking business with a guy who's got his dick hanging out."

Joe looked down and realized he was completely naked. He grabbed the towel hanging over the curtain rod and pulled it down, wrapping it around his waist.

"Okay, so who are you?"

The man smiled. "How about I tell you my last name and you tell me if that rings any bells."

"Okay."

"Ventimiglia."

Joe tried to play it cool. "That supposed to mean something to me?"

"Look, you can't bullshit me, because I already know you killed my uncle and all those other fucks in that hotel."

"What makes you think so?"

"Because you left the surveillance videos in the machine, Einstein. If I hadn't taken those tapes and killed the desk clerks, you'd be in jail already."

"Why'd you save my ass?"

"I didn't do it for you," the man said. "It's my job to track you down. If you end up in jail, then I'm not gonna be able to catch you."

"Are you gonna kill me?"

"We'll get to that. Now you're obviously not a criminal master-mind, so I wanna know why you killed those guys."

"Four men broke into my house last week and took my wife and I at gunpoint," Joe said. "They demanded that I murder your uncle."

The man cocked his head. "Why *you*?"

"No one ever gave me a good reason. They said it was 'almost random.'"

"Who were they working for?"

"I don't know yet."

The man nodded, taking this in. "Go on."

"They murdered my wife and kidnapped my eight-year-old daughter."

"So you go and kill Carlo and those other guys to get your daughter back?"

"Yeah. Only thing is, they never gave back my daughter."

"Really? You do all that, and you don't get your daughter back?"

"Right."

"That's fucked up. So what do you do? Call the cops?"

"I can't go to the cops. I mean, I killed a bunch of people. So I've been tracking these men down myself."

"And?"

"I've located two of them so far."

"And you've met with them?"

"I met with the first one."

"How did that go?"

"He's dead now."

"You killed him?"

"He didn't die of old age."

The man nodded. "You gettin' pretty good at this killing thing, Joe. So what about the second guy?"

"I was gonna visit him today."

"That puts us in an awkward position," the man said.

"How's that?"

"Because I'm here to kill you now."

Joe thought about it, and to his surprise, realized he really didn't care all that much. Without Denise and Emily in his life—and there was a good chance he'd never see Emily again—he had nothing to live for. "Tell you what, how about you wait a couple days and you let me talk to these people—"

"By talk you mean kill."

"Semantics."

"And then what?"

"You let me finish what I started and then you kill me when I'm done."

The man nodded. "I could help you track down these guys and get to the bottom of all this. Then I could find out who's responsible for killing my uncle Carlo." He looked up at Joe. "Besides you, I mean."

Joe shrugged. "Sorry. It wasn't personal. I didn't even know the guy."

"It's okay. He was a hard-on anyway."

"Yeah?"

"Yeah, so don't worry about it," the man said. "I'm gonna have to kill you either way. I mean, an example has to be made, but Carlo was no big loss to me."

"Good. So we've got a deal."

"Yeah, we got a deal."

Joe put his hand out for the man to shake, but the man declined. "You're still naked under that towel, my friend. I ain't shakin' hands with no naked guys."

* * *

After Joe got dressed, he and Carlo Ventimiglia's nephew sat down at the table and drank coffee with whiskey and downed a few Eggo waffles with maple syrup.

"We gotta lay down some ground rules if we're gonna do this," the man said.

"Okay, you name 'em."

"Rule number one is you don't try to get cocky and either take a shot at me or try to escape. You do either one of those things, you're gonna be as dead as Michael Jackson. Second rule, you don't try to be my long lost buddy. No matter how friendly we get, I'm still gonna kill you when this is all said and done. *Capice*?"

"That it? Those are the rules?"

The man stared at him. "There will be more rules to come. I think of any more, I'll pass 'em along."

"Fair enough," Joe said. "So what do I call you?"

"Sir, if you're smart."

"No, seriously. What's your name?"

"I guess it can't hurt to tell you my name. Who are you gonna tell? It's Vinnie."

"Vinnie, I got a rule for you."

Vinnie couldn't believe his ears. "Really? *You* got a rule for *me*?"

"Yeah."

"Okay, let's hear it."

"Tracking down these assholes is my thing, not yours. So when we go busting down these fuckers' doors, I lead the way. It's my show. I do the talking."

Vinnie thought about it for a minute. "Okay, what the hell. Sure, it's your show." He ate a big mouthful of waffles before speaking again. "But I got another rule, too. From now on, we take my car. You ride shotgun."

DAY SEVEN

PART TWO

Jonesy's apartment sat atop a dusty, junk-filled pawn shop. Joe and Vinnie took the stairs, guns out, and were surprised to find a note on Jonesy's door that read: "COME ON IN, SWEET THING. DOOR'S UNLOCKED." Vinnie smirked at Joe and said, "I don't think this note's for us." Vinnie took the note down and crumpled it, dropping it to the floor.

Joe opened the door, gun still out, prepared for whatever. Inside he discovered a clean, well-decorated apartment with scented candles lit all around. The scents of baked apple pie, vanilla, coffee, cookies, and probably a dozen other aromas combined with burning incense to create a smoky smell that was at once welcoming and sickening. Some light old-school R&B song—Joe thought it might be Teddy Pendergrass—filled the room.

Jonesy was nowhere to be seen.

Joe led the way through the apartment. He turned a corner and found Jonesy sitting at a table, dressed only in a fluffy pink robe and a black do-rag, snorting cocaine through a ceramic straw from a small mirror. Jonesy looked up, eyes watering, and saw the two white men standing there with their guns out. "What the fuck?"

Vinnie grinned. "And you must be Mr. Jonesy, I presume?"

Jonesy didn't pay much attention to Vinnie. Instead he stared at Joe uneasily, either recognizing him and wondering why the fuck he was here, or wondering exactly where he'd seen him before.

"You're Gibson," Jonesy said, pointing the ceramic straw at him. "The writer."

"And you're the fuckhead who helped kill my wife and kidnap my little girl."

Jonesy started to get defensive. "Look, that shit wasn't me."

"You telling me you weren't there at my house six days ago? You telling me it was some other skinny asshole with a big fucked-up Don King hairdo was there and not you?"

"Nah, of course not. I'm saying I ain't have shit to do with any of that. That wasn't my thing. I was just there on a job, nothing more. The man called and said he needed me to go along and harass some guy and his old lady, said he'd pay me two thousand in cash to stand there and act tough. So that's exactly what I did."

"You don't look so tough to me," Vinnie said, prodding the guy. "You got a friggin' pink bath robe, for Chrissakes."

Jonesy looked irritated. "You ain't got no style, man. This shit is in right now."

Vinnie laughed. "Bullshit. Even Rick James wouldn't have been caught dead in that shit, and that was during disco. Hell, pimps wouldn't even wear a get-up like that."

Jonesy started to disagree. Joe straightened his arm, pointing the Smith & Wesson in Jonesy's face, letting him know he meant business. "Who called you about the job?"

"White guy by the name of Nicky Needles. He was there, at your house."

"Was he the skinny one or the one with all the pockmarks on his face?"

"The skinny, cheese-eatin' little bastard, look like a rat or somethin'."

"Who was he working for?"

"He didn't say."

"You did the job and didn't know who you were working for?"

"I get a lot of jobs like that."

"And you don't ask?"

"The streets don't work like that, homie. My need for money outweighs my need to know who the fuck is hiring me. At the end of the day, I don't give two shits who's behind the job just as long as my black ass gets paid."

"Did you know either of the other two guys who were there that night?"

Jonesy nodded. "Sure. Hector, big Mexican goes by the name Gonzo? We go way back. We did a stretch together at Lewisburg."

"I'll bet you two were lovers," Vinnie said.

Joe ignored this. "The other white guy—the one who shot my wife? He was in Lewisburg, too. Right?"

"Yeah, he was there. Ran with the Aryans, sold dope. But I didn't know the guy. Just used to see him around. Looked like an asshole. Something about him... He looks like a cop to me, and I don't hang around Aryans or cops."

"What's the guy's name?" Joe asked.

"Damned if I know. He was just another silly-ass white boy to me." Jonesy looked up at Vinnie, squinting his eyes, trying to look tough. "And all y'all ofay motherfuckers look alike to me."

Vinnie grinned. "You're a funny guy, huh?" He reached back and backhanded him with the Glock, leaving Jonesy's nose and mouth bloodied.

Jonesy looked up at Vinnie. "Who the fuck you supposed to be, anyway?"

"I'm Mr. Gibson's attorney," Vinnie said. "I represent Mr. Gibson in such matters as these."

Jonesy smiled. "You gonna serve me with some papers, take me to court?"

Vinnie nodded. "Something like that."

"Maybe I need a lawyer like you."

"You won't after today." Vinnie winked.

Joe broke up this exchange. "Do you know where they took my little girl?"

"Nah, man, I don't. I didn't even see the little girl. I was driving when we went to the bus stop. I know they put her in the trunk, but that's all I know."

"Why would they want to keep my little girl?"

"They *kept* her?" Jonesy asked. "I didn't even know that. I figured when you capped that old linguine-eating greaseball they'd give you your kid back. That's fucked up."

Vinnie nodded in agreement. "Gives honest criminals a bad name."

"Do you have any idea what they would want with a little girl?" Joe asked.

"Hate to break this to you," Jonesy said, "but there are people who would buy a little girl like that. There are places on the other side of the border where dirty old men would pay good money for a little piece of white tail like hers."

Joe was shaken, didn't move.

Vinnie stuck the Glock right up against Jonesy's nose. "You think you could be a little more tactful, asshole?"

"I'm sorry," Jonesy said. "I thought you wanted the truth. Next time I'll just tell you some lies."

Joe said, "Tell me about Nicky Needles."

"What you wanna know?"

"Anything and everything."

"He's an asshole," Jonesy said. "I can't stand that dude. And he's got bad breath, smells like he been eatin' cat shit. I've worked with him a couple of times now, and it's always the same. Dude thinks he knows everything about everything and he can't wait to tell you 'bout it. It's like, 'If you so smart, man, why the fuck you been to prison so many times?'"

"Any idea why he went to prison?" Joe asked.

"Shit," Jonesy said, "which time? Nicky Needles been to prison more times than Carmen Electra's had rock star dick in her. I think the last time he went upstate was for cars. Apparently he was part of some big auto theft ring across the bridge. Another time he got caught with a truck full of stolen merchandise. Furniture, I think. Love seats and ottomans. And they say he went up for rape once—an old woman, I think. Someone's grandma. At least that's the talk around the campfire."

Joe nodded. "Any idea who might employ a guy like that?"

"A guy like Nicky Needles? He works for anyone who'll have his dumbass. I sincerely doubt anyone's got him locked down full time. A guy like that, he's a freelancer all the way. But you find that other guy—the cop-lookin' motherfucker with all the bumps on his face? I'd bet you two blowjobs and a partridge in a fuckin' pear tree he's connected with somebody. You see how he handled shit that night?

He just kind of took over, let it be known he was runnin' the show. And who was it that shot your old lady? That same cop-lookin' motherfucker. I'm telling you, you catch him and make him talk, you find out who planned that job."

"I guess we're done with you then," Vinnie said. "No reason to keep you alive now, is there?"

"Look, man," Jonesy said, "I'm telling you, I didn't have nothin' to do with any of that crazy shit happened that night. My black ass was just there to get paid, end of story. They didn't tell me nothin' about no kids, and they damned sure didn't tell me they were planning on murdering someone. I'm on parole. I don't need to be mixed up with no stupid shit like that. Besides all that, now I got you two crazy-looking peckerwoods standing here pointing guns in my face."

Joe smiled at this. "You don't enjoy this?"

"Hell no, I don't like it. To tell you the truth, all this drama is making me a little sick to my stomach."

Vinnie opened his mouth and started to talk some more shit, but the girl walked in. She was young, white, dressed in skimpy clothes with so much eyeliner on that she looked like a raccoon, and scared out of her drugged-out mind. "What the hell is this?" she asked, a stupid, confused look plastered across her pierced-up face.

Joe aimed the Smith & Wesson at her. "And you must be Sweet Thing."

She still looked confused. "What?"

"What's your name?" Vinnie asked.

Sweet Thing said nothing.

Now Vinnie had his Glock aimed at her face. *"I asked you what the fuck your name was, princess."*

"Traci."

Joe turned back to Jonesy. "What if I do to her what you sons of bitches did to my wife?"

Jonesy shrugged. "Fuck do I care? I don't even know this junkie bitch. I met her at the taco stand."

Traci wasn't listening. She could have been a million miles away. Stoned, transfixed by the lines of coke in front of Jonesy.

"Musta been quite a date you had planned here," Vinnie said. "What was on the agenda? A little date rape, a little cocaine?"

"We were gonna shoot some smack and watch *New Jack City* on cable," Jonesy said. "Then later, maybe have some sex. But not until after *New Jack City*. Wesley Snipes is my man in that shit."

Vinnie ignored the Wesley Snipes talk. "You got smack, huh? Of course. I mean, you can't have coke without a little smack, too."

Joe asked, "Where's the heroin?"

Traci snapped out of her trance. "It's in my purse."

"Well, get it out," Vinnie said. "Let's see it."

Traci took out a syringe, a bent spoon, and a baggy filled with powder, sitting them on the table beside Jonesy's coke.

Joe repositioned the Smith & Wesson against Jonesy's face, bending the tip of his nose a little. "I need to know how to get ahold of Nicky Needles."

"You ain't got to put that gun all in my face, man. I don't give a damn about no Nicky fucking Needles. I'll give you that information without the gun, partner. That creepy little bastard hangs out at a bar in the Bronx. It's called The Rabid Rabbit. It's a real dive—nothing but crazy-assed crackers and outlaw country songs about lynchin' niggers and whatnot."

"They make country songs about lynchin' niggers?" Vinnie asked, completely serious.

"How the fuck do I know? All that shit sounds alike to me. I hear that shit, I know it's not for me, the man talkin' about pickup trucks and drinkin' Old Milwaukee."

Joe spoke. "You sure he's gonna be there?"

"Unless he's in prison, which he's apt to be any day now, he'll be in that dingy little shithole. I think he may have some sort of deal going with the owner, like maybe he's getting a percentage of the till or something. I dunno, but he's *always* there. It's like his office."

Joe looked at Vinnie and Vinnie nodded. Joe picked up the syringe. "I'll cook you up a batch of heroin," Joe said, turning and leaving the room.

Vinnie pressed the Glock to Jonesy's temple. "I want you to snort another line of that coke."

Jonesy looked up incredulously. *"Really?"*

"Yeah."

Jonesy grinned. "You ain't got to tell a nigga twice."

Jonesy leaned forward, putting the ceramic straw up to his nose, and started snorting up a line of coke. Jonesy was halfway through the line when Vinnie smashed his head forward against the table, the ceramic straw jamming up his nose. Jonesy started screaming and thrashing around, blood pouring from his nose.

Joe returned from another part of the apartment, holding up the syringe. "Hold his arm steady," Joe said. Vinnie grabbed Jonesy's arm—Jonesy still thrashing around—and pulled up the sleeve of the robe. Joe injected the syringe's contents into Jonesy's vein. Within seconds Jonesy thrashed around even harder than before. He fell to the floor, thrashed around some more, and then went silent.

"What did you inject him with?" Vinnie asked.

"Drain cleaner."

Vinnie laughed.

Traci started freaking out. "You *killed* him?"

Joe nodded, a smile on his lips. "Yeah."

Traci looked at Jonesy's body. "You sure he's dead?"

"He ain't sleeping."

Vinnie pointed the Glock in Traci's face. "I'm sorry to do this, but this is a classic case of you being in the wrong place at the wrong time."

Her eyes got big. "You're gonna shoot me?"

"Unless you want my friend Joe to serve you up one of those drain cleaner cocktails."

"Please don't," Traci begged.

Joe thought of Emily. He looked at Vinnie. "Why don't we let Traci go," he said. "She doesn't even know this guy. I'm sure if we let her go she'll keep her mouth closed about what she saw here."

"That's right," Traci said. "I won't say shit to anybody."

Vinnie shrugged. "You're a lucky girl, Traci. If it was just me, you'd be dead already."

"What are you saying?"

"I'm saying you better start running, and you'd better not stop until you get home. *Capice?*"

And Traci was gone.

DAY SEVEN

PART THREE

True to Jonesy's word, The Rabid Rabbit was a dark, smoke-filled shithole. The place smelled of cheap cigarettes, stale beer, and body odor. The clientele, what little came out in the afternoon, looked like something out of *Deliverance*. The jukebox—a vintage model that still played records—played a tune by David Allan Coe called "My Wife Ran Off with a Nigger."

As Joe and Vinnie were walking in, Vinnie heard a few lines of the song. "Well, what do you know? Jonesy was right. They really do sing songs like that."

Joe scanned the place, searching for Nicky Needles, but saw no sign of the Ichabod Crane-looking motherfucker. As Joe and Vinnie made their way toward the bar, Vinnie spoke again. "I think we're a little out of place here. I think the two of us have more teeth than all of these sons of bitches combined."

A mean-looking fat man with pork chop sideburns, a graying flat-top haircut, and a leather vest eyeballed them from behind the bar. "You boys lost?"

Vinnie and Joe looked at each other. "We're looking for an associate of yours," Vinnie said. "Guy by the name of Nicky Needles."

The bartender looked at them like they were cops. "You two friends of his?"

"What makes you say that?" Vinnie asked. "Do we look like a couple of assholes?"

The bartender put his hands up. "Look, guys, I don't want any trouble here. Why don't you two just go back out the same way you came in?"

Vinnie's hand went for the Glock, but a door opened up behind the bar and Nicky Needles emerged. He looked up from some receipts and he saw the two men. He recognized Joe and stopped dead in his tracks. "Why are you here?"

"Why do you think I'm here?" Joe asked.

Nicky said nothing.

"You hear about Gonzo and Jonesy yet?"

"No," Nicky said. "What about 'em?"

Vinnie grinned. "They're waiting for you."

"Where?"

"In hell."

An expression of concern washed over Nicky's face. He went for his gun—a .38 police special tucked into his waistband—but Joe had the big Smith & Wesson trained on him before he could get to it. The bartender came up from behind the bar with a pump shotgun, but Vinnie shot him in the shoulder with the Glock before he could do any damage. The shotgun fell to the ground and the bartender moaned in agony.

"Pick up that shotgun and give it to me," Joe said.

The bartender sheepishly gave him the gun.

Vinnie held up the Glock, showed it to everyone sitting in the bar. "Anyone else wants to get involved, you'll get shot, too. I got plenty of bullets, so come on up." No one moved or said a word.

Joe stood there, shotgun slung over his shoulder, Smith & Wesson out, staring at Nicky. "You and I are gonna have a little talk."

Nicky grinned. "You're just sore cause I kicked your ass."

"I'll bet money you're not so tough when you don't have a pistol in someone's face," Joe said. "I don't think you'll be kicking my ass today."

"Where you wanna talk?"

"You're leaving with us," Joe said.

Vinnie yelled out to the bar's patronage again. "Nicky Needles is not worth losing your life over. Anyone says shit to the cops, I'll come back here myself and kill every one of you motherfuckers. Got it?"

As they were walking out, the jukebox started playing another David Allan Coe ditty about black people. Joe racked the shotgun once and shot the jukebox, effectively ending the music. Joe turned to the bartender, "Next time get better music."

* * *

A few minutes later the three men were in Vinnie's Lincoln Navigator. With Vinnie driving, Nicky rode in the passenger seat. Joe sat in the back, his shotgun aimed at Nicky's head.

"Why are you doing this?" Nicky asked.

"Two reasons," Joe said. "To find out about my daughter, and for good old-fashioned revenge."

"You gonna kill me?"

"What do you think?"

Nicky's eyes were as big as saucers. "What if I tell you what you want to know? Will you still kill me?"

"Now isn't the time for this," Joe said. "We can talk about this when we get where we're going."

"Please," Nicky said.

Joe pushed the barrel of the shotgun against the back of Nicky's head. "Just shut up and ride."

* * *

Within minutes Joe, Vinnie, and Nicky were walking along the pedestrian walkway of the Whitestone Bridge. Nicky walked out front, with Joe and Vinnie behind, their pistols still out. Cars and trucks passed by, their passengers no doubt seeing the guns, but everyone pretended to see nothing and went on their merry way.

"How far we gonna walk?" Nicky asked.

"Just keep walking," Joe said.

Vinnie added, "We'll let you know when we get there."

"You guys must be nuts," Nicky said. "You gonna kill me out here in the middle of the fucking Whitestone suspension bridge? You're out of your fucking minds."

"Shut up and keep walking asshole," Vinnie said.

"Let's talk about this," Nicky said. "Tell me what you want to know."

Irritated, Joe said, "What I want to know is whether or not you can walk to the middle of this bridge without talking."

Vinnie chuckled. Nicky took the hint and kept his mouth shut.

Finally when they were close to the middle of the bridge, Joe said, "Stop here."

Nicky looked down at the water. "How high you figure we are?"

"I'm gonna say about a hundred and fifty feet," Vinnie said.

"Nah," Joe said. "It's one hundred and thirty-eight feet."

"How you know that?" Nicky asked.

"I read, asshole. But I'm not here to discuss the fucking bridge."

Nicky nodded. "What do you wanna know?"

"Who hired you?"

"For what?"

"The job at my home."

"Ronnie Gates, the guy with all the acne scars on his face."

Joe looked out over the water. "The one that looks like a cop?"

"Yeah," Nicky said, nodding. "He used to be NYPD, but he went to jail for selling meth and stealing evidence. Now he's the Greek's go-to-guy. He does hits and oversees day-to-day operations for the Greek."

"Who the fuck is *the Greek*?" Joe asked.

"Nikos Panagakos," Nicky said.

"Small-time gangster and Mafia wannabe," Vinnie said. "Has operations in several cities around the U.S., but calls New York home."

Joe bit his lip. "So this job was ordered by this guy, the Greek?"

"I can't say for sure," Nicky said, "but I would imagine so. Ronnie called with the job and I didn't ask any questions. He just told me to round up some guys and I did. I figured a job's a job."

"Any idea how they picked my buddy Joe here for the job?" Vinnie asked.

"No idea. I thought it was kind of weird, since Joe was just a writer, but I figured they knew what they were doing. And I guess it worked. I saw on TV you killed the old greaseball in that hotel."

"My uncle Carlo," Vinnie said. "Carlo Ventimiglia."

Nicky looked around nervously. "Uh, sorry. I didn't know he was your uncle."

"I'll try to remember that," Vinnie said.

Joe spoke up. "What about my little girl?"

"What about her?"

"Where is she?"

"They didn't bring her back?"

"No."

"That's crazy. That doesn't make any sense."

"Right. So you don't know where she is?"

"No idea," Nicky said.

"Were you there when they took her from the bus stop?"

"Yeah. I was the one who put her in the trunk."

Joe raised the Smith & Wesson to Nicky's head. "Strike one, asshole."

"Sorry," Nicky said, sweat pouring down his face. "I didn't hurt her. I swear."

"Well, that's a plus."

"You know these kinds of people better than I do," Joe said. "Why would they kidnap a little girl?"

"If I was gonna do it, I'd do it for the ransom money," Nicky said. "But they didn't do that, so I'm not sure. I hear there are brothels down in Mexico who buy little girls. I've also heard tales of drug smugglers hollowing out the insides of little kids and using them as mules. They say they fill their insides with drugs."

Nicky realized who he was talking to and stopped talking. "Sorry," he said.

Joe started to lose it. He found himself on the verge of tears, the gun shaking in his hand.

"How do we find Ronnie Gates?" Vinnie asked.

"Ronnie's not hard to find," Nicky said. "His office is in the back of this little tattoo parlor in the Village."

"How many people are usually working in there?" Vinnie asked.

"One or two ink slingers, and Ronnie's bodyguard."

"Ronnie got a bodyguard?"

"Yeah, big Samoan sonofabitch."

"You know the address of this tattoo parlor?" Joe asked.

"No," Nicky said, "but it's in the book. Murder Ink Body Arts."

"Anything else you can tell us about that night at Joe's house?" Vinnie asked.

Nicky looked at Joe. "I swear I didn't know they were gonna kill your wife."

Joe looked up, his expression intense. "Really?"

"I swear, man."

"The way you kept kicking the shit out of me and laughing, I really doubt you would have had any trouble with them murdering Denise."

"Denise?" Nicky said. "Her name was Denise?"

"Yeah," Joe said, sticking the Smith & Wesson in Nicky's face. "And you don't get to say her name."

Vinnie moved toward Nicky, pushing him back against the railing. He pressed the barrel of his Glock against Nicky's left cheek. The barrel of Joe's Smith & Wesson already rested against Nicky's right cheek.

Tears started trickling down Nicky's cheeks. "There must be something I can do or say..."

"No," Joe said. "There's no way to talk your way out of this."

"Why?"

"You bastards didn't give Denise the opportunity to talk her way out of it."

Vinnie grinned slightly. "Any last words, scumbag?"

Nicky thought for a second and then said, "I'm sorry."

Joe nodded. "Duly noted."

Joe and Vinnie looked at each other and then back at Nicky. They pulled their triggers simultaneously. Nicky's body fell back and flipped over the railing of the bridge, and he fell into the East River.

Vinnie looked at Joe and said, "You hungry?"

Joe was tired as hell but said, "I could eat."

DAY EIGHT

PART ONE

Joe toiled in the garage, listening to a Billy Joel CD on repeat and modifying the shotgun he'd taken from the bartender at The Rabid Rabbit. It was only 9 a.m. and he'd already removed the stock from the rifle and sanded it down smooth. Now he had the barrel of the shotgun clamped in a vise and used a panel saw to cut the barrel down to size. This would make the shotgun easier to conceal and would also remove the choke, giving the pellets a wider spread when fired.

Joe took a drink of his beer. Billy Joel was singing *Big Shot* when Vinnie stepped into the garage.

"I thought maybe you tried to make a run for it," Vinnie said.

"Nah. I just thought I'd modify this shotgun before we go after Ronnie Gates."

"And the Greek. Let's not forget him."

"You planning on going after them both today?"

"No time like the present."

"Sounds good to me."

"So, you like Billy Joel?"

"Yeah. You?"

"Not really. My old man was a big Billy Joel fan though. His favorite was *Scenes from an Italian Restaurant.*"

Joe nodded. "Good song." He went back to sawing the shotgun barrel.

"I'm gonna go in and take a shower. I figure we'll go see old Ronnie boy in maybe thirty, forty minutes."

"Sounds like a plan."

"You got another beer in the fridge?"

"Help yourself."

"Thanks." Vinnie turned and walked back toward the house.

Joe and Vinnie pulled up in front of the tattoo parlor and parked the Navigator right there on the street. The shop's windows had a light tint on them, so Joe and Vinnie couldn't see how many people were inside. Joe and Vinnie both had their pistols out already, Joe with the sawed-off shotgun down beside his right leg.

Vinnie led the way. A bell jingled when he opened the door. There were two tattoo artists—a man and a woman—goofing around in the shop, but no one paid Vinnie any mind. The man tinkered with one of the tattooing chairs, his back to them, and the woman sat in the corner, reading a magazine. After they were both inside the store, Vinnie said, "Get the sign," and locked the front door. Joe went to the neon "OPEN" sign and unplugged it from the wall beneath the window.

Now the tattoo artists were looking at them. "What do you think you're doing?" asked the guy. Joe thought he looked like a retarded, tatted-up, Henry Rollins. He wore a sleeveless shirt to show off his muscles. He probably thought this would be intimidating as he moved towards Joe and Vinnie. When Joe racked the shotgun, however, Retarded Henry Rollins stood down. He put his hands up, palms out. "Whoa, hold it there, partner," he said.

Vinnie aimed the Glock at him. "You keep your mouth shut and do as you're told, you just might live through the day. Where's Ronnie?"

The guy played dumb. "Ronnie who?"

Joe pointed the shotgun at him, and suddenly the guy remembered. "Oh, *Ronnie*," he said. "Ronnie's in the back."

"Hey, you," Joe said to the girl, still reading her magazine.

"Yeah?"

"You got any tape?"

She looked at him like he was an idiot. "What kind of tape?"

"You know, the thick, silver kind."

"Duct tape?"

"Yeah, duct tape."

"Why the fuck would we have duct tape?"

"I need something to tie you up with, so we can keep you out of the way."

"I don't think it matters much," Retarded Henry Rollins said.

Vinnie looked at him. "What makes you say that?"

"I'm pretty sure they already know you're here."

"What makes you say that?"

Retarded Henry Rollins pointed to a surveillance camera mounted on the ceiling in the corner of the room.

"Good Christ," Vinnie said. He looked at the girl. "How many people are back there?"

The girl rolled her eyes, started to say something smart, but the door to Ronnie's office opened and the big Samoan came out firing a .45, a shot hitting the girl square in the temple. She fell to the floor in a bloody mess. Retarded Henry Rollins started towards her. "*Adrian!*" he shouted, as a bullet hit him in the side of the head, just beneath his ear.

Vinnie moved to the left side of the hallway where the Samoan shot from. Joe moved to the right, a bullet just missing his head as he did so. Vinnie peeked around the corner, seeing the Samoan in a mirror hanging in the hallway. He wore oversized hip-hop clothing and a big gold chain around his neck. The Samoan fired another shot from his .45, nearly hitting Vinnie's face.

For a moment there was silence. Vinnie said, "Stop shooting. We just want to talk." Another .45 shot rang out from the hallway, the round striking one of the swiveling tattoo chairs.

Joe looked at Vinnie. "Here goes nothing." Joe jumped into the mouth of the hallway, shotgun out, and fired the thing right at the Samoan. The blast from the shotgun struck the big sonofabitch in the chest and sent him flying back through the semi-closed door behind him. As he fell, the Samoan fired off one last shot into the wall beside him.

Joe moved quickly towards the door. As he did so, he switched the Smith & Wesson and the shotgun from one hand to the other. Now he had the Smith & Wesson up, ready to go through the door. Vinnie came right behind him.

"Come out, come out, wherever you are," Vinnie said.

A single shot came through the door in response.

"Seriously. Put the fucking gun down or we're gonna kill you."

It was dead silent for a moment before Ronnie spoke. "You're not gonna kill me?"

"Not if you tell us what we wanna know."

"How do I know you'll keep your word?"

Joe spoke up. "Ronnie, it's Joe Gibson. I'm not a criminal. I'm a normal guy. I don't like you at all. In fact, I fucking hate your guts. But I'm a man of my word. You put the gun down and talk to us, I promise I won't kill you."

"What about the other guy?"

Joe looked at Vinnie. "I promise you that neither of us will shoot you."

"You *promise*?"

"Scout's honor."

Vinnie became impatient. "You gonna put the gun down or what, asshole?"

"I'm putting it down," Ronnie said.

"It's down now?"

"It's down."

Joe started toward the door. "We're coming in. So help me God if you shoot at me—"

"You shoot at him," Vinnie said, "and I guarantee you that you're dead."

"No, no," Ronnie said. "The gun is down, the gun is down."

Joe stepped over the Samoan's body and found himself inside the ugliest office he'd ever seen. The walls had been painted red, and there were framed photographs of Ronnie with all types of celebrities, from Joe Montana to Christopher Lloyd. Ronnie knelt behind the big oak desk, his .45 sitting on top of it.

"You've met a lot of famous people," Joe said, looking at the photos.

Ronnie beamed. "I'm pretty proud of these."

Joe was looking at a photograph of Ronnie shaking hands with Bob Barker when Vinnie said, "You wanna meet any more celebrities—living ones, at least—you'll tell us what we need to know."

Ronnie nodded his head like a bobble-head doll. "Anything, guys, anything."

"Stand up," Vinnie said, "and sit in the chair so we can talk like normal human beings."

"Okay." Ronnie stood up and sat in the chair.

"Who was behind the job at Joe's house?" Vinnie asked.

Ronnie didn't hesitate. "It was the Greek. The Greek sent us there, told us to take the little girl, told us to tell Joe to kill Ventimiglia."

Joe's Smith & Wesson was trained on Ronnie. "The Greek tell you to kill my wife?"

Ronnie looked around nervously. "Yeah."

"Why?"

"He wanted you to know we meant business."

"Why'd he pick me for this little caper?"

Ronnie shook his head. "I really don't know. I've been curious about that. I asked him once, but he said, 'Don't worry about it,' told me to mind my own fucking business. But yeah, I thought it was weird."

"I never hurt anybody in my entire life…"

"You sure hurt the fuck out of old man Ventimiglia," Ronnie said.

Joe and Vinnie exchanged a knowing glance.

"And Denise, she sure as hell never hurt anybody."

Joe straightened his arm, repositioning the gun in Ronnie's face.

Ronnie put his hands up. "I thought you said you wouldn't kill me."

"You tell him what he wants to know, he ain't gonna kill you," Vinnie said.

"Why'd the Greek want my daughter?" Joe asked.

"She was supposed to be insurance—to make you do what the Greek wanted you to do."

"So why didn't he give her back?"

"He didn't expect you to succeed, and he really didn't expect you to survive. He sold the little girl to some backwoods bayou brothel before you even went to that hotel."

"Where is she now?" Joe asked, the tears starting to come.

"I don't know. I'm sure she's in Louisiana by now, turning tricks or whatever."

"Do you want to live?" Joe asked.

Ronnie said he did.

"Then you pick up that telephone."

"Who am I calling?"

"The Greek. And so help me, if you tip him off in any way, I'll blow your fucking head off."

Ronnie picked up the phone. "What do I tell him?"

"Tell him you're coming to see him."

"Today?"

"Now. And you better put on a swell performance. I mean, it better be a dandy, because if I get so much as an inkling of an idea that you're selling us out, your brains are gonna be all over these walls."

Ronnie dialed the phone. He listened for a moment and then said, "Yeah, this is Ronnie. Lemme talk to the boss." Ronnie listened silently for about thirty seconds before saying, "Yeah, Boss. I gotta talk to you about some things, but I don't wanna do it over the phone. If you don't mind, I'm coming over." Another pause and then Ronnie said, "I'm on my way."

Ronnie hung up the telephone. "Now what?"

Vinnie said, "Now we go meet the man."

* * *

Mertis Whitlock stopped by Joe Gibson's place just after eleven. Gibson's Ford Expedition sat in the driveway, so Mertis figured he was home. Mertis climbed out of the Crown Vic, lit a cigarette, and made his way up towards the porch. He knocked on the door several times but no one answered. He walked down around the porch. He could hear music—sounded like Billy Joel—coming from the garage, some ten feet further up the driveway beyond the Expedition.

As Mertis made his way around the house, he saw the garage door standing open. He envisioned Gibson back there tinkering around at his workbench.

"Mr. Gibson?" Mertis said.

No answer.

Billy Joel sang "We Didn't Start the Fire," a song that Mertis didn't particularly care for. Mertis noticed the can of beer sitting there on the workbench. He touched it to see if it was still cold, but found it to be warm. Mertis was about to call out for Gibson again when he noticed the sawed-off shotgun barrel clamped in the vise.

"Shit," Mertis said.

At once he knew Gibson was out for revenge against the bastards who'd taken his little girl. Mertis couldn't fault him for going after the kidnappers, but he also knew that the law was the law. At least for now, until after he'd spoken to Gibson about all of this, Mertis decided not to say anything to anyone about what he'd discovered.

DAY EIGHT

PART TWO

The three men took Ronnie's Cutlass Supreme to see the Greek. When Vinnie started the car, Conway Twitty's *Hello Darling* came blaring from the speakers. Vinnie quickly rectified this by ejecting the CD and tossing it out the window. At first Ronnie objected, but Vinnie reminded him that he was lucky to even be alive.

"You sure the Greek's gonna be home?" Vinnie asked.

Ronnie nodded. "He does all his business there. He never leaves."

"How many men does he have with him?"

"He keeps a small army in there."

"How many men?"

"I'm not sure."

"Guess."

Ronnie rubbed his chin, thinking. "I'd say twenty, maybe more."

Vinnie laughed.

"How can you laugh?" Joe asked from the backseat. "We could get killed in there."

"A guy's gotta die some time, Joe. Besides, what do you care? Your time is coming pretty soon either way."

Ronnie thought about this for a moment. He started to comment, but Joe pressed the Smith & Wesson against the back of his head. "Mind your own business."

* * *

Nikos Panagakos, also known as the Greek, lived in a swanky neighborhood on the Upper East Side. He had a mansion that looked like the kind of place a hip-hop music mogul would own. At once both stately and gaudy, the Greek's home had the Spanish structural design that was much more prevalent in California. There it would likely have been surrounded by palm trees. Here it was only surrounded by the Greek's goons, standing guard. There were two of them out in front of the place, on opposite sides of the yard. Their guns weren't out, but they were obviously packing.

Vinnie pulled the Cutlass into the driveway, parking behind four black Cadillacs.

"Let's run through this," Vinnie said. "We're gonna have our guns holstered, Ronnie. But so help me God, you pull any shit, you die. Simple as that."

Ronnie chuckled. "You must be pretty quick on the draw."

"I'm Wyatt fucking Earp," Vinnie said, chewing on a toothpick. "Don't try me."

"You guys promise you're not gonna kill me?"

"We won't kill you," Joe said. "All you gotta do is go through the motions, act like it's business as usual, and get us inside that house."

"That shouldn't be a problem."

The three men got out of the car. Ronnie led the way up the driveway, with Vinnie and Joe right behind. One of the goons patrolling the yard called out to Ronnie, "Hey chief, how's it going?"

Ronnie played it cool. "Not bad. And yourself?"

"Another day, another dollar."

Ronnie smirked and nodded, walking up the steps to the front door.

"You guys ready for this?" he asked.

"Ready as I'll ever be," Joe said.

Ronnie knocked. A man opened the door just a crack, peering out through the chain-lock.

"It's me," Ronnie said. "The boss is expecting us."

"Gimme a minute."

The man called someone on a walkie-talkie. "Ronnie's here. Got two guys with him." He waited for a few seconds and then a voice said, "Send 'em on back." The man said "Okay," and unlocked the door. When he did, Vinnie turned and fired on the goon who'd said "another day, another dollar" to Ronnie. The bullet struck the man center mass in the back, and he dropped. Vinnie whirled around and fired on the second goon, shooting him in the face.

Joe followed right behind Ronnie. He reached over Ronnie's shoulder and fired into the doorman's face. Joe then grabbed Ronnie from behind and shoved him into the doorway, firing upon the Greek's men from around his body. First he shot a man to the left, and then he shot a goon just to the right. Ronnie started to blurt something out about not being able to hear anything due to Joe's gunshots next to his ear, but a hail of bullets struck him from the front. As Ronnie fell dead to the ground, both Joe and Vinnie came up firing from behind.

Vinnie shot a big Latino with a .45 standing on the stairway in the chest. The man lost his balance and toppled down the stairs, landing in a bloody heap. A large Italian man in a bright blue and orange Hawaiian shirt sat at a table to their left. Joe fired on the man before he could reach for his weapon. The bullet struck him in the nose, and the man's face slammed forward into the bowl of Fruity Pebbles he'd been eating.

A heavyset black man with a Beretta emerged from a hallway at the back of the room. "What the fuck goin' on out here?" Vinnie shot him in the chest. The man staggered for a second, looked around with an expression of confusion, and finally fell, taking a small decorative table down with him.

No one else was visible in the two front rooms. Joe and Vinnie moved quickly, making their way toward the bowels of the estate. An attractive woman, probably twenty-five or so, emerged on the stairway just above the dead Latino. Joe raised the Smith & Wesson, but decided to let her go since she wasn't one of the Greek's soldiers. As he lowered the pistol, the woman pulled out a snub-nosed .38 and aimed it at Joe. Vinnie fired on her before she could shoot, hitting her in the forehead, and she flopped down the stairs.

Joe looked at Vinnie. "Thanks."

"Don't mention it," Vinnie said. "We'd better reload while we can. Me first, then you."

The two men took turns reloading their weapons. They then moved quietly into the hallway from which the black man had emerged. Joe led the way, with Vinnie watching their rear. Joe came to a couple of rooms, pushing their doors open, and finding no one inside. Joe saw a closed door at the end of the hall. He crept toward it. He saw a movement in the light beneath the door, realized what was happening, and said, "Oh Jesus." He managed to dive out of the way just in time, as a shotgun blast splintered the door to pieces.

The guy inside, another Latino, made the mistake of peering out through the hole in the door. When he did, Vinnie shot him square in the face, and the man went down.

"You all right?" Vinnie asked.

Joe raised himself up from the floor. "Yeah."

Joe led the way again, and the two men entered the room at the end of the hallway. There was no one inside other than the dead Latino with the scatter gun. The room looked like a sort of break room for the Greek's men—bare with only two picnic tables in the center of the room. A refrigerator and a microwave were the room's only adornments. A small television sat in the corner, an old black-and-white western on the screen, a shoot-out taking place between a gang of outlaws and a pursuing posse.

When Joe opened the door on the other side of the break room, he found himself in another hallway. A door ahead and to the left opened and a heavyset man with a pistol emerged. The man spotted Joe and raised his gun, but Joe shot him in the throat.

"Nice shootin', Tex," Vinnie said.

Before the words were out of Vinnie's mouth, a Puerto Rican popped up behind him. Joe saw the guy, but couldn't move fast enough to stop him from shooting Vinnie in the left shoulder. So the Puerto Rican popped off his shot, and then Joe shot him in the cheek, blowing his brains out.

"You all right?" Joe asked.

"Fuck no," Vinnie said. "It hurts like a sonofabitch."

"You'll live?"

"Yeah, I'll live. But I could sure use a smoke right about now."

Joe turned and pushed the next door open, finding no one inside. He then moved on to the next door, on his right, and looked inside. A bathroom, no one inside. The next door he came to was the one from which the heavyset man had emerged. It was a bedroom, and it was empty.

Joe stepped over the body and moved toward the closed door at the end of the hallway. He carefully opened it and found a large rec room. It had a bar on one end, a pool table and an air hockey table in the center, and a variety of vintage arcade games lining the walls. At the far end of the room, near the bar, a young black guy listened to loud music in headphones and played Ms. Pac-Man, completely oblivious to all the ruckus. The guy completed another level on the game when Joe stepped up behind him, pushing the barrel of the Smith & Wesson against the back of his head.

The guy jumped, startled. "Fuck you doin'?" he asked, his eyes big and crazy. The gun in his face now, he pulled off the headphones. "Who the fuck are you supposed to be?"

Joe nodded towards the game. "You're pretty good."

"Yeah, well, I play a lot."

"That what you do for the Greek, play video games?"

The guy shrugged. "It passes the time."

Vinnie said, "Here's one for you, Einstein. Imagine you were in here playing your stupid fucking game and listening to your music, and the house was overrun. I bet you wouldn't even know." He looked at Joe. "What do you think?"

"Nah," Joe said. "I doubt you'd have even the slightest clue."

The guy looked shocked. "You guys overran the house?"

Vinnie nodded.

"How many people are dead out there?"

"All of 'em," Joe said.

"Everyone we saw, anyway," Vinnie added.

"Damn," the guy said. "So now you gonna kill me?"

"Depends," Joe said.

"On what?"

"On how much you cooperate."

"You say *everyone's* dead?"

Vinnie nodded again.

"Shit, I don't wanna die. You ain't gotta ask me twice. What you wanna know?"

Joe and Vinnie looked at each other, grinning.

Joe said, "We can't find the Greek."

"You didn't see him while you were playin' *Wild Bunch* out there?"

"Un-uh."

"Shit, he's probably locked away down in the safe room."

"Can you get in?" Vinnie asked.

"The safe room?"

"Yeah."

"Sure. That all you need?"

Vinnie laughed. "You'd give up your boss' life to save your black ass?"

"Nigga, I'd give up my *mama's* life to save my black ass."

∗ ∗ ∗

The guy, who identified himself as Tyrone, led them through a series of hallways and stairs. On the way, Tyrone said, "Can I ask you a question?"

"Anything," Vinnie said.

"While you guys were shootin' up the place, you happen to notice a fat bastard in an ugly-ass Hawaiian shirt?"

"Yeah," Joe said. "The guy with the cereal."

"You guys kill him?"

"Yeah. Why?"

"That nigga Chuck still owes me twenty dollars."

Joe ignored this. "What's the safe room like?"

"It's just an empty room with nothing in it but a bed, a table, and a refrigerator. It's got concrete and steel-reinforced walls. The Greek says you'd have to have a bazooka to get inside."

"We won't need a bazooka," Vinnie said.

"Nah," Joe said, looking at Tyrone. "We got you."

"My lucky day," Tyrone said.

Finally Tyrone brought them to a closed steel door with an intercom system next to it, two levels beneath the ground.

"This is the safe room?" Joe asked.

Tyrone nodded. "This is it."

Vinnie pointed his .45 at Tyrone. "Do your thing, buddy."

"Put that motherfuckin' gun down and I will. I don't do shit with a gun in my face."

Vinnie gave Joe a "fuck this guy" look and lowered the pistol. "Go to it."

Tyrone pushed the button on the intercom.

"Who is it?" asked a husky voice.

"It's Tyrone. Let me in the goddamn door, Jake."

"What's the password?"

Tyrone looked at Joe and Vinnie, shaking his head. "Kumbaya, my Lord."

There was a moment of silence and then the door opened. Jake, a big burly guy, stood there looking stupid just before Vinnie shot him in the chest.

This left only the Greek, a heavyset, old man with liver spots who reminded Joe of Anthony Quinn. The Greek looked at Tyrone. "What the hell did you let them in here for?"

"What?" Tyrone asked. "And get *my* ass killed? Hell no."

Tyrone started to talk some more shit when Vinnie raised the .45, pointing it at the back of his head. "Sorry, Tyrone," Vinnie said, pulling the trigger.

Noticeably perturbed, the Greek said, "Fuck you do that for?"

"To get your attention," Vinnie said.

"Trust me, you got my attention when you wiped out all my men."

Joe stuck the Smith & Wesson in the old man's face.

"Watch where you put that thing," the Greek said. "I'd hate to have to stick it up your ass."

"Big talk for an old man sitting in front of a .45 and a great big Smith & Wesson," Vinnie said, looking at Joe. "What do they call that thing?"

"The Governor," Joe said.

"I've got to say, I never imagined you getting this far," the Greek said. "The way you took out Ventimiglia and all his guys—"

"And all *your* guys," Joe said.

"Right," the Greek said, grinning. "Very impressive. In another life, who knows? You coulda been one of us."

"Why the fuck did you pick *me* to go after Ventimiglia?" Joe asked. "I've never understood that."

"Yeah," Vinnie said, nodding. "That shit don't make sense."

The Greek smiled. "You sure you want to hear this?"

Joe looked at Vinnie, then back at the Greek. "Let's hear it."

"Well, we were having problems with Ventimiglia. We were trying to expand to Chicago, but he kept fucking with us. So, I decided, the old bastard had to go. I didn't want me or any of my guys connected to the hit. Who needs that kind of shit storm raining down on their head? So, I decided to have a regular guy—a, uh, *regular Joe*, if you will—" The Greek laughed at his own joke. "I decided to have him kill Ventimiglia for me. I figured it would be easy—all I'd have to do is threaten to take away their loved ones and they'd do it. I got the idea from that movie—"

"The one with Johnny Depp?" Vinnie asked.

"No. It was an older movie with, uh, Ben Gazzara in it. You seen it?"

Vinnie shook his head. "No, I don't think so."

Joe didn't care about any of this. "So why *me*? How the fuck did you select *me* for this little adventure?"

"You'll love this," the Greek said.

"Somehow I kinda doubt that."

"I was reading one of your books. It was *No Rest for the Wicked*. Pretty good book. At least the first half. I didn't care much for the conclusion. Seemed kind of contrived."

Joe pressed the barrel of the Smith & Wesson against the Greek's nose. "Go on."

"Anyway, I was trying to figure out how I would go about selecting someone for the job. Then, I look down at the book, and lo and behold, there's your picture on the back. And your bio said you lived in New York City with your wife and daughter, and I thought, 'Well, shit, it's my lucky day.'"

Joe couldn't believe what he was hearing. "*That's* how you selected me?"

The Greek smiled big, obviously quite proud of himself.

Joe swung the Smith & Wesson hard across the Greek's face, pistol-whipping the old man. The Greek's head rocked sideways and a mixture of blood and teeth flew from his mouth. He shook his head, trying to clear his vision, blood dripping from his lips.

"Nice swing, kid," he said.

Joe wasn't laughing. "Why'd you kill Denise?"

The Greek looked confused. "Who the fuck is Denise?"

"My wife, asshole!" Joe swung the Smith & Wesson again—harder this time—and managed to knock out a few more of the Greek's teeth.

"Sorry," the Greek said, still grinning. "Your wife... Well, I just wanted you to know we meant business."

"You took my daughter," Joe said. "I think I would have known you meant business without your killing my wife."

"We had to be sure we had you by the *cojones*. We had to know you wouldn't go to the cops."

"Well, I didn't. And I did what you wanted. So why didn't you bring back my daughter?"

"Who knew you'd make it out of there alive? The odds were a million to one. So I figured, hey, I'd make some money off the little girl. Sold her to a couple of brothel owners down in Louisiana, go by the name of the Kleek brothers."

There were tears in Joe's eyes again. "Where is she now?"

"Like I said, I sold her to the Kleek brothers. I suspect she's down there in Louisiana, working in that brothel."

Joe started shaking. Badly. He repositioned the pistol, pressing it right between the Greek's eyes.

"Before I kill you," Joe said, "I have to know one thing."

"Which is?"

"How much money did you get for my little Emily?"

The Greek smiled, his mouth a bloody mess. "Ten thousand."

"You sold my eight-year-old daughter for ten thousand dollars?"

"Yeah."

Joe pulled the trigger, and the Greek was no more.

DAY EIGHT

PART THREE

Dewayne and Arturo had been watching the little girl for a week now, and the shit had gotten old fast. Someone was supposed to have come to pick her up two days ago, but there had been a delay. Dewayne was starting to miss the outside world. He'd been cooped up in the little house for the past seven days, with no one to keep him company but Arturo and the old black-and-white television. This sucked, as Arturo didn't talk much and the television only picked up two channels.

Dewayne had started watching the little girl—really paying attention to her—about three days ago. He couldn't say exactly when he'd developed the taste for little girls—maybe during his stretch in Lompoc—but it was certainly there now. Try as he might, he couldn't get the thoughts of that little girl and all the things he could do to her out of his head. So far it hadn't been a problem, as he hadn't had more than two minutes alone with her. But today would be different. Today Arturo announced that he was going out for food.

"I'm sick of eating ramen noodles every meal," Arturo said.

"What's wrong with ramen noodles?" Dewayne had asked.

"Fuck ramen noodles. I've eaten so many ramen noodles this week that I've got 'em coming out my ass. If I never eat another ramen noodle again, it'll be too soon."

And Arturo left.

* * *

Emily was scared and she missed her parents. She didn't know what exactly was happening to her, but she knew it was wrong. The two guys—the one with the brown skin and the one with the white skin—were nice enough to her, but she sensed that this wasn't supposed to be happening. "We're gonna watch you until your Mommy and Daddy come home," the brown-skinned one had told her.

"Where did they go?" she asked.

"Mommy and Daddy had to go on a trip. It was real urgent and they didn't have time to tell you goodbye. But they asked us to watch you until they get back."

The brown-skinned man was okay, but the other one—the one who told her to call him Uncle Dewayne—was much nicer. Emily couldn't put her finger on it, but she sensed there was something wrong with him. The way he looked at her. Something was weird about it.

Emily sat on the bean bag in the room they had given her, watching *The Flintstones* on an old VHS tape. She had already seen this episode many times over the past week, but watching it beat doing nothing.

The door opened, and the one who called himself Uncle Dewayne entered. And Emily knew at once there was something different about him.

"You and I are gonna play," he said.

Emily looked at him. "Can we play with the toys?"

"What toys?"

"The ones in the closet."

"There are toys in the closet?"

Emily pointed at the closet. "Way up at the top, on one of the shelves. You can see *Monopoly* and some other games up there, and there are toys stacked on top of the boxes—a teddy bear and some other stuff."

Dewayne rubbed his chin. "I wonder why those are up there."

Dewayne walked to the closet and looked inside. Looking up, he said, "Sure, I'll get 'em down. One of those games is *Twister.* Have you ever played *Twister?*"

Emily said she had not.

"Well," Dewayne said, "you and I can play us a game of Twister. I think you'll like it."

He winked at her.

He then stood up and walked out of the room. He left for about thirty seconds, and then returned with a wooden crate.

"I'll just climb up on this and get those toys down. Then we can play *Twister.*"

Dewayne climbed on top of the crate, but still had difficulty reaching the toys. He stood on his tip-toes, and managed to pull down the stack of games and toys. Just when he retrieved the toys, however, the crate caved in and Dewayne came crashing down to the floor, hitting his head in the process.

Emily picked up an *Etch-a-Sketch* that had fallen with Dewayne, and looked at it for a moment. Dewayne blinked and tried to focus his eyes, but Emily smashed the *Etch-a-Sketch* over his face as hard as she could. Dewayne made a moaning sound when the toy struck his face, and he was out cold.

Emily turned and ran through the open door, and then ran out of the house.

* * *

Mertis Whitlock sat at his desk, looking over crime scene photographs of the Hyperion Hotel massacre when Johnson, a uniformed cop, approached his desk. Mertis didn't look up.

"Detective Whitlock?" Johnson asked.

"Yeah, what is it?"

"I've got something you're gonna wanna see."

Mertis looked up and saw the teary-eyed little girl standing beside Johnson.

"I don't understand," Mertis said.

"We found her wandering around in an alley, crying and lost. They said we should bring her to you."

"Why is that?"

"Her name is Emily Gibson."

DAY EIGHT

PART FOUR

Vinnie and Joe were back in Vinnie's Navigator listening to some obnoxious song by Public Enemy that Joe neither liked nor understood. They were two blocks from Joe's house when Vinnie said, "I like you, Joe, but I'm still gonna have to kill you. Business is business."

Joe's grip tightened on the Smith & Wesson. "I'm afraid that's not gonna happen."

Vinnie looked at Joe, a smirk on his face. "Oh yeah? You don't think so?"

"Look," Joe said, "I just found out my little girl is alive and working in some goddamn brothel down in Louisiana. I'm gonna have to go find her. If you wanna kill me after that, then so be it. But I have to go get Emily."

"I get what you're saying, but I don't have that kind of time to wait."

Joe pulled the pistol up from beside his legs, sitting it on his lap. He gripped it tightly, making no effort to conceal the fact. "So how do you want to do this?"

"I really wanna let you go, honest I do. But if I go back to Chicago without your head on a platter, I'll be the one gets killed. And I can't have that, Joe. So I'm thinking—in about a minute we're gonna be right in front of your house. Suppose I let you run in the house and wait ten seconds to come in after you. Then, I kill you, you kill me, whatever..."

Joe looked at Vinnie and realized he'd come to like him. "I don't want to kill you."

"But I'll kill you. I'll kill the fuck out of you, Joe. I like you, but it ain't shit to me. So you gotta look at this as self-preservation. It's kill or be killed, eat or fucking be eaten. Which one are you, Joe:

are you Jaws or are you some dumb motherfucker on the beach that gets eaten by Jaws?"

Joe really didn't want to do this, but he played along. "I guess I'm Jaws."

"That's what I wanna hear."

Vinnie parked the Navigator in front of Joe's house.

He grinned and put out his hand for Joe to shake, and Joe shook it.

"You'd better get out now," Vinnie said. "Because I'm gonna start couting. Ten...nine..."

Joe opened the door, got out, and ran like a motherfucker.

＊ ＊ ＊

Joe was crouched behind the couch when Vinnie got to the front door. Vinnie was angry and yelling about the door being locked. "Fuck you lock this door for, Joe? You really think that's gonna slow me down?"

Joe braced himself, arm over the couch, pistol trained on the front door.

Vinnie kicked the door open and started to step inside. The shot from Joe's Smith & Wesson just missed his head, and Vinnie ducked back out the door.

"Jesus Christ, Joe, you coulda killed me," Vinnie said, laughing at his own joke. "You wouldn't want to kill me, would you? I'm your buddy."

Vinnie stayed out of sight, and Joe kept the pistol trained on the doorway.

"What if you just stayed there with your gun aimed at the door," Vinnie said, "and I ran around the house and came in behind you through the back door? That would be something, huh?" Vinnie sounded irritated that Joe wasn't responding. "What's wrong, Joe? Cat got your tongue?"

Joe said nothing.

Vinnie took the hint and stopped talking. There was a long moment of silence—Joe thought it was maybe two, three minutes—before Vinnie came diving through the door. It took Joe a millisecond to realize what was happening, and he fired late, missing Vinnie by a foot or so. Vinnie hit the ground and sort of rolled behind the wall to the stairs, where Joe couldn't see him.

"You like that?" Vinnie asked. "That looked like something out of a John Woo movie, didn't it? I took tumbling for two years as a kid. Always knew that would come in handy someday."

Joe fired into the wall, hoping to hit Vinnie.

Vinnie screeched. *"Oh shit, I'm hit!"*

Joe waited a few seconds before speaking. "You're hit?"

"Yeah, you hit me in the chest."

Joe didn't know what to say. "Is it bad?"

Vinnie sounded irritated. *"I'm hit in the fucking chest. Yes, goddammit, it's bad! How the hell could it possibly be good?"*

"Call this whole thing off, and I'll drive you to the hospital."

Joe could hear Vinnie sobbing. "I don't wanna die, Joe."

"Come on. We don't have to do this. You could just put down your gun and we could get you some help."

"I dunno."

"What's to know? If you don't get help, you're a dead man."

"Yeah," Vinnie said, "but if I let you go, I'm gonna die anyway."

"Maybe we can work that out together. Just put your gun down."

"And you'll put yours down, too?"

"Yeah. You put your gun down, I'll put my gun down."

"Okay, my gun is on the floor. Is yours?"

"Yes," Joe lied. "My gun is on the floor."

"Now what?"

"Now we take you to the hospital and get you patched—"

Vinnie came walking out from behind the corner, his pistol out. He fired once, his shot hitting the couch and just missing Joe by about an inch.

Joe still had his pistol trained on the corner where Vinnie was. He returned fire immediately, his shot striking Vinnie in the same shoulder he'd already been hit in at the Greek's place. Vinnie cried out in pain and spun around, falling out of sight.

"What the fuck?" Vinnie said. *"You lied!"*

"Well, you lied, too! You said your gun was down. And you said you were hit."

"You said *your* gun was down, goddammit!"

"I kind of figured you were gonna pull that shit," Joe said.

"You knew I was faking?"

"It seemed like something you would do. Hell, I would have done it."

Joe could hear Vinnie laughing. "I taught you well, my friend."

"Now what?"

"I guess now we get into some gangster shit, and we have us a good old-fashioned shoot-out."

"I was afraid you'd say that."

Joe turned and sprinted, heading for the kitchen.

Vinnie fired, his shot hitting the China cabinet ahead of Joe, just before Joe rounded the corner. Joe ran through the dining room and into the kitchen, ducking behind the cabinet island in the center of the room.

Vinnie was now in the dining room, hiding around the corner.

"Come on out, Joe," he said. "Why not make this easy for everybody?"

"Now what fun would that be?"

Vinnie fired into the kitchen, his shot hitting a frying pan hanging above Joe's head. The shot caromed off the pan and zipped into the wall.

"If you were me, what would *you* do?" Joe asked.

"Thank God I'm not you. But if I were you, I'd fight back. I'd fight back real hard, and I'd hope like hell that I won this little gunfight so I could go and save my little girl, Joe. That's what I would do."

Joe couldn't help himself—he actually liked this sonofabitch trying to kill him. "Yeah, that's pretty much where I'm at."

"Only problem with that," Vinnie said, "is that you can't beat me, Joe."

"Why is that?"

"I told you—I'm Wyatt fucking Earp."

Vinnie and Joe both laughed at this.

"You got your cigarettes on you, Joe?"

Joe wondered where this was going. "Yeah, why?"

"There's a real good chance at least one of us is gonna die, right?"

"Yeah."

"So what say you and I take a break and we each smoke a cigarette? Then, just as soon as we're both done with our cigarettes, we'll get back to killing one another."

This sounded like bullshit. "You fuckin' with me again, Vinnie?"

"No, I'm dead serious. I swear on a stack of Bibles. I swear on the Virgin Mary herself."

"You're Catholic?"

"I'm Italian, Joe. We're all Catholic."

"And you wanna take a break and smoke a cigarette?"

"I just wanna take a time out."

"A time out, huh?"

"Yeah, why not? I mean, I know it sounds silly, but it's just you and me here. Who's gonna know? Especially if we end up doing what we came here to do when we're finished with our cigarettes."

"You're serious?"

"As a heart-attack."

"Something is seriously wrong with you, my friend," Joe said. "And it's no small thing."

Vinnie laughed. "So we gonna do this, or what?"

Joe shrugged. "What the hell? A cigarette sounds pretty good right now."

Vinnie pulled the pack of Winstons from his jacket pocket, put one to his lips, and lit it. "I really do like you, Joe. I figure, if I gotta kill you, maybe we can just kind of sit here and shoot the shit for a few minutes first."

Joe lit his Pall Mall. "Shoot the shit, huh?"

"Yeah."

"What do you wanna talk about?"

"Why don't you tell me about Denise?"

Joe took a drag from the cigarette and exhaled. "Where do I begin? Denise was my life. I would have done anything for her."

"It shows."

"How so?"

"Look at all the people you've killed."

Joe smiled. "If you'd have told me two weeks ago that I would have killed all those people, I would have said you were crazy."

"Grief makes a person do strange things."

"I guess," Joe said. "How about you? You got a woman back home?"

Vinnie laughed. "I got lots of women back home."

"But no one special?"

"What are you talking about, Joe? They're *all* special. They're special for a night, and then they get dressed and they go home in the morning."

Joe laughed at this, and took another drag from his cigarette. "Don't you ever get lonely?"

"Nah, not really. I'm the kind of person who really likes being alone. I like being able to do what I want, when I want."

Joe nodded. "How'd you get into this line of work?"

Vinnie chuckled. "'*Line of work*,' huh?"

"Yeah."

"You know, it was the family business. My uncle was the fucking boss of Chicago. I never really had a choice." Vinnie took a drag of his cigarette. "How about you—how'd you end up becoming a writer?"

"It's all I ever wanted to be. For as long as I can remember I always wanted to write. When I was a kid I used to write stories about the characters in the books I read."

"What kinds of books?"

"*Treasure Island*, *Superman* comic books, shit like that. The usual."

"It wasn't usual for me," Vinnie said. "I hated to read when I was a kid. Only thing I ever read was a racing form."

"That's too bad. Did you ever want to be anything else besides a gangster?"

Vinnie thought about it for a minute. "Well, I really wanted to play shortstop for the Cubs. I wanted to be like Shawon Dunston. I had his poster hanging over my bed and everything."

"So what happened?"

Vinnie chuckled. "I couldn't hit the breaking pitch, that's what happened."

Joe laughed.

Vinnie stubbed out his cigarette against the wall. "I'm finished with my cigarette."

"Me too."

"You ready to do this?"

"Not really."

Each of them counted to ten in their heads before moving. And then they both emerged, pistols blazing. Vinnie's shot struck Joe in the chest. Joe felt a burning near his heart. He gasped for air, but found it difficult to breathe. He staggered backwards in shock.

Shit, he'd really been hit.

Vinnie stood there for a moment, also in shock. Joe looked down at the bleeding wound, and then looked back up at Vinnie. Joe raised the Smith & Wesson and fired again, this time hitting Vinnie in the chest. The shot knocked Vinnie off his feet, and he was out cold.

Joe slid down against the cabinet. Breathing had become difficult, and Joe knew he was going to die. His shaking hands pulled out the pack of Pall Malls again, and he put one to his lips. He fumbled with his lighter for a moment before managing to light the damned thing.

He thought about his little Emily, and he closed his eyes.

CONCLUSION

Mertis hadn't gotten much out of Emily. She couldn't tell him exactly where she'd been kept, or who her keepers were. She'd given him the name "Dewayne," but had nothing more to offer. Mertis had then attempted to call Joe Gibson, but the phone went straight to voice mail. Probably out killing bad guys, Mertis thought. Hopefully he was wrong about Gibson. After all, little Emily was going to need her father.

They were driving in the Crown Vic, with Emily sitting in the backseat. She didn't speak at all on the drive over. Mertis tried to talk to her, but the little girl was having none of it. She just sat there in silence.

Mertis parked in the driveway behind Gibson's Expedition. There was also a black Navigator parked at the curb. Mertis sensed that something was wrong. He looked up and saw that the front door to the house was hanging open.

Then he heard gunshots.

He grabbed the CB and called for backup. Then he heard another shot.

He turned to the little girl. "Emily, you stay here. I'll be right back. Whatever you do, don't get out of this car until I get back here."

Mertis pulled out his .38 and ran onto the porch. He moved carefully into the house.

"Mr. Gibson?" he yelled out. There was no answer.

Mertis made his way through the house. He saw the broken China on the floor. He moved around the corner and saw what looked to be a dead man lying on the floor, a pistol next to him. He moved towards the body, but then heard a moan coming from the kitchen.

"Gibson?" he called out.

"Yes?" the voice answered weakly.

Mertis moved carefully into the kitchen and around the cabinet island. There was Joe Gibson, leaning against the cabinet. He was a bloody mess. He was barely alive and smoking a cigarette. There was a big Smith & Wesson lying on the floor beside him.

Joe Gibson looked at him through squinted eyes.

"Hello, detective."

Mertis started to say something, but Vinnie's shot caught him in the throat. Mertis reached for the wound. Vinnie's second shot caught him in the chest, and Mertis fell to the floor.

"You didn't have to do that," Joe managed. "He was a really nice guy."

"He was a cop."

Vinnie dragged himself across the dining room and into the kitchen, leaving a trail of blood in his wake. He finally made it around the cabinet island.

"You gonna kill me now?" Joe asked.

"No offense, but I think I already did. And you definitely killed me. You and me, we're gonna sit here and die together."

Vinnie pulled himself up against the cabinet, and sat next to Joe.

"I should have worn a bulletproof vest," Vinnie said.

Joe forced himself to smile. "Me too."

* * *

Emily was tired of waiting. She had already waited a week to see her Mommy and Daddy, and she was ready to go into her house. She opened the car door and climbed out. She made her way up the steps and onto the porch. She looked at the broken door, but didn't understand what she was seeing. She went into the house and looked around for her parents. She saw the bullet hole in the wall beside the stairs, but didn't know what had caused it. She made her way into the dining room and saw the broken China all over the floor.

"Mommy?" she said. "Daddy?"

She looked down at the trail of blood which reached across the dining room carpet and onto the kitchen linoleum. She followed it.

When she came around the cabinet island, she saw her daddy lying there hurt.

"Daddy," she yelled. *"Daddy, wake up!"*

* * *

Joe opened his eyes. It was blurry, but he saw his Emily standing there.

"Daddy?" she said, crying.

The voice sounded like it was far away.

Joe couldn't see much, but he could feel her nestling up against his bloody chest.

"Daddy, please," she sobbed.

And the voice was even farther away this time.

This, Joe thought, must be heaven, where people reunited with their loved ones. Here he would be with his little Emily again.

Would Denise be here, too?

"Please, Daddy, please."

The voice was so far away now.

Joe smiled and closed his eyes.

$CRILLA

In memory of Elmore Leonard.

ONE

Charlie Grimes had lost his mojo. He'd already been in Los Angeles for three days and had yet to get laid. He knew what the problem was—the women here were too damn hot. He considered himself a pretty good-lookin' dude, but these LA girls were way the fuck out of his league. Not even the same sport. Girls who rated a ten back in Chicago weren't more than fives, maybe sixes out here.

He'd already hit on more than a few women, but none of them seemed the least bit interested in what he had to offer. These were women with aspirations of being actresses and models, and they longed for the companionship of movie moguls, millionaires, and oil men. Charlie figured they could smell the musky ordinariness on him a mile away.

Tonight he was giving up on women. Tonight he was just gonna sit in this bar—the creatively named *Doc's Tavern* —and down a few bottles of beer. He was sitting on his stool, taking the occasional swig from his Budweiser, and nodding his head to some kind of electronica garbage he absolutely hated. But, Charlie figured, when in Rome...

He took out a pack of smokes and pulled one out. He put it to his lips and lit the fucker about thirty seconds before a waiter appeared asking him to extinguish it.

"Sorry," he said. "I keep forgetting it's illegal to smoke here."

A voice came from behind. "Silly, isn't it?"

Charlie turned to face the voice and saw a stunning brunette, about his age, probably forty or so, standing behind his stool.

"What's that?" he asked.

She smiled a smile that made all seven inches of Charlie's dick stand on end. "It's silly you can't smoke in a bar. I mean, bars are for smoking. Right?"

"I take it you're not from around here?"

Charlie sized her up as he spoke. She was a Chicago ten for sure, maybe even a twelve, but here she would only rate as a seven or eight. That was fine by him. Fuckable was fuckable, and she was that in spades.

"I'm originally from Detroit," she said.

"You always creep around listening to other people's conversations?"

"Not *all* the time."

Sensing there was more to this girl than just great tits and a nice ass, Charlie decided right then and there he liked her.

"My name's Charlie."

"You don't see many Charlies in LA."

"What do you see?"

"Dicks," she said. "Lots and lots of dicks."

"Would you like to sit?" asked Charlie, motioning towards the open stool.

"Sure," she said.

"You got a name?"

"Candace."

"That's a nice name."

"My parents thought so."

A waiter who slightly resembled one of the Duran Duran twinks approached the table. "How are you tonight?"

"We'll have a couple more beers," said Candace.

"Budweiser?"

Candace nodded. The waiter scurried off, and Charlie grinned. "Beer, huh?"

"Like I said, Detroit."

"I woulda pegged you for a martini drinker. Something more cosmopolitan."

"Sometimes I drink martinis," said Candace. "But tonight I'm drinking beer."

She crossed her legs, and Charlie looked down at her knee-high black leather boots.

"Those are some interesting boots."

"Interesting good or interesting bad?"

"You either look like a pirate or a hooker. I don't know which."

"You're a forward one, aren't you?"

"It doesn't pay to beat around the bush."

"So you think I look like a pirate hooker?"

"No," said Charlie. "I said you either look like one or the other—not both."

"Which implies that it's possible for me to be both a pirate and a hooker, which pretty much makes me a pirate hooker."

Charlie threw his hands up. "I give up."

"So you're saying I *am* a pirate hooker?"

Charlie said, "I forgot how hard it could be to talk to a woman."

"You speak like a man who's been married a time or two."

"Something like that."

"How many times?"

"Three."

"What happened?"

"Didn't take."

"I like you, Charlie."

"Now who's being forward?"

She smiled. "Tell me something I don't know about Charlie."

"I've got heart disease."

Her expression fell away. "What kind?"

"The bad kind."

"Is there any other?"

"No," he said. "Not really."

"But you look healthy. I mean, you just tried to smoke a cigarette."

"I am healthy."

"All things considered," she said.

"All things considered."

"How long have you had it?"

"I was twenty-one when I was diagnosed."

"Really?"

"Surprised?"

Candace said, "Kind of."

"Because you figured I'd be dead by now?"

"Yeah," she said. "I guess so."

"Nope. Still here."

"How do you deal with that?"

"I smoke and I drink. How do you think I deal with it?"

She nodded. "You don't."

"I've got a defibrillator in my chest," he said, thumping it with his finger.

"What is that, like a pace-maker?"

"Sort of," he said. "When my heart stops, it shocks me and my heart starts beating again."

"Oh," she said. "Has it ever gone off before?"

"A time or two."

"What happened?"

"My potassium was low and it caused my heart to stop."

"I didn't even know that was a thing."

"What's that?"

"Potassium could stop your heart."

"Neither did I."

The waiter returned with their beers.

"Put it on my tab," she said.

The waiter nodded and left.

"You come here often?" he asked.

"Too often."

"You always pick up guys like this?"

She smiled. "Who says I'm picking you up?"

"I was certainly hoping."

"Where you from?" she asked.

"Chicago."

"Let me guess—you were a cop."

"What gave it away?"

"Must have been your designer clothing."

"Musta been," said Charlie, feeling slightly embarrassed.

"The cowboy boots."

"Oh yeah?"

"And the goatee."

"Now what's wrong with my goatee?"

"Look around the bar."

Charlie scanned the place.

"You see anyone else in here with a goatee?"

"Look," he said. "I see a lot of people do a lot of crazy shit in LA, and I don't do any of that either. What they do or do not do in LA doesn't concern me."

She laughed.

"You don't like my goatee?"

"It makes you look like a cop."

"I've never heard that before—a goatee making someone look like a cop."

"I guess you have now."

"I like my goatee."

"Well, I like my boots."

"Yeah, but I actually like your boots, too."

"I'm a Nineties girl, Charlie. I still like guys with goatees, and I still listen to indie alt bands from back then."

"Like what? Nine Inch Nails?"

"Radiohead."

"I don't think you'd ever make it in the music world."

"Why's that?" she asked.

"Because these kids today hate anything that wasn't created in the next twenty seconds."

"What kind of music do you listen to?"

"Old stuff."

"Gee," she said, "that really narrows it down. Like Beatles old stuff or Beethoven old stuff?"

"I listen to a lot of Seventies music."

"Like who?"

"Electric Light Orchestra."

"Nice."

Charlie perked up. "You like ELO?"

"Not really."

"Then why'd you say '*nice*'?"

"Because you at least listen to *real* music."

Charlie nodded at the speakers overhead. "Not like the pulsing, throbbing shit that passes for music here."

Candace smiled. "You wanna go somewhere?"

"Where?"

"To get a drink."

"I thought we were having a drink."

"Nobody goes to just one bar in LA."

"They don't?"

"You have a lot to learn, Charlie."

* * *

The second bar they went to was the *Brown Rooster.*

"Fuck does that mean?" asked Charlie.

"Hell if I know."

Charlie didn't see any roosters. In fact, the only brown things he saw were brown people. Lots and lots of brown people.

Candace asked, "You uncomfortable?"

"I'm gonna lie and say no."

"Goodie."

The two of them made their way to an empty booth in the corner, the sounds of funky Seventies' music filling the place.

"You can smoke here," she said.

"I thought it was illegal."

"It is, but they do it anyway. Management doesn't mind."

Charlie looked around, saw a lot of the bar's partrons smoking, and immediately started to like this place a whole lot more.

A waiter came over to the table.

"What can I get you?"

"Two Budweisers," said Charlie.

The man smiled. "We ain't got Budweiser."

"What kind of beer do you have?"

"Colt 45."

Charlie looked at the man to see if he was serious.

He was.

"Okay," said Charlie. "We'll take two Colt 45s."

The waiter left.

"So why aren't you a cop anymore?" asked Candace.

Charlie took his time to answer, lighting a cigarette. Finally he said, "You want the official reason, or you want the truth?"

"Let's try the truth."

"I shot a guy."

Candace looked impressed. "He die?"

"Deader than a Kennedy."

"What was the story?"

"It was either gonna be him or me, and I knew right then it wasn't gonna be me."

"So you shot him."

"I shot him."

"Did they have a hearing?"

"Yeah," said Charlie, drawing on his cigarette. "It was ruled a clean shoot."

"So what was the problem?"

"Truth?"

"Yeah."

"He was black."

"And?"

"The media had a field day with it—white cop shoots black teenager."

"Why do I get the feeling there's more to this?"

Charlie grinned.

She asked, "What haven't you told me?"

"It was my second shooting."

"In how long?"

"Three months."

"You're shitting me," said Candace.

"I shit you not."

"That one ruled a clean kill, too?"

"Yeah."

"Was he a black guy also?"

"Nah. Spoiled white kid who wanted to play with guns."

"You killed him?"

"What do you want me to say? He pulled a Glock on me."

Candace reached for the pack of smokes. "Mind if I have one?"

"Help yourself." This was moot as Candace was already opening the pack. This was a girl used to getting her way. If he didn't watch himself, he might end up falling for her, and that was out of the question. No more serious relationships for Charlie Grimes.

"So they ran you out of Chi Town?"

He nodded. "On a rail."

The waiter returned with two mugs of Colt 45 and stood there waiting to be paid.

Charlie reached into his pocket and pulled out a ten. He handed it to the man, who smiled and walked away.

Charlie looked at Candace. "They don't give change here?"

"They do that sometimes."

"This is an odd place."

"Maybe you're an odd guy."

"No two ways about that."

Charlie was about to talk some more shit, but their conversation was interrupted by a commotion in the center of the room. They both looked to see what was happening. Music still blaring, a big Puerto Rican dude had pulled a gun on a little scrawny black guy. The PR's mouth was moving fast. Charlie couldn't make out the words over the blaring Funkadelic record, but he was pretty sure it was a threat.

Charlie was out of his seat before Candace knew what was happening.

He moved towards the two men, the barrel of the big PR's .45 resting on the little guy's forehead.

As he moved closer, Charlie could make out their words.

"I swear I didn't know she was your girl," the black guy was saying.

The PR wasn't having it. "You're dead, motherfucker."

The Funkadelic record came to an abrupt stop, and everyone watched the two men.

Charlie pulled out his own .38 and leveled it at the PR.

"Drop the weapon," he said.

The PR looked at him like, *What the fuck?,* but didn't drop the gun.

Charlie kept moving forward until he was right up on the dude.

The PR attempted to raise the .45 in Charlie's direction, but Charlie was too fast, the barrel of his .38 crashing down across the bridge of the man's nose. And just like that, the big PR was lying there unconscious in a puddle of his own blood.

Charlie looked at the black guy. "This is the part where you thank me for saving your ass."

"Man, you're crazy," the guy said.

* * *

A few complimentary Colt 45s later, and Charlie and Candace had a good buzz going.

"You told me the real reason you got fired," she said. "You never told me the bullshit reason they gave for firing you."

Charlie said, "Guess."

Candace bit her lip, mulling it over. "I dunno."

Charlie tapped his chest again.

"Your heart?"

"Right."

"Even though you'd had the disease for—"

"For as long as I was a cop," said Charlie.

"Ain't that a bitch."

"A bitch it is."

"If I didn't know any better I'd say you had a death wish."

"You think?"

Candace nodded. "You could've been killed here tonight."

"I could die in my sleep. So what?"

"I have to admit, it did turn me on, though."

Charlie grinned. "Mission accomplished."

"I'll bet you do that on all your dates."

"Disarm Puerto Rican thugs in black bars?"

"Exactly."

"I think you got me all figured out," said Charlie.

* * *

The two of them staggered out back to where their cars were parked.

"Where we going?" she asked.

"My place, I guess."

"Sounds good. I'll follow you."

Charlie climbed into his Dodge pickup and started it up. He looked back at Candace, parked behind him, in a fucking Beamer. He'd have to ask her what the hell she did for a living, he thought. He pulled out of the lot, and she followed.

* * *

When they got to his shitty little one-room apartment, they started kissing at once. It wasn't smooth like in the movies, but it wasn't completely awkward either. Charlie was on top of her, both of them still fully clothed, pushing her down into the soft couch. He raised up for a moment. "Should I turn on some music?"

"Not if it's ELO."

And they went on making out without any musical accompaniment. Soon they were both naked on the questionable shag carpet, and Charlie was inside her. He managed to not tell her he loved her or anything stupid like that, but he knew as he was making love to her that he was falling hard.

* * *

It was just after seven when Charlie woke up alone on the futon. He reached over, but found that Candace was gone. He got up and looked for a note, but there wasn't one. Shit, he thought. A good one had slipped through his fingers.

"Easy come, easy go," he told himself as he fixed a screwdriver.

Candace was like every other woman he'd ever known—she was gone.

TWO

Loop and Bugs were sitting in the lobby at Pronto Records, waiting to see the label's chief exec, Davis Cartright. Usually they met with their A&R guy, an Asian cat named Mikey, but this was different. Loop was leafing through a tattered copy of *Rolling Stone*. "What you think the man wants to see us for?"

"Damned if I know," said Bugs. "I hope it's to pay us the money they owe us for the last record."

Loop nodded. "Hopefully."

"These guys are all crooks."

"Pimps," said Loop.

"Right, they're the pimps, and the artists are hoes."

"I don't like bein' nobody's hoe."

"Me neither," said Bugs. "Me fuckin' neither."

Bugs looked over at Loop. "Whatcha readin'?"

"An article about Majestyk."

Bugs rolled his eyes. "I'm tired of hearing about that nigga."

"Yeah, that should be us on there."

"If the label put a tenth of the resources they put into Majestyk into us, we'd be big stars, too."

Loop nodded.

"What do they say about Majestyk?"

"They say he's the savior of hip-hop music."

Bugs rolled his eyes again. "Fuckin' Majestyk, the goddamn second coming."

"You shouldn't say shit like that."

"Like what?"

"It's blasphemous to compare our Lord Jesus Christ to that punk nigga Majestyk."

Bugs pulled out a pack of menthol cigarettes. He lit one.

"Ain't no smokin' in here," said Loop.

"Fuck 'em."

"Fuck 'em?"

"Yeah," said Bugs. "As much money as they owe our black asses, they can put up with a little smoke."

He looked over at the receptionist, giving him the stink eye but saying nothing.

Finally, after another two cigarettes, the receptionist called them. "Mr. Cartright will see you now."

* * *

Davis Cartright had no business being in gangsta rap. He was a sucker, a privileged yuppie white kid making his money off the blood, sweat, and tears of black men. In Bugs' mind, he was no better than a goddamn plantation owner in the slave days.

Loop was in awe, looking around the man's office.

Fuckin' Loop.

"How are you fellas today?" asked Davis Cartright.

"We're good," said Loop.

Bugs didn't say shit.

"I'm sure you're wondering why I asked you here."

Bugs said, "The thought had crossed my mind. I'm hoping it's to tell us you're finally gonna pay us for the last album."

Davis smiled. "We still haven't recouped our investment."

"Which means?"

"You still owe *us* money."

Bugs squinted. "We owe *you* money?"

"You know how the business works," said Davis. "We put up the money for the tours, the videos, the clothes, the remixes."

"What remixes?"

"We hired a few producers to remix your songs for the last single."

"We didn't authorize that shit," said Bugs.

Loop was still looking around the man's office.

"You didn't have to," said Davis. "It was our call."

"Whose call exactly?"

"Mine." Stupid motherfucker sitting there, all smug, not afraid of them at all.

"Then how do we owe you for remixes we didn't want or know about?"

"That's the way it works. Look at your contract."

"How much did you pay for these remixes?"

"Fifty, sixty thousand dollars each."

"Tell me you at least got Premo."

"We couldn't afford Premo."

"So who'd you get?"

"A rock producer named Benton Michaels."

"A *rock* producer?"

"We did some rock remixes."

"We ain't no rock band."

"We wanted to broaden your fanbase."

"So what happened to the remixes?"

"We weren't happy with them, so we shelved 'em."

"You're not even putting 'em out, but we owe you hundreds of thousands of dollars for them?"

Davis nodded. "Yeah." Smug little bastard, sittin' there in his goddamn Brooks Brothers suit.

"That's bullshit."

"But none of that is why I called you here."

"It's not?"

"No."

"Then what?"

"When you operate a record label, you have to make a lot of very difficult decisions..."

"Okay," said Bugs.

Davis said, "We've decided as a label to part ways with the Road Dogs."

"What's that supposed to mean?"

"We're dropping you from the label."

"The fuck?" asked Bugs.

"Frankly the sales haven't been there."

"But the label has hardly put any money into us. If you put a tenth of the money you put into Majestyk into us, we'd be big time, too. We'd be on the fucking cover of *Rolling Stone*."

Davis looked at him like, *I don't know what to tell you.*

"So now what?" asked Loop.

"Now what *what*?" asked Davis.

"Where do we go from here?"

"You're free agents. Do whatever you want. Go sign with Def Jam."

"But what about the tour with Majestyk?" asked Bugs.

"You've been dropped from the tour."

"Man, I really wanted to see Europe," said Loop.

Fuck this guy, thought Bugs. And fuck Europe, too, the motherfuckin' tea-drinkin', croissant-eatin' sons of bitches.

"How could you do this to us?" asked Bugs. "We been loyal to you."

"And we've been loyal to you, but we can't sustain these kinds of losses annually."

"You're telling me you haven't made any money off us?"

"Not a dime," said Davis.

"Man," said Bugs, "That's some questionable math you usin'."

"How you figure?"

"We had a hit single. *Pump It Up* hit number thirty-seven on the black charts. Our video was number six on BET."

"But we never recouped our investment."

"Word?" asked Loop.

"Fuck this," muttered Bugs, lighting a joint.

"You can't smoke that in here," said Davis.

"Like hell I can't. If you can drop us from the label, I can smoke this goddamn spliff."

"Please extinguish that now."

"Or you'll do what?"

Davis shook his head. "Fucking studio gangstas."

"What?" asked Bugs. "What did you call us?"

"Studio gangstas."

"You're questioning our street cred?"

Davis stared at him. "Get the fuck out of my office."

* * *

Booby was driving the Escalade, and Loop and Bugs were in the back.

"What the fuck we gonna do now?" asked Loop.

"No shit," said Bugs. "We just bought a goddamn mansion. How we gonna pay for that shit?"

"Maybe we could sign with another label."

"Maybe, but that's gonna take time. We'll lose the house before that."

"You think?"

"Yeah, man, I do."

"How much we got in the bank?"

"$45,000."

"That's it?"

"That's it."

"That's fucked up."

"I wish there was something we could do."

And that's when Booby spoke up. "Y'all really wanna do something?"

Bugs asked, "You got something in mind?"

"Well," said Booby, "you could kidnap the white boy."

"Who?"

"Davis Cartright."

"And what, hold him for ransom?"

"Nah, man, just make him sign over five million dollars."

"He got that much?" asked Loop.

"Shit, nigga, he got hundreds of millions," said Bugs.

"Yeah, I seen it in *Forbes*," said Booby. "He's worth over 300 million dollars."

"So what's five mil' to a guy like that?" asked Loop.

"Exactly," said Booby. "Small potatoes, nigga."

"You really think we could do that?"

"With my help, sure."

Bugs and Loop respected their bodyguard's street smarts. Booby used to run with the gangs and he'd done a dime up at Lompoc for bank robbery. Booby knew what the fuck he was talking about.

"How would that work?" asked Loop.

"We just roll up on the motherfucker and we snatch his punk ass," said Booby.

"Then what?"

"Then we coerce him to go to the bank and get us five million dollars."

"What's that?" asked Loop.

"What?"

"*Coerce.*"

"It means we beat the shit outta that nigga."

Bugs nodded. Beating the shit out of Davis Cartright sounded real good.

"Do we let him know who we are?" asked Loop.

"Shit no," said Bugs. "We cover our faces with pantyhose."

"How about a mask?" asked Loop.

"What's the difference?"

"I don't like pantyhose."

"Why's that?"

"One time I robbed a liquor store over on Sepulveda with pantyhose on. I didn't like that shit."

"How come?"

"I'm pretty sure the bitch I got the pantyhose from had crabs."

"So you got crabs? On your face?"

"Itched like a motherfucker. That's why I shaved my beard."

"Okay, so a mask," said Bugs.

"What kind of mask?" asked Loop.

"Maybe a mask of the president's face."

Loop nodded. "Or maybe a Michael Myers mask. That would be scary as hell."

"You know the Michael Myers mask was a Captain Kirk mask turned wrong side out?"

Loop said, "Maybe we could get a Frankenstein mask."

"Don't matter what kind of mask, nigga," said Booby. "You just gotta have a mask."

"Maybe a zombie," said Loop.

"You really think this might work?" asked Bugs.

"Shit yes," said Booby. "I knew a nigga up at Lompoc did the same thing."

"And he went to prison for it?"

"Nah. He murdered some nigga out in the Valley."

"Okay," said Bugs, nodding. "So we take this motherfucker."

"That's how you get your money out a sucker like that."

"He called us studio gangstas," said Loop.

Booby said nothing. He thought they were studio gangstas, too.

"Fuck that nigga," said Bugs, rolling another spliff.

"So we gonna do this or what?" asked Booby.

"Shit yes," said Bugs.

And that's how the whole thing started.

THREE

Bugs and Loop were sitting at the bar in the kitchen when Booby came back from the costume shop. They were watching curling on ESPN.

"How can y'all watch this shit?" asked Booby.

"What?" asked Bugs. "You don't like sports?"

"Of course I like sports. I just don't be watchin' this peckerwood stuff y'all be watchin'."

"It ain't too bad," said Loop. "Especially when you're high."

Bugs looked at Booby. "You ever watched curling?"

"Hell no, I ain't never watched no damn curling."

"Then how you gonna talk shit if you don't know nothin' about it?"

Booby turned off the little TV. "There's lots of things I don't know nothin' about, but that don't mean I'm missing out."

"For instance?"

"Gettin' fucked in the ass," said Booby. "I ain't never done that and I'm pretty sure I'm not missin' out."

Loop grinned. "Says the guy who just got out of prison."

Bugs didn't laugh. Neither did Booby.

Booby reached for the the .45 tucked into his velour track pants. "The fuck you say, nigga?"

Loop could tell from the look on Booby's face, the tone of his words, he wasn't fucking around.

"I'm sorry," said Loop, doing his best to backpedal.

"Yeah," said Bugs. "He's sorry. You know how this dumb nigga get when he's been smokin'."

"Yeah, I say dumb shit," said Loop.

Booby relaxed a little, but didn't take his eyes off Loop. "Don't let your mouth write a check your dumb ass can't cash."

Loop played it smart and kept his mouth shut.

Booby was still staring at him when Bugs said, "You go to the costume shop?"

"Yeah, I went," said Booby.

"What'd you get?"

"Masks, nigga."

"What kind of masks?"

Booby smiled, lifting the big sack up to the counter. He opened it and reached in.

"You get a zombie mask?" asked Loop.

"Nah," said Booby.

"You get a Michael Myers mask?"

"Nope."

"What'd you get?"

Booby took out a rubber mask and pulled it on over his head. It was a Barack Obama mask.

"You feel me?" asked Booby.

Loop nodded. "That could work. That could definitely work."

Still wearing the mask, Booby reached into the sack and grabbed a second mask, tossing it to Bugs. Bugs pulled it over his head, and he, too, was Barack Obama.

Loop was smiling big, ready for his own mask.

Booby pulled out a third mask and tossed it to Loop. Loop held it up and looked at the thing. "Who the fuck is this?" asked Loop. "This Elvis?"

"Nah, nigga," said Bugs. "That's Ronald Reagan."

"Dumbass motherfuckers, that's Richard Nixon," said Booby.

"Who the fuck is that?"

"He was the president."

"Of what country?" asked Loop.

Booby looked at him. "What the fuck country you think?"

"I don't remember him."

"It was before you was born, dummy," said Bugs.

"Well shit," said Loop. "We ain't smart like you, Booby. We didn't go to prison."

Loop was arguing with Bugs and Booby, both still wearing Barack Obama masks.

"Why the fuck I gotta wear this cracker-ass motherfuckin' mask?" asked Loop.

Booby said, "You're the one said we gotta wear masks."

"But I wanna be Obama."

"They was all out of Obama," said Booby. "They only had two."

"So why you get to be Obama?" asked Loop.

"Cause I bought the motherfuckers, that's why."

Loop looked at Bugs. "How about you?"

"How about me what?"

"Trade me."

"Trade you, shit. I got it first."

"What's that got to do with anything?"

"Finders keepers, nigga."

"Bullshit," said Loop. "This some straight up bullshit."

Loop pulled the Nixon mask on over his head, still fuming inside it. He took out a joint and lit it, inhaling through the mask's little mouth holes. He started to cough.

The two Barack Obamas laughed their asses off at Richard Nixon, standing there pouting in a cloud of weed smoke.

* * *

Booby was driving the stolen Suburban. Bugs was in the passenger seat, Loop was in the back. They were listening to the radio when Majestyk's new song came on.

"Oh, hell no," said Bugs. "Turn that shit off."

"What's wrong with Majestyk?" asked Booby.

"That motherfucker got half the talent we got, but the label gives him ten times the push."

"So what you saying?"

"Majestyk ain't shit," said Bugs.

Booby liked Majestyk's shit a hell of a lot more than he liked these two idiots' music, but they paid his bills, so he kept his mouth shut.

"The radio station hardly ever plays our song," said Loop.

"Payola, nigga," said Bugs. "Money talks."

Booby pulled up along the curb about a half a block behind Davis Cartright's Beamer, parked out front of a little out-of-the-way diner.

"You sure he's in there?" asked Bugs.

"He eats here same time everyday," said Booby.

"This whole week you been watchin' him?"

"Every single day."

"How you know he's in there?"

"Cause that's his Beamer right there."

"The white one?"

"Yeah," said Booby. "The big expensive-looking rich boy motherfucking white Beamer."

"And they just let him park there—right in front of the place?" asked Bugs.

"You got as much money as Davis Cartright, you do whatever the fuck you want."

"I guess."

"Ain't no guessin' to it, man. You see where the nigga parked."

Bugs was fiddling with the stereo knob, trying to find something to listen to. Finally he came to a Run-DMC song and let it play.

"Old school," said Booby, nodding his head.

"Yeah."

Loop said, "It don't get no better than that."

Bugs was in the middle of agreeing with him when the record ended and the Majestyk song came on.

"Goddammit," said Bugs. "Fucking Majestyk."

"Maybe we shoulda kidnapped that nigga," said Loop.

"Nah, man," said Booby. "Majestyk ain't got the kind of bread Davis Cartright got."

"He's rich as a motherfucker," said Bugs.

"Yeah, but he's nigga rich."

"So what's Davis Cartright?" asked Loop.

"White boy rich."

"There's a difference?"

"Oh, yeah," said Booby. "Nigga rich is like MC Hammer, all bankrupt and shit. You got some money, but you got debt, too."

"And white boy rich?"

"White boy rich is like Paul McCartney. *Beatles* rich. A motherfucker like Paul McCartney owns islands and shit."

"Does he really?" asked Loop.

Booby looked at him in the mirror. "What?"

"Own islands."

"How the fuck do I know? I'm just saying—"

Bugs cut him off. "There go that motherfucker right there."

There was Davis Cartright, getting into his car.

"If he's so rich, why the fuck he drive himself?" asked Loop.

"A motherfucker with real money don't have to flaunt it," said Booby. He turned and looked at Bugs and Loop, but neither of them caught that he was talkin' about them. Dumb ass niggas.

"We gonna take him or what?" asked Loop.

"Nah," said Booby. "Not here."

"Then where?"

"Everyday when he leaves he goes to the same place."

"Where's that?" asked Bugs.

"He got a girlfriend lives right off Cahuenga."

Loop asked, "She hot?"

"Nigga got three hundred million dollars."

Bugs nodded. "He ain't gonna have no ugly bitch."

"Three hundred million dollars means no more ugly bitches ever," said Booby.

Bugs laughed. "Shit, Loop could have all the money in the world and he'd still be fuckin' around with them fat bitches."

Loop shrugged. "So what? I like big bitches."

"Let's get our game faces on," said Booby.

Davis Cartright's white Beamer pulled away from the curb, and Booby stayed about a half a block behind. Loop was in the backseat talkin' about fat bitches, and Bugs was fuckin' around with the stereo again. Booby was getting pissed.

"You niggas gonna straighten up and fly right?"

"What?" asked Bugs and Loop in unison.

"I ain't going back to the pen because of y'all niggas."

"You got your masks?" asked Bugs.

Loop looked down at his Nixon mask, pissed all over again.

"Why the fuck I gotta be the white dude?"

Bugs said, "Ain't no time for that now, Loop."

"Get your masks ready," said Booby. "When I say put 'em on, you put the motherfuckers on."

Loop muttered something under his breath about the mask.

Booby took his eyes away from Davis Cartright and gave Loop a look in the mirror.

Loop shut the fuck up.

"When we snatch the white boy, y'all let me do all the talkin'," said Booby.

"Why?" asked Bugs.

"What?" asked Loop. "You the boss now?"

Booby ignored it. "Davis Cartright don't know my voice, but he damn sure knows yours. Unless you wanna spend a decade in prison having dicks double-parked in your asshole, I'd shut the fuck up right quick, nigga."

"Good thinkin', Booby," said Bugs.

"We almost there."

"We gonna snatch him right in front of his girl's crib?" asked Loop.

"Yeah," said Booby. "Easy fuckin' peezy."

"I don't know why the fuck I gotta be Elvis," said Loop.

Booby looked at him again. "You ain't Elvis, dumbass."

"Then Ronald Reagan."

Booby wanted to smack this motherfucker. "Richard Nixon, motherfucker! You're Richard goddamn Nixon. Got it?"

Loop looked hurt back there, big spoiled-assed fucking baby.

Booby really wanted to knock the shit out of him.

"Game time," said Bugs.

Davis Cartright was pulling up into a driveway.

"That her place?" asked Bugs.

"It is," said Booby. "Masks on now."

Loop gave his Nixon mask one last look of disdain, shook his head, and then pulled the thing on.

Booby stopped the Suburban behind the Beamer, and the three men were out in a flash.

Davis Cartright was distracted, talking on his goddamn cell phone. He never saw them coming. He opened the car door and was immediately flanked by two Barack Obamas and a Richard

Nixon, all wearing black Adidas track suits. One of the Obamas stuck a pistol in his face.

"*What?!*" asked Davis Cartright.

Booby took the phone from him, put it to his ear, and said, "He's gonna have to call you back."

"Who the fuck are you?" asked Davis.

Booby smacked him across the face with his .45, drawing blood.

"I'm the nigga tellin' your dumb ass what's what," said Booby.

Loop snatched the white boy's arm and practically dragged him to the Suburban, shoving him inside.

Davis looked at Loop. "Who are you supposed to be? Ronald Reagan?"

Booby felt himself losing his temper. He got right up in the white boy's face. *"That's Richard Nixon, motherfucker! Don't you know anything?"*

"I know you stupid sons of bitches are all good as dead," said Davis. "Nobody does this to me and gets away with it."

Bugs delivered an uppercut to Davis' midsection, and the shit felt good. So good, in fact, that he punched him again.

"We ain't got time for that," said Booby. "Get in the goddamn car."

* * *

They were driving back to the mansion, a backwards ski mask over Davis's face now, shielding his eyes. Booby, Loop, and Bugs all had their masks off.

"Is this about the call girl I killed in Atlantic City?" Davis asked.

"What call girl?" asked Booby.

"Never mind then."

"You killed a call girl?"

Davis clammed up.

"Hit that nigga," said Booby.

Bugs punched the white boy again, real hard this time, and Davis spit up blood inside the ski mask.

"I repeat: you killed a call girl?" asked Booby.

"Yeah, but it was legit."

"How so?"

"I paid her boss a hundred grand."

"So you could kill her?"

Davis stopped talking again.

"You wanna punch this motherfucker again?" asked Booby.

Before Bugs could strike him, Davis started talking. "Yeah, I paid him a hundred grand to let me kill her."

The three kidnappers looked at one another.

"The fuck you do that for?"

"I get off on it," said Davis.

"You've done it before?"

"What I did to her..."

"Yeah?" asked Booby.

"What I did to her," he repeated, "ain't shit compared to what I'm gonna do to you stupid porch monkeys. Don't you know who the fuck I am?"

Booby looked in the mirror, exchanging a glance with Bugs. Bugs backhanded Davis.

"You're Davis motherfuckin' Cartright," said Booby. "That's why you're here."

"What the fuck do you want?"

"We don't want much. We just want a little of your money."

"How much?"

"Just five million dollars."

Davis paused for a moment before saying, "I'll kill every last one of you black sons of bitches."

And Bugs went to work tuning up the white boy. Davis' blood got all over the seat, and Bugs was happy as hell the vehicle wasn't his. Getting blood out of the upholstery could be a real bitch.

FOUR

Charlie was sitting on the couch, a beer between his legs, playing *Call of Duty 3* when someone knocked on the door. He got up, spilling Budweiser on his jeans as he did. He sat the beer on the coffee table. They knocked again.

He opened the door and there was Candace, looking fine as ever.

"You look surprised," she said.

"I didn't figure I'd see you again."

She smiled. "Can I come in?"

"Sure," he said, moving out of her way. She walked in, kind of looked at the couch where they'd made love, seeing it for the first time in daylight, and sat down.

"Aren't you a little old for video games?" she asked.

"Age is only a number."

"Yeah?"

"You're only as old as you feel."

"And how old do you feel?"

"Pretty fucking old. You want a beer?"

"No thank you," she said.

"What's up?"

"You don't think I came by just because I wanted to see you?"

Charlie just looked at her.

"The other night you mentioned the possibility of going to work as a private investigator," she said. "I think I might have a job for you, if you're up for it."

"I'm pretty busy. *Call of Duty's* not gonna play itself, you know."

"It's my boss," she said.

"What about him?"

"He's missing."

"You never even told me what you do for a living," he said.

176

"I work in the music industry."

"Really?"

"Yeah," she said. "I'm an exec at Pronto Records."

"What kind of music?"

"Gangsta rap."

Charlie made a face.

"I know, I know," she said. "It offends your ELO-loving sensibilities."

"You're an exec?"

"Second from the top."

"No shit?"

"My boss' name is Davis Cartright. Ever hear of him?"

"No," he said, "But then I'm not really a gangsta rap aficionado."

"He's kind of a big shot," she said. "He's worth hundreds of millions of dollars."

Charlie nodded. "Plum gig."

"He inherited the job."

"Nepotism?"

"Right," she said. "His father started the company."

"I see," said Charlie, taking a swig of his beer.

"Davis is missing."

"So why not go to the cops?"

"It's complicated," she said. "I've been asked not to. It looks bad, panics the shareholders."

"So you thought of me."

"I thought of you."

"So this isn't a social call?"

"Depends on how you look at it," she said.

"There's money in it?"

"I'll give you five grand to poke around and see what you can find out."

"Off the books?"

"Completely," she said.

"I don't know, I'm awfully busy," he said, looking at the video game.

She smiled. "So you'll do it?"

"I gotta pay rent somehow."

"Good."

"Tell me about your boss."

"He's an asshole."

Charlie said, "So you've slept with him?"

She smiled. "You think I sleep with every asshole?"

"That a yes?"

"Only twice," she said.

"He any good?"

"Not really," she said. "Itty bitty cock, great big ego."

"His place nicer than mine?"

She smiled again, looking around. "It's close."

"Fair enough," he said.

"So now what?" she asked.

"You go to dinner with me."

"You don't wanna skip right to the sex?"

"Nah, it's more fun this way."

"Where do you wanna go?"

"Where do you usually eat?" she asked.

"Strip club buffet."

"Really? They have a buffet at the strip club?"

"I'm told it's the best around."

"By who?"

"Strippers."

"I'm sure they wouldn't lie."

"So really, where would you like to go?" he asked.

"You're not taking me to the strip club?"

He grinned. "The strippers might get jealous."

"Must be the goatee," she said.

He rubbed his beard. "Must be."

* * *

A half hour passed and they were at Bazongas, a strip club Charlie already considered his second home. Charlie led Candace to a table in a darkened corner. A couple strippers waved and said, "Hello, Charlie" as they made their way through the room.

Candace said, "They really know you here."

"They're the only people I know in LA."

"You know me."

"You don't count."

"Why's that?"

"You left without leaving a note."

She turned her head and gave him a sad expression. "Did I hurt your feelings?"

Charlie grinned.

"I'm serious. I think I hurt your feelings."

"I'll live," said Charlie.

Candace said, "I promise I'll leave a note next time."

"What makes you think there'll be a next time?"

"Wishful thinking?"

Charlie pulled out his cigarettes.

"They let you smoke here?"

Charlie grinned. "Enough shit goes down in here that the smoking ordinance is the least of their worries."

Candace nodded. "Can I have one?"

"Knock yourself out."

"So what's the allure of this place?"

"The buffet."

"I'm serious."

Charlie pointed towards the center stage, where a naked girl was writhing around on a pole. "That's the allure."

"Tits?"

"And ass."

"You actually eat here?"

"Sure. They have great meatloaf."

"Is it...sanitary?"

"That depends on your definition of the word sanitary, I guess."

"My definition is clean," she said.

"Then no, probably not."

"So why eat here?"

"The meatloaf," said Charlie.

"It's that good?"

"Like mother used to make."

She grinned. "Your mother didn't dance around the kitchen naked, did she?"

"Hey," he said. "We had a very progressive household."

"So you really wanna eat here?"

"Sure."

At that moment they were interrupted by a shapely young blonde with basketball-sized implants. "You want a lap dance?"

Charlie nodded towards Candace. "She'll take one."

The stripper smiled.

"No lap dance for me," Candace said.

The stripper made a pouty face. "Hey, it's only ten bucks."

Charlie handed the stripper a ten. "We're good here, Jasmine."

The stripper smiled. "You sure?"

Charlie nodded, and the stripper moved on to the next table.

"So you're gonna snoop around, see what you can find out about Davis?"

"Who's Davis?" asked Charlie.

"My boss."

"Oh, missing guy. Right."

"Think how many lap dances you could buy with that five thousand dollars."

"Five hundred. I've already done the math."

"If you go into business for yourself, you should just open up your office here."

"Who says I won't?" asked Charlie.

Candace drew on her cigarette. The song changed from bland electronica to Prince's *Pussy Control*.

"Classy place, Charlie."

"Nothing but the best for you, my lady."

She smiled. "That what I am? Your lady?"

"Let's not get carried away. It was one time."

"Hey, you're Mr. Sensitive, not me."

Charlie stubbed out his cigarette and lit another.

"Tell me about Davis Cartright," he said.

"Like I said, he's a huge dick."

"He got enemies?"

She laughed.

"What?" asked Charlie.

"The man breeds enemies like your apartment breeds cockroaches."

"Hey," he said. "I resent that comment."

"To know Davis Cartright is to loathe him."

"Sounds like a swell guy."

"He's a smarmy little bastard with the personality of a snake."

"I can see how he seduced you then."

"That bother you, Charlie?"

"No, but it sounds like it should bother you if he's half the creep you say he is."

Candace nodded. "I'm afraid he is."

"When'd he disappear?"

"Day before yesterday."

"Where was he last seen?"

"He left his car parked in front of his mistresses' house."

"I should probably talk to her."

"You gonna fuck all his women?"

"Give me time," said Charlie.

"I hear she's got great tits. I know how you like tits."

"And ass," said Charlie.

"Right," she said. "Can't forget ass."

"Has anyone ever threatened the guy that you know of?"

"We work for a gangsta rap label. Every artist we got thinks he's Ice Cube. They always threaten us when they don't get what they want. They're like giant babies who carry Glocks."

Charlie nodded. "I know the type."

"Ever miss it?"

"What?"

"Being a cop."

"Every single day," he said.

"Maybe you could be a cop out here," she said.

He grinned, knowing where she was going with this.

"I hear they don't mind an officer who's not afraid to shoot a few black guys," she said.

"Hey," he said. "I only shot one black guy."

"So now what?"

"Act two."

"You're kind of old for act two. I think you mean act three."

"Act two and a half," said Charlie.

Candace lit another cigarette. "Why don't you buy cloves?"

He looked at her. "Why don't you buy your own cigarettes?"

She smiled. "The million dollar question."

"And the answer?"

"Because I quit smoking."

"No," he said. "You quit *buying*. There's a difference."

She took another drag.

Charlie said, "Anyone threaten your boss lately?"

"A rapper named Majestyk, practically runs the label."

"How's that?"

"He sells more than everyone else. Multi-platinum. He was on the cover of *Rolling Stone* a while back."

"Nifty."

"Yeah," she said. "He actually pulled a gun on Davis a few weeks back."

"For what?"

"They were negotiating the terms of his new deal."

"Hell of a negotiating tactic."

"Like I said, everybody wants to be Ice Cube."

"The guy from the kiddie movies?"

"He wasn't always in kiddie movies."

Charlie took a drag from his cigarette, watching a nubile nineteen year old blonde shaking a red, white, and blue g-string filled with dollar bills. Candace looked at the girl. "She your type?"

"She's everybody's type," said Charlie. "Tell me about Majestyk."

"He's one of the only guys on the label who actually has a street rep."

"Yeah?"

"He's been to prison a couple times."

"For what?"

"I can't remember, but I wanna say drugs."

"I guess I'll have to talk to him."

"What makes you think it's someone who's got a beef with Davis?"

"Because they haven't tried to get a ransom."

"You're pretty good at this."

"I know, right?" he said. "It's almost like I was a cop or something."

"Who you gonna talk to first?"

"The mistress."

Candace rolled her eyes.

"Do you wanna find this guy or not?" he asked.

"Personally, I could give a shit less."

"But you *need* to find him."

"Sadly, yes."

"Okay then," Charlie said. "Let's get some meatloaf."

FIVE

Booby, Bugs, and Loop were sitting in the living room, half-ass watching music videos and getting high. It was all good until the new Majestyk song came on and Bugs started getting heated.

"Fuck Majestyk," he said.

Booby didn't say shit, just sat there rolling a blunt.

"Don't you ever get tired of talking about that dude?" asked Loop.

Bugs stared at him. "Hell yes, I get tired of talkin' about him."

"Then why do it? It's a waste of time and energy."

"Can't you see he's the reason we're in this mess in the first place?"

Loop cocked his head. "How you figure that?"

"If Davis Cartright and the rest of them pencil-pushin' motherfuckers at the record label had paid half as much attention to us, we'd still have a record deal. We'd be as big as Majestyk."

"Woulda, coulda, shoulda," said Loop. "That's what my mama always said."

Booby liked that. Good for Loop, speaking up and saying something to the nigga for once.

"Majestyk is the reason that white boy is tied up in the goddamn basement," said Bugs. "Think about it. If the label hadn't paid so damn much attention to him, we'd have gotten our due. Then there'd be no Davis Cartright tied to a lawn chair right now."

Booby got tired of hearing this same old tired shit. In prison, every cat he had ever known had a story about why he was in prison. And guess what? It was always somebody else's fault. That's exactly what these niggas was like—prison cats. But Booby knew they'd never make it on the inside. Bugs would pop some shit and get killed on day one, and Loop would be somebody's bitch before the sun went down.

High, Booby nodded his head to the Majestyk song.

Bugs stared at him. "What? You *like* this shit?"

Booby shrugged. "It's alright, man."

"Nah, that shit is garbage."

Booby being Booby, he didn't let Bugs get to him. He just let the nigga run his big, stupid mouth while he sat there lighting up that blunt. He inhaled deep, and then blew the thick smoke out slowly, trying to let it linger there so he'd look cool.

"What we gonna do with the white boy?" asked Loop. "It's already been a day, and he ain't even close to giving that money to us."

Bugs said, "We just gotta talk to him some more."

"Nah," said Booby. "Talk time is coming to an end. It's time for action."

"What kind of action?"

Booby looked at him. "What kind you think?"

"You mean like hurtin' the dude?" asked Loop.

Booby nodded. "Whatever works."

"Bugs already kicked his ass, and that didn't work."

"There's more kinds of violence than just kickin' a guy's ass."

"Like what?"

"There's some things a man can't walk away from. He fears he's gonna get real fucked up, he's more likely to play ball."

Bugs nodded. "Booby's right. We gotta make that white boy give us our money."

Loop asked, "You got any ideas?"

"Nothing specific," said Booby. "Not yet, but I've done some work with a blowtorch in the past that proved to be just the trick. You put a blowtorch on a dude's balls, man, he'll tell you whatever you wanna know, and right fast, too. Shit, he'll tell you anything. If he don't know the answers you want, he'll just start makin' up shit." Booby took another drag and said, "We gotta get a blowtorch. Write that down on the shopping list and we'll go to the hardware store this afternoon."

"That's fucked up," said Loop. "I didn't want it to be like this."

"You kidnapped the man. What the fuck did you think we was gonna do? Give him milk and cookies, let him bang our girlfriends and become pen pals?"

"I been prayin' about this, and I don't think this is what our Lord Jesus Christ would want."

"You been talkin' to Jesus?"

"I talk to Jesus every day except on Saturday."

"Why not Saturday?"

"I get busy on Saturday, forget to talk to him's all."

"On account of partying and whatnot?"

"Right," said Loop.

"And what's that nigga Jesus say about all this?"

"It's mostly one-sided conversations."

"He don't speak to you?"

"Not directly."

"Then how you know he's there?"

"I just know it," said Loop. "I can feel him."

"And how did your buddy Jesus Christ feel about you kidnapping the dude in the first place?"

"He wasn't too happy about it."

"You don't say."

"I don't think he liked it."

"Nobody put a gun to your head, Loop. Nobody made you kidnap that man. But now you done did the damn thing, and there ain't no going back. Once you start something like this, you gotta go the full way, see it through till it's done."

"I didn't know it was gonna be like this."

Booby asked, "You want out?"

"It's just that I—"

"I said do you want out, nigga?"

Booby not giving him any wiggle room.

"No."

"Good. I don't wanna have to dig two holes for sorry niggas instead of one when this is all over with."

"You think it's gonna come to that?" asked Bugs.

"What?"

"Diggin' a hole?"

"It very well might, but not until we get our five million dollars first," said Booby. "I hate digging holes. Five million is about what it'd be worth to me to dig that motherfucker. That shit is hard work."

Booby looked at Loop and held up his glass. "I'm out of Scotch."

Now the shoe was on the other foot, and Booby was the one in charge. Booby wondered if they understood that yet. If they didn't like it, fuck 'em. What were they gonna do about it? They no longer had any income, so they weren't really his employers anymore, and if Booby played his cards right he might just get all Davis Cartright's money for himself.

Loop stared at Booby for a moment, and then got up and fixed him another Scotch.

✳ ✳ ✳

It took all of five seconds for Booby to convince Bugs and Loop that he should go down and talk to the white boy alone.

"He don't know you," said Bugs. "It's safer this way."

"And I don't wanna put that goddamn hot-assed mask on no more," said Loop.

"You gonna hurt him?" asked Bugs.

Booby said, "I ain't gonna hold his hand and sing Kumbaya."

"Yeah, it's better that you go by yourself," said Loop. "I don't wanna watch you hurt the man."

"Better to be a part of the atrocity and not have to actually see it," said Booby.

Loop nodded. "Right."

"Spoken like a true Christian."

Booby put on the Obama mask and went to the basement door. He looked back at Bugs and Loop, but they were already off in their own worlds. Booby unlocked the door and started down the stairs. Halfway down, he could see the empty lawn chair just sitting there, knew he was in for some fucked up shit. About the moment he came to this realization, the white boy jumped out and smacked him in the head with a shovel.

Fuck, that hurt.

Booby reached back and pulled out the .45, aiming it at Davis. "Put down the shovel."

Davis Cartright stood there for a moment, shovel in hand, weighing his options. Finally he realized he had none and dropped the shovel.

Booby motioned towards the lawn chair. "Back in the chair, white boy."

Booby tied him up again. As he did he said, "Let's get this straight—you are not to untie these ropes anymore. If you do, you are not to fucking attack us. We will always have guns. You do that shit again, you see what happens. I'll shoot you deader than a motherfucker, man. I promise you that on my mama, nigga."

"I'm sorry," said Davis. "I won't do it again."

"I'm gonna leave that gag off for now, too. As long as you show that you can do the right thing, it'll stay off. *Capeesh?*"

Davis nodded.

"I got a question," said Davis.

"Okay, shoot."

"Tell me the truth..."

"What is it?"

"Did Majestyk put you guys up to this?"

Booby sat there for a long moment before answering. "How'd you know?"

"It had to be him."

"Why's that?"

"He's the only person I associate with who has the balls to try something like this."

"Oh, yeah?"

Davis said, "We made him a star, and this is how he repays me?"

"That's fucked up," Booby said.

"Why would he do that?"

"Man told me he just wanted your money."

"Well, he's not gonna get it."

"We'll see about that," said Booby. "The day is still young, white boy."

"What does that mean?"

"My job is to get you to give us that money."

"And?"

"I'm good at my job."

"I hope you won't be offended if I don't root for you," said Davis.

"It ain't got to be so hard, man."

"What? Just hand over the money?"

"Pretty much."

"How do I know you'll let me live even if I give you the money?"

"The truth is, you don't," said Booby. "You gonna have to trust me."

"Why would I ever trust a kidnapper?"

Booby thought it over for a moment. Then he took off his mask so Davis could see his face.

"That doesn't inspire trust," said Davis.

"How's that?"

"Now that I've seen your face, you have even more reason to kill me."

"Nah," said Booby. "You don't know me."

"What do you mean?"

"I'm not worried. What are you gonna tell the police sketch artist? That I had curly black hair, dark skin, brown eyes, and big lips? I know we all look alike to you."

"I think I'd know you."

"What if I was to tell you that we've met on at least three occasions prior to this?"

"Is that true?"

"I dunno," said Booby. "Is it?"

Davis sat there thinking about it.

"I'm fucking with you. We ain't never met before."

Davis just sat there.

Booby said, "You're a smart motherfucker, aren't you?"

"That's why I make the big bucks."

"And there I thought it was on account of your rich music mogul daddy."

"Who told you that?"

"I read it in *Forbes*, when they did that profile on you last year."

"You know, they exaggerated about how much I'm worth."

"You don't get it. Whether you got one million dollars or $700 million, you're rich to a motherfucker like me. Hell, I can't even afford to buy that issue of *Forbes*, and you're in the motherfucker."

"Haves and have-nots," said Davis.

"Right," said Booby. "You have, and I have not."

"So if I give you the money, you're gonna let me live?"

"Depends. You gonna tell anyone Majestyk was behind this?"

"Like who? The cops?"

"Yeah."

"Hell no," said Davis. "I've got other ways of taking care of Majestyk."

"Such as?"

"You don't know who I work for."

"You work for Pronto Records."

"But who do you think owns Pronto Records?"

"I thought you owned it."

"Nope," said Davis. "I'm just the front-man."

"So you're telling me, what? The Mafia owns the label?"

"Something like that."

"If that's true, then why aren't they out looking for you?"

"I'm sure they are," said Davis. "They make a lot of money off us."

"Is that shit true, that the Mafia owns the record label?"

Davis looked at him. "What do you think?"

SIX

Davis Cartright's mistress was a cute little brunette, with legs that went on forever. Her name was Kismet, and she opened the door with a .22 aimed at Charlie's midsection.

"Cute gun," Charlie said.

"Cute, huh?"

"Cute as a beagle in a bathtub."

"I hate dogs. I'm allergic."

"I know the feeling. I'm allergic to people aiming guns at me."

She wavered, started to put down the pistol. "Who are you? You a cop... or are you one of them?"

"Depends on who *them* is, I guess."

"The bad guys."

"Nope, no bad guy here."

She put down the gun. "Who are you?"

"Name's Charlie Grimes."

"You look like a cop."

"I've heard that before."

"I think it's the goatee."

"So do I."

"But you're not a cop?"

"Not anymore."

"What does that mean?"

"It means I used to be a cop. Now I'm not."

"So what are you doing here, Charlie Grimes?"

"I'm unofficially investigating the disappearance of your boy-friend."

She made a face.

"What?" he asked.

"Davis isn't my boyfriend."

"He's not?"

"No. He pays for all this, but I'm free to see whomever I like."

Was she making a pass at him? Was she telling him this for a reason? No way of knowing, but Davis hoped for the best.

"You wanna come in?" she asked.

"Sure."

They entered the house.

"You want a drink?"

"It's only, what, ten in the morning?"

"I usually start drinking around eight," she said.

"Girl after my own heart."

"So what'll you have?"

"You got beer?"

"I got domestic, and then there's the nasty-tasting import shit Davis buys."

"As tempting as that sounds, I think I'll just have a domestic beer."

She went to the kitchen. Charlie looked around at the walls, covered with art deco crap, paintings that looked like a four-year-old had done them with finger paints, and sat down on the couch. A moment later Kismet returned with a bottle of Bud Light.

"So what does 'unofficial investigation' mean?" she asked.

He started to speak, but then she said, "You work for the label?"

"Something like that," he said.

"Those guys from the label came by yesterday."

"What guys?"

"Three big guys."

"Black?"

"No. They looked like rejects from a *Sopranos* casting call."

Charlie nodded. "And they were from the label?"

"That's what they said."

"You ever see 'em before?"

"No," she said. "But then I've never seen you before either."

"True enough," Charlie said, taking a swig of his beer. "Kismet. That's cute. Is it your real name?"

"It is now."

"What was it before?"

"Less cute."

"Come on, tell me."

"Roberta."

Charlie looked at her. *"Roberta?"*

"Sounds like an old woman's name, right?"

"So now you're Kismet."

"Now I'm Kismet."

"And what is it you do, Kismet? Let me guess—you're an actress."

"Am I that big a cliché?"

Yes, she was.

"No, of course not," said Charlie. "You're an attractive young lady, and this is Los Angeles. It only makes sense."

"I guess so."

"So what've you done that I might've seen?"

"I've mostly been in pilots, but none of them have gone anywhere."

"Oh yeah?"

"Yeah," she said. "I was in one with that comedian... what's his name? The one with the funny hair?" She thought for a moment. "Hell, I can't remember his name."

Charlie asked, "That one didn't work out?"

"There's a reason I can't remember his name."

Charlie nodded. The girl had a point.

"I was on *Days of Our Lives* once," said Kismet.

"Really?"

"Yeah. It was a hospital scene. I stood there in the background holding a scalpel."

"No lines?"

"No," she said. "But I was a featured extra. It looks good on the resume."

"What's a featured extra?"

"It means I didn't get any lines, but they showed my face real clearly."

"That's pretty cool."

"I thought so."

"So when was the last time you saw Davis?"

"It's been, what? Five days now? He was supposed to come by and see me three days ago, but I found his car parked out in the drive."

"No Davis?"

"Not a sign."

"Keys still in the car?"

"The door was open," said Kismet. "The radio was on. It looked like he left in a hurry."

"So you figure it was a kidnapping?"

"Davis is worth a lot of money."

"I bet he never stops reminding you of that."

She smiled. "So you know him?"

"I know the kind. How long have you known him?"

"Going on two years now."

"What were your initial thoughts when you saw the car sitting there like that?"

"Can I be frank?"

"Be whomever you like."

She said, "I was afraid of losing all this."

"You don't care much for Davis?"

"He's okay, but I have special needs."

"Such as?"

"I'm the kind of girl who comes to expect certain things...to live a certain way. And I don't wanna lose that."

He nodded. "I understand. Seems like a pretty good thing you've got here."

"It's not bad. Sure, I got to have sex with the man once or twice a week, but it could be worse. I mean, there's kids starving in Africa. I bet they'd give anything to have this deal."

Charlie said, "You think those starving kids are dreaming of giving blowjobs to Davis Cartright?"

"You know what I mean."

"This gives you time to pursue your acting career."

"It beats working at Starbucks," said Kismet. "And Davis knows a lot of important people."

"He get you the gig on *Days of Our Lives*?"

"He's friends with one of the show's line producers."

"What's he like?"

"The line producer?"

"No, Davis," said Charlie. "How's he treat you?"

"He doesn't treat me bad, *per se*."

"*Per se*, huh?"

"I mean, he doesn't beat me up or make me sleep with his friends. No S&M, no shit like that. He just talks down to me. But he's rich. What are you gonna do? It's part of his deal. He's an asshole."

"So I keep hearing."

"But he's really likeable as far as assholes go."

"I didn't know there was any such thing as a likeable asshole."

"You haven't been in Los Angeles very long, have you?"

"Good point," said Charlie.

Now she turned the tables on him. "Where you from?"

"Chicago."

"You were a cop there?"

"Yeah."

"What made you quit and come out here? I doubt you decided to become an actor at your age."

"I'm not that old."

"No," she said, grinning seductively. "You're not."

"How old do you think I am?"

"Thirty-five?" she asked.

"Exactly," he lied.

"I'm pretty good at guessing."

"So I see."

"You were a cop?"

"A good one."

"Is there any such thing?"

"I like to think so."

"I always thought cops were racist douche bags."

"Well," said Charlie. "I might be a douche bag, but I'm not a racist."

"So you quit?"

"Something like that."

"They fired you?"

Charlie shifted uneasily. "There's the rub."

"Why would you wanna be a cop anyway?"

"You know how it is, kids in Africa and all that."

"Yeah."

"So Davis is married?"

"Yeah, but they don't love each other."

"Isn't that always the way?"

She looked at him. "You judging me, Charlie Grimes?"

"Not at all. Him, maybe. You, not at all."

"Why's that?"

"A girl's gotta do what a girl's gotta do."

She smiled. "I like you, Charlie."

"I've got one of those faces."

"Except for the cop thing."

"Yeah, except for that."

"What else you wanna know?" asked Kismet.

"You said Davis doesn't love his wife."

"I did say that."

"Does he love you?"

She grinned. "What's not to love?"

"But you don't love him?"

"That's not part of our deal," she said. "I don't have to love him."

"Sounds like you've got it all figured out."

"I'm a smart girl," said Kismet. "I'm more than just a pretty face."

Charlie made a point to scan her body from head to toe. "I see that."

She smiled. "What do you really want to ask me?"

"Is there something you'd like me to ask you?"

She stood up. "Would you like to see the rest of my house, Charlie?"

He stood up and she led him straight to the bedroom.

He looked at the walls, covered with gaudy framed Marilyn Monroe portraits.

"I love what you've done with the place," he said.

She pushed up on him, and stuck her tongue into his mouth. He thought—*briefly*—about Candace, but remembered that they were not in a relationship. What the hell? When in Rome...

He kissed Kismet hard, pulling back.

She started unbuttoning his shirt. She looked up at him with beautiful brown eyes.

"So this is what 'unofficial investigation' means," she said.

Charlie said nothing.

"Is this how you interview all the girls?" she asked.

And Charlie kissed her again.

"What would Davis Cartright think of all this?" asked Charlie.

"I guess it's a good thing he's kidnapped. He doesn't have a say."

* * *

A half hour later it was all over, and Charlie was lying in the big plush bed next to Kismet.

"Are you worried about Davis?" he asked.

"No," she said matter-of-factly. "I'm just worried about losing all this."

He nodded. "I can see how that might be a concern."

"What should I do, Charlie?"

"Not much you can do, but sit back and wait. Hope they return your boyfriend in one piece."

Kismet made a face. "I wish you'd stop saying that."

"What?"

"That Davis is my boyfriend. It gives me the willies."

"If you hate him so much, how can you stand to sleep with him?"

"I don't hate him exactly," she said. "I just don't like him."

"So how do you do it?"

"I compartmentalize, Charlie," she said. "I pretend I'm someone else, somewhere else. I'm not me. I don't know how to explain it any better than that."

"You just try not to think about it?"

"Yeah, that's about the size of it." She lit a cigarette and inhaled. "Do you think they'll kill him?"

"Who knows. Anything's possible. If he's as big a prick everyone says he is, then he may do something that pushes them that way."

"That's kind of what I'm afraid of."

"Would you miss him?"

"Davis Cartright," she said, "is the kind of man nobody would miss."

"Geez, with sentiments like that they probably won't be asking you to give the eulogy."

"You wanna do it again?"

This took Charlie by surprise. "Have sex?"

"Yeah."

"More than anything, but I don't know if I'm up for the task."

"We'll see about that," she purred, reaching down and grabbing his cock. It turned out he was.

SEVEN

Charlie stood out like a sore thumb on the video shoot set. He watched as this guy Majestyk rapped about having flashy cars and fly women and all that other bling-bling bullshit. Most of the film crew was white, but Charlie still stood out. He wasn't cool enough or hip enough to blend in here.

A bikini-clad model with breasts the size of casaba melons stopped the shoot. "I need make-up," she said. "The make-up on my left titty is coming off. See, there's a smudge right there." And the model was whisked away to a corner of the shoot where some lucky make-up artist got to apply make-up to her sizable breast.

The director spoke to Charlie as if he knew him. "We only got two days to shoot this fucker, and we're already behind schedule."

"I hate when that happens," said Charlie.

The sarcasm was lost on the director, who went on complaining about the frugality of Pronto Records when it came to shooting videos. "For a record company that makes as much paper as they do, they really do rush these things. Instead of spending the kind of money—the *right* kind of money—to make a proper video, they just cobble something together and hope the song is enough to interest people."

"There's a concept," said Charlie.

"I've directed so many videos now, and no one at the label will ever take my word for it..."

"How many videos have you directed?"

"How many in-breds are in Arkansas?"

"A lot?"

"You could say that," the director said. "I think this is my seventh or eighth video just for Pronto, and I really don't like working for them. They only pay scale."

"What makes you keep coming back?"

The director turned and grinned. "Majestyk, of course."

"What do you mean?"

"That man is the future of music. He combines the old school boom-bap of guys like KRS-One and Rakim with a futuristic sound that...well, nobody else has even come close to creating yet. He's unique, and his lyrics are first-rate. The part in the song where he says, 'Absolute power corrupts absolutely' is brilliant. The guy is like a fucking prophet."

Charlie didn't have the heart to tell him that line was older than Betty White. He just kept his mouth shut while the director ranted about the brilliance of Majestyk. Personally Charlie didn't think Majestyk was all that great. He sounded just like every other talking-along-to-the-music so-called rap "artist" he'd ever heard, but what the hell did he know? Different strokes for different folks. Some people liked quality music, and others liked shit.

"Majestyk is the Bob Dylan of his generation," said the director.

Charlie nodded. He could actually see that since he couldn't make heads or tails of what either Dylan or Majestyk ever said.

Finally the stripper-turned-model returned before the cameras, her left breast restored to its proper glory.

"Where you want me?" asked Majestyk, all three hundred pounds of him looking intimidating as hell.

"I want you back on your mark—right *there*—and we're gonna pick up at the line 'ain't got no love for these hoes on my nuts.' Sound good?"

"Right as rain, nigga," said Majestyk.

And the cameras started rolling again, the music came blaring to life pronouncing Majestyk's lack of love for the hoes on his aforementioned nuts, and Majestyk became animated again, waving his arms wildly with the music.

The two bored-looking models, one white, one black, both with ridiculously-oversized bosoms, gyrated around next to Majestyk, trying their best to feign enthusiasm. The director continued to shoot, allowing the song to play the rest of the way through. Once the music stopped, he said, "Let's pick up on the line about the licking of the ball sack."

Majestyk held up his hand. "I need a break, son."

"Again?" asked the director. "No offense, Majestyk, but we're behind already."

"Just give me twenty. I gotta get my head right."

The director didn't really like it, but he agreed to the twenty-minute break. After all, what choice did he have? Majestyk was running this show.

Charlie watched as the rapper made his way over behind one of the trailers. He followed. By the time Charlie reached Majestyk, he was already enveloped in thick ganja smoke.

"Hey, homie," said Majestyk. "You want a hit of this?"

Charlie stepped towards the rapper, reached out and took the spliff from him. He put it to his lips, pulled in a drag, and held the smoke there for what seemed like forever.

"You know your way around a spliff," said Majestyk.

"I grew up with this stuff. Of course the weed's better now. We used to smoke skunk weed and we thought we were big shit, but this here... this is the stuff."

"I gotta guy who brings me this shit once a week. I can hook you up if you want. It's even better than the shit from the dispensary."

"No," said Charlie. "I'm good."

"What do you think of the shoot so far?"

"Just seems like the run-of-the-mill rap video to me."

Majestyk looked visibly hurt.

"But what do I know?" said Charlie. "Rap isn't really my thing."

Majestyk nodded. "I get you now. What do you listen to? George Jones and shit? Reba fucking McIntyre?"

"I like ELO."

"Are they like NWA?"

Charlie laughed. "How about Fleetwood Mac?"

"That sounds like some old pimp shit right there."

"It kind of does."

"So what are you doing here?" asked Majestyk. "What's your job?"

"Actually, I'm just here to see you."

"Me? About what?"

"I'm investigating the disappearance of Davis Cartright."

Majestyk took another hit and chuckled. "That stupid pecker-wood."

"You knew he was missing?"

"What can I say? Good news travels fast."

"You don't like the man?"

Majestyk laughed again. "I doubt Davis Cartright's own mother likes that nigga."

Charlie laughed.

"I ain't had nothing to do with his disappearance, but I'm not sad about it either. The guy is a weasel. A certified, bonafide sucker of cocks."

"What does that mean?"

"The guy's a cocksucker."

Charlie grinned.

"He's probably the worst person I've ever met, and I've been to prison twice."

"What makes him so particularly bad?"

"You don't know the man?"

"Never met him."

"The dude ain't got no soul," said Majestyk. "That motherfucker is pure evil, through and through. He cares about one thing and one thing only."

"Which is?"

"That man loves money like white people love Starbucks."

"Don't you care about money?"

Majestyk smiled. "Don't get me wrong, I love to make a dollar just like the next man, but Davis Cartright is just a foul, putrid, uh..." He was searching for his next word.

"Wretched?"

"Right, *wretched*, son of a bitch. I hope he's somewhere getting ass-raped with a pitchfork right now."

"Hate him that much?"

"I could go on about that cat for hours."

"I heard you threatened him."

"You a cop? You kind of look like a cop."

"No, but I get that all the time. I think it's the goatee."

"Who you working for?"

"Interested parties at the label."

"Was it that fine-ass Candace? I'll bet it was her."

Charlie grinned. "Something like that."

"You think she and Cartright were fucking?"

"Nah. Davis Cartright has a mistress."

"The mistress hot?"

"She's pretty damned hot. So you threatened him?"

"I wouldn't say I threatened the man. We came to an understanding."

"Which was?"

"That he either give me my money or I put a hole through his fuckin' head."

Charlie took another drag from the spliff. "And that worked?"

"Like a charm. Besides, they can't afford to lose me. I'm their boy wonder. I'm the highest selling artist in the history of Pronto Records."

"That's impressive."

"Truth is, I ain't seen neither hide nor hair of that nigga. I can't lie to you—I hope he's dead in a ditch somewhere, maggots in his eyes and asshole—but I didn't have anything to do with his disappearance."

"Anyone else come to talk to you?" asked Charlie.

"Like who?"

"I hear there's some wise guys sniffing around."

"As in Mob guys?"

"Yeah."

"Word? You mean the label is connected to the Mob?"

"That would be my guess. Either the label or Davis Cartright, maybe both."

"That sounds about right," said Majestyk. "They are some sneaky, no-good sons of motherfuckers over there."

A moment of silence passed and then a production assistant wearing a "May the Fourth Be With You" t-shirt came looking for Majestyk. "They're ready for you."

Majestyk took one more drag on the spliff and dropped it to the ground. "Time to go make art, nigga."

EIGHT

Candace called just after Charlie finished with Majestyk.
"Yeah?"

"I need you to come to the office," she said.

"You okay?"

"For the moment."

"What does that mean?"

"There are some gentlemen here asking questions."

The mob guys, thought Charlie.

"Italians?"

"Italian as spaghetti."

"Where are they now?"

"Snooping around the building."

"They threaten you?"

"Nothing like that. Not yet anyway."

"I'm on my way."

And Charlie climbed into the Dodge pickup and headed for Pronto Records.

* * *

Charlie arrived at the record label's office fourteen minutes later. He walked in past a bitchy-looking receptionist. "Can I help you?" she said, hate filling her every word.

"I'm here to see Candace."

"She know you're coming?"

"Yes."

By the look on the receptionist's face, this news did not please her. Why? Who the hell knew? "I'll have to call her and tell her you're here."

"Fine. The name is Charlie Grimes."

She kind of rolled her eyes at this, somehow offended by the very utterance of his name, foreign as it was to her. She pushed a button. "There's a Charlie Grimes here to see you?"

The receptionist listened for a second, nodded, and said, "Okay." She looked up. "You can go."

"Which door is it?"

She pointed, third door on the left.

* * *

When Charlie entered Candace's office, there were two *paysans* fiddling around in there, looking at the décor on the walls. They looked up at him, half startled by his appearance. Candace just sat at her desk silently.

"Hi guys," said Charlie. "I take it you're the gangsters?"

One of the guys—a real big, mean-looking sonofabitch who looked like Big Pussy on steroids—turned to him, trying his damnedest to look menacing. "What do you know about gangsters?"

"Only what I've seen on TV."

Charlie took out a pack of gum, sliding a piece from it. He unwrapped it and put it into his mouth. He held his hand out towards them. "Gum?"

Neither of them smiled.

"What makes you think we're, uh, mobbed up?"

"I just took a look at you," said Charlie.

"So you're saying we look like gangsters?"

Charlie couldn't let them get all inflated with ego, so he said, "I wouldn't say gangsters."

"Then what would you say?" asked Man #2.

"Thugs. I'd say you look like cheap thugs."

Neither man appeared to be too happy to be called a cheap thug.

"Just who the hell are you anyway?" asked Big Pussy on Steroids.

"Name's Charlie Grimes."

"You a cop?"

"No, why?"

"You just kind of seem like one," said Man #2.

"I'm a private eye."

"So what are you doing here?"

"Looking for Davis Cartright."

Man #2 did a kind of peering thing with his eyebrows. "Who hired you?"

"Wouldn't you like to know?"

"I would."

"And just what are your interests here?"

"We, uh, work for a very interested party."

"Interested in what?"

"Finding Davis Cartright."

"Is he missing?" asked Charlie.

"What do you mean?"

"Well, no one ever filed a police report, which seems suspicious."

"We wouldn't want to worry the stock holders," said Big Pussy on Steroids. "What do you care anyway?"

"I don't. Was just curious is all."

"You find out anything interesting about Mr. Cartright?" asked Man #2.

"Just that he's apparently a huge dick."

The two thugs looked at each other.

Man #2 stepped towards Charlie.

"You want me to tune him up?" he asked.

Big Pussy on Steroids said, "Go for it."

Man #2, stout in his own right, reached out to grab Charlie. The fucker moved so slowly he appeared to be moving in slow motion. Charlie ducked and came up with an uppercut to his doughy midsection. *"Unnnnggg,"* said the man, spinning now. He took a step back, caught his breath, and lunged towards Charlie. This time Charlie caught him with a solid blow to the chin, knocking the son of a bitch unconscious.

Charlie looked at Big Pussy on Steroids. "We done here?"

Big Pussy looked like he wanted a fight, but didn't try anything.

"There's no reason for all this," said Charlie. "We can work together."

"I'll tell you what I know if you tell me what you know."

"Like, I'll show you mine if you show me yours? What if mine turns out to be bigger than yours? Then you're gonna be upset."

"Stop screwing around," said Big Pussy on Steroids. "What do you know?"

"Sadly, not much. What do you guys know?"

"I think Majestyk nabbed him."

"I don't think so."

"What makes you say that?"

"I already talked to Majestyk."

"What'd he say?"

"Exactly what you'd expect him to say."

"Which is?"

"That one, Davis Cartright is a jerk, and two, that he had nothing to do with his disappearance."

"And you believe that?"

Charlie nodded. "I do."

"He got an alibi?"

"I don't know."

Big Pussy gave him a look. "What kind of cop are you?"

"I told you, I'm not."

"I can see that."

"So where do we go from here?" asked Charlie.

"Do you wanna work together?"

"No, but thanks for the offer. I just got out of a relationship, and I'm not sure I'm quite ready for another one."

"You're a smug fucker, aren't you?"

"You know, I've heard that once or twice before."

Charlie looked at Candace and winked just as a third *goomba* wandered into the office. The guy looked at his partner, laid out on the floor. Then he looked up at Charlie. "Who the hell is this?"

"Charlie Grimes," said Charlie.

"That supposed to mean something to me?"

"Ask your wife."

NINE

Davis Cartright was trying to talk his way out of his situation.

"Maybe we could work something out, just me and you," he said.

Booby grinned. "You and I might be able to work something out, but you still ain't walking away from this for anything less than five million."

"That's a lot of bread."

"You got a lot more where that came from."

"I worked hard for that money."

"I'm working hard for it, too, nigga," said Booby.

"I can't do it. I'm sorry, but I just can't."

"What is your life worth?"

"Somewhere south of five million."

"How much?"

"I dunno, but not five million."

"Money's that important?"

"It's the *most* important thing," said Davis Cartright.

"But you need to ask yourself this—how you gonna spend it if you dead?"

This was a good question. Davis mulled it over.

"I can give you $250,000 if you let me go now."

Booby looked at him like he was stupid. "Are you joking?"

"I'm dead serious."

"Well, you better get a whole lot more serious before you get a whole lot more dead."

"$300,000."

"Stop with that," said Booby. "Stop right now."

"What?"

"Your ass ain't gonna nickel and dime me on this. The cost for your life—and your balls—is five million, and not one dollar less."

"Why do you keep talking about my balls?"

"Trust me when I tell you you don't want this to go there."

"What would you do?"

"Maybe put out a lit cigarette or two into them."

Davis looked horrified.

"That would just be the beginning," said Booby.

"Come on, man."

"You ever seen what a blowtorch'll do to a man's balls?"

Davis didn't say anything. He just stared up at him.

"And that ain't the end of it."

"It's not?"

Booby looked up at the wall. "Look over there."

Davis looked.

"You see those gardening prunes?"

"Are you serious?"

"That's the *piece d' resistance*."

"No," said Davis. "I don't want that."

"Five million dollars and you get to walk away, balls intact."

"What if we turned the tables around here?"

"How so?"

"What if I paid you to kill Majestyk?"

Booby looked at him. "You serious?"

"Yeah."

"For five million?"

"I was thinking two."

"Two million to kill Majestyk?"

"Right," said Davis. "What do you think?"

"You do know you could have that kind of thing done for a whole lot cheaper?"

"I don't care. You bring Majestyk here, in front of me, and you kill him, I'll give you two million dollars."

Booby didn't know what to think. For two million dollars he would kill a whole bunch of motherfuckers, so killing one dude didn't seem all that serious. But two million wasn't five million. Still, it was a lot more money than Booby had ever seen in his life. And who knows? Maybe he could come up with a way to get more of the man's money later.

"Let me ask you this," said Booby.

"What?"

"Isn't Majestyk your big earner? I mean, how you gonna pay to have him killed? Won't the label lose money if he goes missing?"

"I don't want him to go missing. I want him to go dead."

"I got that."

"I hate to lose the Majestyk money, but there's no way I can let this stand. That coon," Davis stopped himself. "Sorry."

Booby nodded. "Go on."

"He's gotta go."

"And I get to walk away scot-free if I have him killed?"

"Free as Django."

"Why?"

"Why should I have you killed? You're just doing your job. But Majestyk... that's another story altogether. He betrayed me. He betrayed the label. Besides, you would be doing work for me, which would make this a completely different matter altogether."

"I'll do it," said Booby. "For $2.5 million."

Davis grinned. "Holding out for more money now?"

"No. The terms have changed. I'll get Majestyk down here and kill him in front of you for $2.5 million. If you say 'no,' you die. Simple as that."

Davis nodded. "Then you won't get to spend the money."

"Neither will you."

"And I get to walk away, as you say, scot-free once you get the money?"

"Free as Django."

* * *

When Booby got back upstairs, Bugs was high, watching an Arnold Schwarzenegger flick where Arnold was gunning down dozens of soldiers with a machine gun, and Loop was passed out on the couch.

"You seen this movie before?" asked Bugs.

"I dunno. Those movies all look the same."

"What do you mean?"

"Arnold kills a hundred dudes without getting a scratch on him... Even if I haven't seen the movie, I've seen the movie. You know what I mean?"

Bugs nodded. "I guess you're right."

"Turn that shit off."

"What?"

"The TV, nigga. We gotta talk."

"What about Loop?"

"Wake that nigga up. He needs to be in on this, too."

Bugs switched off the television and shook Loop awake.

"What?" said Loop, startled.

"Wake up," said Bugs. "Booby needs to talk to us."

Loop looked at him through hooded eyes, still half asleep. "About what?"

Booby said, "Your boy Davis Cartright."

"What about him?"

"He's offering to pay us."

"That's what we wanted, right?" asked Bugs.

"Yeah, but the terms have changed."

Loop looked at him. "What does that mean?"

"It means we gotta do something for the man in exchange for the money."

"What we gotta do?"

Booby said, "We gotta kill Majestyk."

"I ain't never killed nobody before," said Bugs.

Loop piped up. "Me neither."

"Killing's easy. You just raise the gun and you pull the damn trigger. Nothing to it."

"You killed someone before?" asked Loop.

"What is you," asked Booby, "scared?"

"Hell yes, I'm scared," said Bugs. "I ain't never been to prison, and I damn sure don't wanna go now. I'm too old to go to prison now."

"But you hate Majestyk, right?" asked Booby.

Bugs nodded. "Yeah."

"And you need to ask yourself—do you wanna keep this mansion and all them cars, or what?"

"Of course I do."

"So what's one dude's life compared to your happiness?"

Loop said, "I gotta pray about this."

Booby got pissed. "I'm running this show now. You wanna pray..." He pulled his pistol on Loop. "Pray about this."

"There's no need to be rash," said Bugs. "I'm sure we can work this out."

"Y'all niggas talk about how hard you are, but you're afraid to overcome one little obstacle to get what you want."

"This ain't no small obstacle," said Bugs.

"It's a man's life," said Loop.

Booby stared at them, pistol still trained on Loop. "Whose life is more important—yours or Majestyk's?"

"Obviously mine," said Bugs.

Booby looked at Loop. "And you?"

"I guess I'm in. But I'm still gonna pray about it."

"Let me ask you this," said Booby. "Do you think Jesus would let one life stand in the way of something he wanted to accomplish?"

"No, I guess not."

"Hell no, he wouldn't."

"So now what?" asked Bugs.

"We gotta get Majestyk over here, preferably by himself."

"How do we do that?" asked Loop.

Booby said, "I got a plan."

TEN

"I still got that nigga's number," said Bugs, dialing up Majestyk on his phone. He hit the button and the call went through. Majestyk answered on the third ring.

"Hello?" he said.

"Majestyk?"

"Yeah?"

"This is Bugs."

Majestyk hadn't a clue. "Bugs who?"

Bugs really didn't like the dude.

"Bugs," he said. "From the Road Dogs."

"What up, Bugs?"

"I wanted to talk to you."

"You ain't wantin' to borrow no money is you?"

"Why the fuck would I want to borrow money?"

"Well," said Majestyk. "I heard you got dropped from the label."

"Nah, it ain't a bad thing. We wanted out of our contract anyway."

"Yeah?"

"Fuckers wouldn't pay us what they owe us," said Bugs.

"Davis Cartright?"

"One in the same."

"That dude is slime, pure fucking slime."

"Word."

"I'm glad he's gone."

"Gone?" asked Bugs. "Where'd he go?"

"Nobody knows. White boy just up and disappeared."

"Really?" Bugs hadn't heard a word about Davis Cartright's disappearance, and had actually believed maybe no one had noticed.

"Yeah," said Majestyk. "So what you wanna talk about, dog?"

"I want to collaborate."

Majestyk chuckled. "Now why would I wanna do that?"

"What does you mean?"

"You need this collaboration more than I do. So how much you gonna pay me?"

"It's like that?"

"Definitely. Money talks, bullshit runs the marathon. It's like *Goodfellas*, you know, 'Fuck you, pay me.'"

"How much you want?"

"How much you got?"

"Give me a number."

"A number?" asked Majestyk.

"A dollar figure."

"I don't think you can handle my dollar figure."

"Any number," said Bugs.

Majestyk thought for a moment. "$750,000."

Bugs nodded. "We can do that, but only if you can convince Premo to do the track."

He had piqued Majestyk's interest. "You can do 750?"

"As long as Premo does the track."

"I can get Premo, but you know he's gonna cost another 500 or so."

"Not a problem," said Bugs. "Why don't you come by tonight and get your 750, and we'll iron out the details."

"Give me your address and I'll be right over."

"Good. One more thing."

"Yeah?"

"Come by yourself."

Majestyk frowned. "Why?"

"This is a top secret deal. We don't need every nigga and his mama knowin' about it."

"Cool," said Majestyk.

* * *

Majestyk got off the phone and looked at his boy, Reggie, who was playing *Grand Theft Auto IV* on the 100-inch TV. Reggie was wearing headphones and a microphone, talking shit to some thirteen year old from Nebraska. "Take that, you little punk-ass *maricon*," he was saying.

"Reggie," said Majestyk.

But Reggie didn't hear him; he was off in his own little world of shit talk and video games.

"How you like them apples, you sorry little son of a fuck?" Reggie asked the kid.

Majestyk was growing impatient. *"Reggie!"*

Reggie looked up, saw that Majestyk was speaking to him, and removed his headphones and mic. "What up, son?"

"Get up off there. We gotta go see a man."

"What man is that?"

"A nigga named Bugs."

Reggie squinted. "Who the fuck is Bugs?"

"Dude from that group the Road Dogs."

"Ah," said Reggie, nodding. "He's a little candy-ass, and their music is wack as a Vanilla Ice tribute show. The fuck we goin' to see him for?"

"He's got some money for us."

"Money's always good."

"He wants to record a song with me and Premo."

Reggie nodded. "Yeah, that would be dope. At least you and Premo would be dope. Them niggas are hot garbage."

"Thing is," said Majestyk, "I think he's up to something."

"Up to something? Like what?"

"I dunno."

"What makes you think that?"

"He told me to come alone, like it was some kind of drug deal or something."

"That's weird."

"Yeah," said Majestyk. "I gotta funny feeling about this."

"So we goin' now?"

"Yeah."

"Can I play my music on the way?" asked Reggie.

"Shit no."

"Why?"

"I don't wanna hear none of that Marvin Gaye bullshit you like to play."

"You don't like Marvin?"

"You play it too much. I go to sleep, I still hear that nigga in my dreams, and that shit ain't right. The only nigga I wanna hear in my dreams is myself when I'm having sex with a hottie."

Reggie smiled. "We ready to go then?"

"Off to the Batmobile, son."

* * *

The three wiseguys were parked down the street watching the house when Majestyk and Reggie pulled the Escalade out of the drive.

"So now what?" asked Dante.

"We follow 'em," said Jimmy.

"Follow 'em?"

"What? You think we're just gonna sit here and stare at this empty fuckin' house? Maybe the coon's gonna lead us to that spoiled fuckin' rich kid, Davis Cartright."

"You think so?"

Jimmy nodded. "I do."

"What makes you so sure this fucking eggplant took Cartright in the first place?"

"I just got a hunch," said Jimmy. "And my hunches ain't never wrong."

Dante thought about this for a moment. "What about when you lost all that money in that card game in Atlantic City last year?"

Jimmy shook his head. "Okay," he said. "My hunches are *almost* never wrong."

"And what about the four times you been divorced? Your hunches ain't have shit to say when you married those broads?"

Now Jimmy was getting heated. "Just drive the fucking car and keep your goddamn observations to yourself."

"I'm just saying," said Dante.

"Yeah, and I'm just saying shut the fuck up and drive."

* * *

Charlie was driving down by Culver City, smoking a cigarette, Electric Light Orchestra playing just as loud as you please. The band was singing "Evil Woman," and Charlie was in a good mood. He was driving along, lost in his own thoughts, when he spotted Majestyk go past him in a Black Escalade. *Small world,* he thought. Then, about two seconds later, he spotted Big Pussy on Steroids and the *Sopranos* casting call rejects following closely behind in a tan Caddy. *Well, shit,* he thought. He pulled the wheel and flipped a U-turn right there. Something was going down, and he'd be damned if he wasn't gonna find out what.

As he followed, ELO still singing about that vile woman, Charlie's phone rang. He looked down and saw that it was Candace.

"Hello," he answered.

"How's tricks?"

"Pretty damn good right now."

"How so?"

"I might be close to finding douchebag."

"What douchebag?"

"Davis Cartright."

"Really?"

"Yeah, I'm following those *goombas* from the office right now. And guess who they're following?"

"No clue."

"Majestyk."

"What?" she asked. "You're following the Italians, and they're following Majestyk?"

"Right."

"In cars?"

"No," he said sarcastically. "In go-carts."

"You're a funny guy, Charlie."

"I know."

"So how the hell did this happen?"

"Fate," he said. "Must be Kismet."

"You would have to mention that skank's name."

"I guess Kismet was still on my lips."

"Goddamn you, Charlie Grimes," said Candance. "You really are a bastard."

"And then some."

"No two ways about it."

"And that's why you love me," he said.

This was met with a moment of awkward silence before Candace finally said, "Charlie..."

"Yeah?"

"Be careful. Take care of yourself out there."

"I always do."

And he hung up.

* * *

"This here's the address," said Majestyk, pulling into the driveway.

"Nice crib," said Reggie. "I didn't know being wack got you nice shit like this."

"Niggas lost they record contract. This shit isn't gonna last long. Soon it's gonna dry up and blow away in the wind."

"Word?"

"That corny-ass Bugs tried to spin it to me that it was a good thing, but them muthafuckas is sweatin' bullets. I figure that's why they want me to do this song with 'em. They're desperate."

"And you're gonna do the song?"

"I'll at least take their money," said Majestyk.

"Right on," said Reggie, raising his fist for Majestyk to bump. Majestyk bumped it.

* * *

"Park right down the street there," said Jimmy.

"Over there?"

"Yeah, right there."

"Who's house is this?" asked Dante.

"Damned if I know, but I'll bet you this shit's got something to do with Davis Cartright."

"A hunch?"

"A hunch."

"Fair enough," said Dante, pulling the car over to the curb just down the street from the Road Dogs' mansion.

* * *

Seeing Majestyk park in the driveway and the *goombas* park next door, Charlie drove down the street and turned around so he could park on the opposite side of the street. No need to make the mansion look like it was hosting a goddamn Superbowl party. Once he had parked the pickup, Charlie sat and watched the *goombas* watching the house. As long as they sat in the Caddy, he would sit in the truck. He lit another cigarette and hummed along to *Mr. Blue Sky.*

ELEVEN

Majestyk stepped up to the front door and rang the doorbell. He looked down at the "Welcome" doormat, thinking it wasn't very masculine. "Fucking studio gangstas," he grumbled. A moment later, Loop answered the door. Loop put his fist out for Majestyk to bump. "What up, son?" said Loop.

"What up?" responded Majestyk, bumping his fist.

"We just chillin'."

"Where's that nigga Bugs?"

Loop looked Reggie over for a moment, wanting to ask why the fuck he was here, but kept his mouth shut.

Bugs walked in from the next room, Booby following right behind him.

Majestyk put out his hand, and Bugs took it, pulling it to his chest. "How's it goin', son?" asked Majestyk.

"Not bad." Bugs looked at Reggie. "Who's this ol' peanut head nigga right here?"

"This is my homie, Reggie."

Bugs' eyes narrowed. "I told you to come alone. Fuck you bring this entourage cat for?"

"Nah, it's all good," said Majestyk. "Reggie here is my boy. He's in on everything I do. We done lived together, we probably gonna die together."

"No doubt," said Reggie.

Booby and Bugs exchanged a look.

"So where's my money, nigga?" asked Majestyk.

"You in a hurry or something?"

"What? You niggas wanna hang out and have a slumber party?"

Bugs really hated this fucking Majestyk. "I thought we'd at least talk about the song," he said. "Kind of map out what it is we're gonna do, so everyone can get to work writing their verses."

"Sure," said Majestyk. "The song." He looked Bugs in the eyes. "But the question is, do you have my scrilla?"

"Yeah, I got the damn money."

"You know what Big said."

"Big said a lot of things. What you talkin' about?"

"It's all about the Benjamins."

Bugs nodded. "Right. And look where that got him."

"So now what?" asked Loop. Bugs looked at Booby, and Booby made a point to nod towards the basement door.

"We gotta go down to the basement," said Bugs.

Majestyk frowned. "The basement? What the fuck is in the basement?"

"That's where the studio equipment is," said Booby.

"Right," said Loop, getting into it now. "We wanna show you a scratch track. See what you think of it before we bring in Premo."

"I really gotta go," said Majestyk. "I got places to go, honeys to screw."

"Five minutes," said Bugs. "That's all I'm asking for."

Majestyk turned it over in his mind for a moment. What the hell? For $750 grand he could spare five minutes to listen to these wack niggas' wack track.

"Sure thing," said Majestyk. "It's your house. You lead the way."

Bugs led, with Majestyk and Reggie right behind, followed by Booby and Loop. He opened the door and they started down the stairs. Before their guests could see Davis Cartright sitting there, tied to that chair, Bugs turned towards them. Before he could say a word, Booby shot Reggie, leaving a blood mist where his head had been, and the man slumped down the wooden stairs.

"What the fuck?!" asked Majestyk. *"What the fuck is this shit?"*

"I got a gun to the back of your head," said Booby. "Keep walking and don't try no funny shit, nigga."

Bugs led them down the rest of the stairs, and there was Davis Cartright in all his pompous, pain-in-the-ass glory.

"Holy shit," said Majestyk.

"Don't say that," said Loop.

"What?"

"Holy shit. It ain't right. It's like takin' the Lord's name in vain. Jesus don't like that shit, and neither do I."

Majestyk stared at Davis Cartright. "You fuckers kidnapped the white boy?"

"Because you said to," said Booby. Majestyk had no idea what this meant.

Bugs looked at Davis Cartright, staring at him now, and realized they'd fucked up royally.

"Damn!" said Bugs.

"What is it?" asked Loop.

"We forgot to wear our masks."

"Ain't no thing but a chicken wing on a string," said Booby, removing the gag from Davis Cartright's mouth.

"You sons of bitches are in on this, too?" asked Davis.

Bugs looked at Booby, not knowing what to say. Booby spoke up. "They were out of work, needed a job."

"So you went to work for Majestyk?" asked Davis.

"It beat workin' at Popeye's," said Booby. Majestyk started to protest, but Booby fired a round clean through his eye. Majestyk crumpled to the ground, a big fucking hole in his eye socket.

"That's $2.5 million you owe us," said Booby.

Davis Cartright looked at Bugs. "Are you sure that's how this went down? It was Majestyk that kidnapped me?"

"Who else?" asked Booby. "Do you really believe these Road Dog niggas is smart enough to pull off some shit like that themselves?"

Davis shook his head. "No, I don't."

Bugs didn't appreciate that shit, but kept his mouth shut.

"So do we get our money or what?" asked Booby.

Davis' eyes narrowed. "If shit went down the way you said it did, then yeah, you'll get your money."

"And what about that dead nigga there on the stairs?" asked Booby.

"What about him?" asked Davis.

"How much you gonna pay us for killin' that dude?"

"I don't even know who the fuck that guy is."

"The way I see it," said Booby, "he's collateral damage, so you owe us a little extra."

"Really?"

"Yeah."

Davis mulled it over for a moment. "What the hell?" he said. "In for a penny, in for a pound. Can you guys untie me so I can get you your money?"

"Sure thing," said Booby, going to work untying the cracker. As he was untying the hostage, and as Bugs and Loop watched, a voice came from the stairs. "What the fuck is all this shit?"

They looked up and saw a muscular Italian guy standing there, looking stupid.

"Who are you?" asked Loop.

"I'm your worst fucking nightmare," said the man.

"How original," said Booby.

"Jimmy," said Davis Cartright. "I thought you guys'd never show up."

Booby looked up at Jimmy. "You know this cat, Davis?"

"He's one of the guys I told you about."

"The mob guys?"

"One in the same," said Davis Cartright. He looked up at Jimmy, just as Dante and Aldo revealed themselves on the stairs. "Jimmy?" said Davis.

"Yeah."

"Kill these fucking niggers right now."

Jimmy went for his gun, but Booby shot, catching him in the throat, and Jimmy tumbled down the stairs. Dante and Aldo both popped out in full view now, their guns out. Aldo fired wildly, the shot careening off the wall behind Booby.

"We got us a Mexican standoff right here," said Booby.

"Drop your gun, eggplant," said Dante.

"No, you drop your gun."

Now Charlie Grimes stepped out on the stairs, his pistol aimed at the back of Aldo's head. "Now we got a real Mexican standoff," said Charlie.

"Who the fuck are you?" asked Booby.

"Land Shark."

"Real funny, motherfucker. Really, who are you?"

"Name's Charlie Grimes."

"That supposed to mean something to me?"

"Yeah."

"Why?" asked Booby.

"Because it's the name of the man who fucked your mother."

"My mother's dead."

"No shit?"

"No shit."

"Shut up," said Dante. "Both of you."

Dante squeezed the trigger and shot Loop in the chest. Loop fell back, his hands over his chest. "Shit," he said. "I'm hit. He fucking shot me in the chest, right above my Road Dogs tattoo."

Bugs looked down at him. "It's gonna be alright, Loop."

"You tellin' me the truth?" asked Loop. "Am I gonna die, Bugs?"

Bugs looked at him. "I don't know, Loop. Maybe."

"That's not what I wanted to hear."

"What do you mean?"

"You're supposed to make me feel better, Bugs. That shit don't make me feel better."

"Sorry, man," said Bugs. "I thought you wanted the truth."

"Shut the fuck up," said Booby.

Bugs looked at him. "Who the fuck you talkin' to, nigga?"

Booby swiveled towards Bugs, gunning him down. He turned back towards Dante, Aldo, and Charlie. Davis Cartright just sat there watching. "Will you please finish untying me?" he asked.

"Shut the fuck up, white boy," said Booby.

From the ground Loop said, "You shot Bugs."

"Be quiet."

"Motherfucker, I'ma get you. You killed Bugs."

Dante turned his pistol on Loop and squeezed the trigger. The shot caught Loop in the head, spraying his brains across the cement floor.

"Fuck you do that for?" asked Booby.

"He was annoying the shit out of me," said Dante.

Booby nodded. "That was Loop in a nutshell—irritating as all hell."

"So what's the play here?" asked Charlie.

Aldo tried to turn to fire at Charlie, but Charlie shot him in the back of the head. Aldo fell down the stairs alongside his buddy Jimmy. Now Charlie had his pistol trained on Dante.

Booby fired on Charlie twice, catching him in the chest and in the arm. Charlie staggered back up the stairs, falling onto the kitchen linoleum. He was unconscious.

"Now it's just us, eggplant," said Dante.

"I'm getting' real tired of that eggplant shit."

"What you gonna do about it?"

Booby squeezed the trigger, shooting Dante in the chest. Dante fired his gun wildly as he tumbled back, falling down the stairs.

Booby looked at Davis. "Real nice, man."

"What?"

"'Kill these fucking niggers'?"

"I guess that wasn't such a good idea in the grand scheme of things."

"Worst idea since *Waterworld*."

"So you gonna kill me or what?"

"Or what."

"What does that mean?"

Booby said, "I just want my money, Davis."

"Then we gotta go to the bank."

"What bank?"

"Untie me, and we'll go to my bank together and get your money."

Booby finished untying the white boy and then, gun raised, followed him up the stairs. They stepped over the unconscious Charlie Grimes.

"You know that dude?" asked Booby.

Davis Cartright said, "Never seen him before in my life."

"Strange day."

"You can say that again."

"Strange day."

And they made their way out to Bugs' Escalade.

TWELVE

Davis Cartright was driving, Booby's gun leveled at him. The stereo was playing the Road Dogs semi-hit *Pump It Up*.

"Can we please turn this shit off?" asked Davis. "I'm so tired of hearing that shit."

"Pretty wack, huh?"

"It's shit. Pure shit."

"But you're the one who signed them to a contract," said Booby. "If you knew they was wack, why the fuck you sign 'em?"

"I didn't sign 'em. My former A&R guy did."

"Former?"

"He lost his job."

"For signing them?"

"Let's show some respect to the dead."

Booby laughed. "Them niggas was the worst, man."

"Even auto-tune couldn't help them," said Davis.

"You listen to hip-hop?"

"Does it matter?"

"What do you mean?" asked Booby.

"A guy could listen to nothing but polka and still know that this shit was garbage."

Booby ejected the CD and flung it out the window.

"Happy?" he asked.

"As a Republican in a gay bath house," said Davis. "So how'd you get involved in all this mess anyway?"

"I guess a nigga was just in the wrong place at the right time."

"The right time?"

"Hell yeah," said Booby. "I'm getting ready to get paid."

"True enough."

"So what did you do to Majestyk to start all this shit in the first place?"

"He thought I disrespected him."

"How'd you do that?"

"We were negotiating his contract and he wanted more money."

"How much did you offer him?"

"Enough to buy a small African nation."

"And he said no?"

"No," said Davis. "He didn't say no. He pulled a gun on me and threatened to murder me."

"Word?"

"God as my witness."

"That's kind of disrespectful," said Booby.

Davis looked over at him. "Rich coming from a guy who's got a gun on me."

"I can't take no chances. I can't have you jumping out or stopping the cops."

"So what happens after we get your money?"

"You do the right thing, you get to go free."

"Free as Django?"

"Free as Mandela, nigga."

"Mandela's dead."

"Yeah," said Booby, "but before he was dead he was free."

"Three million dollars, huh?"

"Three million dollars."

"I still don't think it's fair that I gotta pay for the dead nigger on the stairs. I didn't ask you to shoot that dude."

"Life's not always fair, Davis."

"When you're as rich as I am, it's pretty fair most of the time."

"So what you gonna do after you get out of this?" asked Booby.

"I'm gonna go fuck my mistress. Maybe in the ass."

"Oh, yeah?"

"Yeah."

"She hot?"

"Hotter than a $20 X-Box."

"Really?"

"She could raise a dead man's dick. And that's just her face."

Booby asked, "Her body is nice?"

"Twelve out of ten."

"That good, huh?"

"For sure."

"How'd an ugly motherfucker like you get that?" asked Booby.

Davis laughed. "Again, when you're as rich as I am, you can have any woman you want."

"Any woman?"

"Any woman, married or single, famous or unknown."

"I suppose three million could get me quite a few bitches."

"No more hood rats for you, my friend."

"Or at least a better class of hood rat," said Booby.

Davis nodded.

"Where the fuck is this bank of yours?"

Davis said, "Couple more blocks. It's up there on the right. We're almost there. How do you wanna play this out when we get there?"

"You go in and fill out the papers," said Booby. "I follow you, pistol in my pocket."

"What if I try something crazy?"

"Then you'll die."

"But you'll die, too," said Davis.

"We'll die together, son. In for a penny, in for a motherfucking pound. Isn't that what you said?"

A couple minutes passed and they were parked on the street in front of the bank. Davis put the Escalade in park. "Do you want me to get out?"

Booby nodded, putting the gun in the pocket of his track pants.

"Remember, you fuck up, you die instantly."

"I remember, I remember. I just want to go home," said Davis.

"And fuck that pretty mistress of yours?"

Davis said, "In the ass."

"Good plan."

Davis Cartright walked into the bank, wearing the same suit he'd been wearing for almost a week. Booby walked a step behind him, his hand in his pocket, fingers curled around the handle of the pistol.

Davis approached a teller.

"Can I help you, sir?" she asked.

"I need to make a substantial withdrawal."

"How substantial?"

"More than you'll earn in a lifetime."

The woman looked irritated by this, but motioned for him to go to a desk at the end of the counter. "Have a seat down there and Mr. Carlson will assist you in a moment."

"Thanks," Davis said, smiling a condescending smile.

"Don't fuck this up," whispered Booby.

"Chill your ass, Sambo."

Davis Cartright and Booby sat down in the chairs in front of Mr. Carlson, the bank manager's, desk. A moment later a portly, balding man emerged from the back.

"Sorry," he said. "I had to go to the bathroom. I had burritos for lunch."

"Thanks for the update," said Davis.

Mr. Carlson ignored this. "So how can I help you?"

"I'm here to make a withdrawal."

"Oh yeah?"

"Yeah."

"What's your name?"

"Davis Cartright."

Mr. Carlson looked up from the form. *"You're Davis Cartright?"*

"I sure hope so, or else I been writing the wrong name on my checks for years."

"I'm so sorry, Mr. Cartright," the man said. "I didn't know it was you. How much money would you like to withdraw today?"

"Three million dollars."

Mr. Carlson looked shocked. "That's a substantial amount of money."

"Not for me it isn't."

"I guess you're right."

"I'm always right."

"Would you like a cashier's check or cash?"

"Cash," said Davis. "Where the fuck am I gonna cash a check for three million dollars?"

"Good point," said Mr. Carlson. "Large bills okay?"

"No," said Davis. "I'd like it in ones and fives."

"Are you serious?"

"No. Of course not."

Mr. Carlson looked relieved. He filled out a form and slid it across the desk to Davis. "I just need you to sign this." Davis Cartright picked up the form. "You got a pen?" he asked. Mr. Carlson handed him a gold-plated ink pen, and Davis filled out the form, sliding it back to the bank manager.

Mr. Carlson looked down at the form on which Davis Cartright had scrawled, "Call the police. This man has taken me hostage."

"Is this some sort of a joke?" Mr. Carlson asked.

Davis looked at Booby.

"What?" asked Booby. "Is *what* a joke?"

Mr. Carlson stood up, staring at Booby. Realizing what was happening, Booby pulled out the pistol and aimed it at Mr. Carlson, squeezing the trigger and shooting him in the chest. Then he turned it on Davis and shot him in the side of the head.

"I told you not to fuck with me, white boy," he said.

Booby turned towards the bank tellers, waving the gun over his head. "Everybody just be cool," he said. "Nobody make a move and everything's gonna be just fine."

The bank alarm started to ring.

Booby knew he was fucked.

He'd be damned if he was going back to prison. When he heard the police sirens approaching, he stuck the pistol in his mouth and squeezed the trigger.

THIRTEEN

Charlie woke up in a hospital bed and he saw Candace's pretty face. "Where am I?" he asked.

"You're in the hospital."

He thought back for a moment. "So I didn't get those guys?"

"No, sweetie," she said. "They got you."

"No bueno."

"How do you feel?" she asked.

"Like shit. How do I look?"

"At least twice as bad as that."

Charlie grinned. "Thanks for your honesty." He looked down. "Where'd they shoot me? Tell me they didn't shoot me in my dick."

"They got you twice."

"In the dick?"

"No, not in the dick," she said. "Once in the chest and once in your arm."

"Good to know my little man's still safe."

"Who was it that shot you?"

"I'm not sure," he said. "It was either the rappers or the mob guys."

"This sounds like a made-up story."

"It does, doesn't it?" he asked.

"I don't know how to tell you this, Charlie, but you died. You were dead."

"I was?"

"Yeah," she said. "You were dead for a minute or so, but..."

Charlie tapped his chest. "The defibrillator saved me?"

There were tears in Candace's eyes. "Yes."

"Best investment I ever made," said Charlie. "Right up there with that Flesh-light."

"What's a Flesh-light?"

"It's a sex toy. You put your dick in it, and..."

"You're the worst. Don't you ever stop joking?"

"I'll stop joking when I die."

"You already have."

"Several times," he said.

"So when you died," said Candace, "did you see anything... strange?"

"Like what?"

"Jesus and his flowing robes and all that?"

"I didn't see shit. I didn't even know I had died until you told me."

"Yeah," she said. "That's what I thought."

"So what happened to Davis Cartright?"

"He got killed when the kidnappers tried to take him to the bank to take his money out."

"Not the smartest kidnappers the world has ever seen."

She smiled. "Not quite."

"So what happened to the rap guys?"

"They all died."

"All of them?"

"Every last one of them."

"And those mob guys?"

"Also dead."

Charlie nodded. "So everyone died but me?"

"Well, technically you all died," said Candace. "You were just the only one who came back."

"You wanna know my secret?"

"What is it, Charlie?"

"It's all that Electric Light Orchestra that saved me."

"Charlie," she said. "Can I ask you a serious question?"

"That sounds like a serious question right there."

"I mean it, Charlie."

"Okay, shoot."

"Where do we stand?"

"What do you mean?"

"You and I, relationship-wise. Where do we stand?"

"You mean are we going steady? You wanna meet after study hall, Candace?"

She smiled. "Yeah, that's what I meant; I wanna meet you after study hall."

"So when we get out of here..."

"Yes?"

"What say we go back to the strip club for some more of that meatloaf?"

"And there I thought you were gonna propose to me, Charlie Grimes."

"Only if I get sex first," he said.

Candace took his hand and kissed it.

About the Author

A ndy Rausch is an American film journalist, author, screenwriter, film producer, and actor. He is the author of several novels and novellas including Elvis Presley, CIA Assassin. He also wrote the screenplay for Dahmer versus Gacy and is the author of some twenty non-fiction books on popular culture.

Word-of-mouth is essential for any author to succeed.
If you enjoyed Riding Shotgun And Other American Cruelties,
please consider leaving a review on Amazon.
Even a couple of lines would make a difference
and would be extremely appreciated.

Crime Wave Press is a Hong Kong based fiction imprint that endeavors to publish the best new crime novels from around the globe.

Founded in 2012 by acclaimed publisher Hans Kemp of Visionary World and seasoned writer Tom Vater, **Crime Wave Press** publishes a range of crime fiction – from whodunits to Noir and Hardboiled, from historical mysteries to espionage thrillers, from literary crime to pulp fiction, from highly commercial page turners to marginal texts exploring the world's dark underbelly.

Crime Wave Press promotes strong voices, exceptional talent and unique points of view in the crime fiction genre.

Visit our website: www.crimewavepress.com
Follow us on Facebook: www.facebook.com/CrimeWavePress

If you like to be among the first to hear about new
Crime Wave Press releases and special **Crime Wave Press**
promotions sign up for our mailing list here.
We promise to never share your email with anyone.
The **Crime Wave Press** Team

www.ingramcontent.com/pod-product-compliance
Lightning Source LLC
Chambersburg PA
CBHW020323200626
46814CB00006BB/2393